The Beautiful Little Things

ALSO BY MELISSA HILL

The Last to Know

All Because of You

Please Forgive Me

Something from Tiffany's

The Guest List

The Charm Bracelet

A Gift to Remember

A Diamond from Tiffany's

The Hotel on Mulberry Bay

The Love of a Lifetime

Keep You Safe

The Summer Villa

The Beautiful Little Things

Melissa Hill

LAKE UNION
PUBLISHING

This is a work of fiction. Names, characters, organizations, places, events, and incidents are either products of the author's imagination or are used fictitiously. Any resemblance to actual persons, living or dead, or actual events is purely coincidental.

Published by Lake Union Publishing, Seattle

www.apub.com

ISBN-13: 9781542033046
ISBN-10: 1542033047

Cover design by The Brewster Project

Printed in the United States of America

With love and thanks to my wonderful parents,
who help me appreciate that the little things in life
really are the big things.

Life isn't a race. It's a relay.

—Dick Gregory

Prologue

The magic was missing . . .

Romy Moore sat at the window chair in her late mother's study and looked out over the nearby woods and forestry trails, appreciating why her mum had always found this spot so peaceful.

The trees wore a light dusting of white, the family home's elevated position in the Dublin Mountains ensuring they always got a bit of proper snow in winter, as opposed to the typically damper stuff on lower ground.

Fittingly beautiful for the season, but also serving merely to highlight the fact that everything felt so . . . wrong.

Romy's world was so out of kilter now that it should be howling gales and driving rain out, not Christmas-card perfection. It made everything even more desperately hollow and painful, and now she understood why some people found this time of year so difficult. The forced festive gaiety, the crippling sense of nostalgia and the idea that everything was supposed to be so bloody *wonderful*. When all she wanted to do right then was pull the covers over her head like it was just another day, a normal day, and she didn't have to pretend to be OK, to try to cheer up and put a brave face on for anyone else's sake.

And most of all, not to have to lie to herself that this time of year, to say nothing of *life*, could ever be the same without her mother.

Romy turned back to the desk and opened up a drawer, seeking a tissue. She found an already open packet of Kleenex and paused a little, reflecting that her mum would've likely used the one just before it, oblivious to the fact that her youngest would be needing the next to grieve her passing.

She wiped her eyes and then blew her nose into the tissue, looking idly through bits and pieces scattered across the desk before coming across a prettily patterned notebook beneath some letters.

Opening the cover, she saw her mother's familiar neat handwriting swirl into focus, achingly comforting, and as she began to read the opening words on the page, Romy quickly realised it was one of her journals.

Her mother loved to write and had kept a journal for as long as Romy could remember – ever the traditionalist at heart, despite her sister Joanna's grand attempt a couple of years back to move her into the twenty-first century with the gift of an iPad.

Feeling like an interloper for even daring to read – these were her mother's private thoughts, after all – she couldn't help but be drawn in, desperate to feel close to her once more.

If you are reading this, then for certain I am no longer with you.

In body at least.

Indeed, it is hard for me to be writing this now, from a place where I am still full of the joys, having just watched you all depart our very last family Christmas together.

While this year's gathering was, in a word . . . eventful, it gives me such joy that all ended happily – just as I'd hoped.

I wish I could imagine how your lives have been since – and, admittedly, I have tried – but when I attempt to imagine any scenarios that have transpired in the interim, I tend to go down a rabbit hole and overwhelm myself.

I cannot control what will happen. Just as I cannot see the future, I have no way of knowing how any of you will handle my passing.

The only thing I can do from this vantage point right this minute is provide my thoughts, my words, and perhaps a little bit of motherly advice.

I'm trying to picture you all together this time next year without me – and truth be told, I struggle with the concept because it feels so foreign.

So bear with me, as I seek to find the words and comb the recesses of my mind for any wisdom or reminders that might be useful as you navigate the festive period without me.

Firstly, it's OK to feel sad . . . but not forever.

And please do not let grief colour the first Christmas where I am absent. Whatever you do, don't allow sorrow to serve as the backdrop.

Because, oh my darlings, it is still the absolute best time of year and as you know has always been my favourite.

So please, for my sake, celebrate this Christmas as if I was still here?

Because I will be, in my own way – in all the little festive traditions we have followed over the years, and recipes and rituals that have become our family's staples.

Yes, of course this will be a Christmas like no other.

But that doesn't mean it has to be a terrible one.

It was like . . . a gift, Romy thought, a lump in her throat; though obviously not for her alone.

Because of course her mother would have understood that the family's first holiday period without her would be impossibly difficult.

Though she couldn't possibly have known just how scattered and broken they'd all become since her passing.

But maybe . . . Romy thought, sitting up straight as an idea struck her, and her mind raced as she flicked through the pages, desperate to read more of her mother's wisdom, or any pointers that might help endure her absence.

Maybe this was *exactly* what was needed to mend things – something to gather up all the little broken pieces that were this family now, and help put them back together?

As Romy continued reading, something akin to hope blossomed within her for the first time all year, as she realised that this was the miracle she'd been searching for.

Thank you, Mum. I think I know what to do . . .

While this family might be sinking beneath the surface at the moment, perhaps, with a little guidance, there was hope for them yet.

Chapter 1

LAST CHRISTMAS

You bring your own weather to the picnic.

That's what my mother used to tell me, and goodness knows you three have heard me repeat it often enough. But now I myself really do need to heed those words and act on that advice.

Because the weather for me lately has been, well . . . unpredictable, to say the least.

But not any more. Now, I finally have a forecast. Not the one that I wanted, but that's life, isn't it?

And like Mr McCartney – another beloved influence in my life – cheerily sang . . . life goes on.

An uncomfortable lyric for me now. Because life does indeed go on; just not for all of us. Everyone's story has an ending.

Of course, I've always been aware of that too, albeit as an abstract concept. A whole different feeling to know for sure that you're facing the conclusion of your own story.

What I need to decide now is the kind of conclusion I want. And I know I do have a say in that, no matter how much it feels like my choices have been taken away.

They haven't – not all of them, at least.

So I want you each to know that I choose a positive outlook – for all our sakes.

Our gang has always loved the festive season – it's always been such a joyful time for us Moores. So much so that I've always felt so sad for anyone estranged or separated from family at this time of year.

Or worse, bereaved.

For how can the season ever again be joyful and magical when someone you love is absent?

Still, it has always been my job to make the occasion special. And I'm determined to make this year one for the memory books. Despite knowing what comes after.

I won't let our time together be dampened or darkened by rain.

So for the moment at least, let us do what we always do: recharge and reconnect, eat and drink as much as we can bear, laugh ourselves silly and just enjoy being together again as a family.

After all, isn't this the time of year for believing . . . in something?

This Christmas, let's try to make the weather perfect.

For it will surely be our last.

◆ ◆ ◆

'Nate, it isn't a race – especially in these conditions. Slow down or you're going to miss the entrance.'

I turned around from the passenger seat of our SUV rental and peered anxiously back at the twins. Both, thankfully, were still sound asleep after the trauma of their first ever transatlantic flight and preceding dash through the chaos of SFO during the holidays. Though maybe not so traumatic when at five months old you get to do it all in business class.

'Jo, I lived in Massachusetts until I was twenty-four – I know how to drive in snow. And this sure as hell isn't snow,' my husband chuckled, looking balefully at the light dusting amid the woodlands either side of the roadway, inching up towards the Dublin Mountains. 'Besides, I'm barely going over fifty.' With twinkling green eyes, he reached across the centre console and patted my knee. 'And the girls are fine.'

I saw him glimpse into the rear-view mirror and smile with satisfaction – Suzy and Katie were snug in their car seats, bundled up in the brand-new Burberry snowsuits I'd changed them into to protect them from the damp Irish winter, in comparison to the California weather they'd known for their short little lives. Yes, I was aware that they would outgrow the suits in no time and that they'd have little need of them back home unless we took them on a ski jaunt, but there was no denying how cute they both looked.

Plus it was their first Christmas *ever*, let alone in Ireland – and I wanted the family pictures to be appropriately Insta-worthy.

As if reading my thoughts, Nate looked at me again and this time he was grinning.

'Should I pull over for a minute? Get another shot of them in all their pink fluffiness with green fields in the background? Hashtag TwinsFirstChristmas Hashtag IrishHomecoming Hashtag IrishFamilyChristmas.'

I couldn't help but laugh. 'You got 'em all.' Then, turning my attention to the outside world, I sighed. 'You know, I always said that I wouldn't miss Irish weather, but now I kinda do. Especially when it looks like this.'

It was a bright, cold December day beneath a brilliant blue sky. Some gentle early morning snow had just fallen, enough to settle at this elevation at least, ensuring the surrounding spruce forest was draped in sheer bright whiteness – like fondant frosting on a skilfully iced cake.

And there was no denying that the tree-lined road we were on just then, winding through the picturesque Dublin mountainside community that was my childhood home, made for a certain charm overall.

Many of the houses on the way were artfully decorated behind their gated entries. And while I knew a great many of the more well-to-do residents had professionals create such aesthetically beautiful winter wonderlands, I still preferred my parents' more modest Georgian pile in the older, rural centre of the community. Where every year my now sixty-something father braved the weather and rooftops – despite my mother's admonishment – to ensure that her home-made holly garlands and all the mismatched lawn decorations and string lighting collected throughout the years were reinstated with care.

'You're in festive mode, though, and forgetting the inevitable mid-morning thaw when everything turns to grey slush,' chided Nate, pulling me out of the picture-perfect holiday postcard I'd been mentally creating.

I snorted a laugh. 'Grinch.'

'Just thought your nostalgia needed a little reframing before you started figuring out a way to split time between Palo Alto and here. I doubt your Manolos would work as well on muddy mountain trails. Nor all the others you're going to buy after the promotion . . .' He winked, expertly steering the rental along the sharp bend on the approach to the house, our tyres cutting a disappointing swathe through the whiteness.

Something that felt uncomfortably like doubt jumped into my throat, and I did my best to shove it back down.

I didn't 'do' doubt.

'That's still not a sure thing, you know,' I replied simply.

'Honey,' he smiled. 'Of course it is. You're a superstar. As soon as you get back from maternity leave and smash the launch, you know they'll make the announcement.'

I swallowed hard, because I knew he was right. About that at least.

Determined to look carefree, I reached over and tickled his cheek; the long day of travel across multiple time zones had allowed just the barest bit of dark stubble to form. Though again, I mused, still feeling the after-effects of all that wonderful Aer Lingus hospitality, we hadn't exactly roughed it.

'I don't know . . .' I took an inward deep breath, trying to choose my words. 'Lately, I keep thinking a lot about Mum – how she raised all of us and how maybe it might be nice to give the girls something like that . . .'

'Sure, but that was a totally different time. Your mum was . . . well, a *mum*.' As opposed to Nate's own less secure upbringing amid the divorced parents he rarely saw. His family situation in general was a million miles from the close relationship I enjoyed with mine, so I couldn't blame him for not really getting it. 'And nothing against that, but, Jo, you are literally the most ambitious person I have ever known.' He side-eyed me curiously. 'Where is all of this coming from?'

I shrugged. 'I don't know really. Maybe it's because I've just begun getting comfortable and actually enjoying the girls now, as opposed to the endless worry and chaos of the early days.'

Nate reached across and took my hand in his, kissing my knuckles. '*Anything* is better than the early days,' he laughed, despite having had very little to do with the night feeds, sleep deprivation, worry and general domestic mayhem that came with a newborn, to say nothing of two at once. 'And while I'm having a hard time picturing you as a full-time mom, I could definitely get used to the idea of coming home to a tidy house and gourmet meal every day. No doubt you'd figure out some brand-new side hustle too – like be a hot mommy blogger or something.'

Laughter was thick in his voice, and I raised an eyebrow. 'A gourmet meal? You'd be lucky if you got fed at all, buddy.'

He rested a hand on my knee. 'You'd be great at whatever you put your mind to, hon – whether it's running a Fortune 500 powerhouse or ferrying the girls to and from ballet, soccer or STEM lessons . . . whatever.'

I smiled and the anxiety I'd been feeling in the pit of my stomach dissipated a little. 'I mean it, Jo,' Nate continued. 'You're the kind of woman who really *can* do it all.'

As if sensing my instantly renewed discomfort, I heard one of the girls stir in the back seat, letting out the tiniest cry, like the whine of a lonely puppy.

'Suzy's waking up,' I murmured, without needing to turn around.

Nate looked in the rear-view mirror. 'How can you tell them apart like that? They both sound the very same to me.'

I shrugged. 'I just . . . can.' And it seemed my body knew too, since my breasts had just begun to ache on cue. 'Watch out. Our entrance is next – just after that holly bush on the left . . .'

'Honey, this isn't my first time at your folks' house.'

'I know, it's just . . .'

'. . . the bush makes it hard to see the drive,' we chorused in unison.

I blew out my lips. Nate was right. Of course he knew where he was going. He didn't need me to guide him.

We turned through the gates and into the driveway, and as always – as if their children wore homing devices – the front door opened and my parents ambled out onto the porch at the top of the stone steps.

They did the very same upon departure, so that my final vision in the rear-view mirror before turning out of the driveway was always the two of them cheerily waving goodbye.

My heart lifted at the sight of them and, again as per usual, Mum and Dad were smiling as they came to greet us, though it struck me all at once that both looked so much older than the last time I'd seen them, in California in the summer – right after the girls were born.

I looked all around at the tacky illuminated lawn ornaments, the colourful lights draped on every inch of the roofline, the twinkling fir tree in pride of place at the living-room window . . . everything just the same as it used to be when I was growing up here.

The familiar sights of an Irish Christmas.

Tears pricked the corners of my eyes, as I realised just how badly I'd needed to be here, back amid my family's warm embrace.

I was home.

'Just as I predicted. You're always the first ones to arrive,' Mum called out happily, as she made her way down the granite steps. Dad would have cleared the ground of any frost earlier, but they were both still carefully watching their footing. 'Welcome home, love.'

Again I caught myself pausing and taking in their appearance – yes, they really *did* look older. Mum had turned sixty-nine in July and Dad would be celebrating his seventieth the year after next. I'd never really thought of my parents as 'old', but it seemed as if they had aged all of a sudden.

Though maybe now because I had children myself, I was more aware of the passage of time?

Still, as I closed the space between us something nagged at me, though I couldn't put my finger on it. Probably just my senses still on high alert after that conversation with Nate in the car. Which, much to my surprise, had in fact gone a lot better than anticipated.

'And I hope you brought our gorgeous granddaughters!' my mother exclaimed as she opened her arms and I sunk into her warm embrace.

'We left them in San Francisco, of course. What, Cathy – you mean you wanted to see them too?' Nate teased as he gave my father's hand a hearty shake.

Mum pulled back and kissed both of my cheeks. 'Motherhood really does suit you, Jo. You're absolutely glowing.' She placed a hand on my face – warm, despite the icy temperature – before she smoothed a lock of my blonde hair behind my ear. 'And you, you divil . . .' She chuckled at Nate before enveloping him in a hug, as I did the same with Dad. 'Are the girls awake? Let us help bring all their stuff in.'

'Mum, you aren't wearing a coat. It's freezing out here,' I reprimanded. She had on a green cashmere cardigan over a red turtleneck – pretty much her festive look for as long as I could remember – but it wasn't enough to protect from today's bitter temperature.

'She's right, let Nate and I unpack. You two should go inside,' commented Dad.

'Nonsense, Bill, we can at least get the girls, can't we?' she argued, and I had a sudden jolt of panic as I realised the twins were still alone in the car.

As if reading my thoughts, Nate smiled. 'It's barely been thirty seconds, honey.'

Moments later, we'd extricated both babies from their car seats. I held a fussy Suzy in my arms, while Mum crooned to a smiling Katie.

'My little warriors,' she said, placing a kiss on Katie's forehead before reaching over to Suzy to stroke her little face, instantly calming my hungry baby with her touch. 'Oh, and look at these adorable snowsuits . . . they look so perfect.' As we turned to head into the house, she gave me one of her famous looks. 'As do you, love. A whole day's travelling with a couple of newborns and your family looks like you've all just walked out of a Brown Thomas catalogue. Anyone else would be ragged.'

I smiled, about to tell her that navigating SFO via the Aer Lingus lounge made flying a breeze, that I'd only changed them into the suits at a service station on the way, and that the car had looked like the aftermath of a hurricane before then.

'But not my firstborn,' she continued proudly. 'Unflappable to the last – so of course motherhood shouldn't be any different.'

'Actually . . .' I cleared my throat, about to confess the behind-the-scenes chaos, but was drowned out by the horn of a Volkswagen Beetle loudly blaring its arrival.

An already irritable Suzy now erupted in an ear-splitting yowl. 'Typical,' I muttered under my breath as I went straight into crisis mode, trying to calm my daughter. My younger brother had always been the harbinger of little else but chaos. 'Will he ever grow up?' I muttered, rolling my eyes good-naturedly.

We all glanced in Matt's direction as he brought the car to a stop and rolled down the window, shouting, 'Merry Christmas! Ho! Ho! Ho!' in the worst Santa voice.

'You know your brother. Always the life and soul . . .'

Thirty-six years old and life was still a huge joke to him, which always had the ability to get under my skin. And probably also because his laissez-faire attitude to everything was in such stark contrast to my own.

Now my brother sprang from the car and headed in our direction. I bounced Suzy in my arms to try to quiet her, but it was clear she was not happy with this entire situation, or indeed her Uncle Matt's gleeful greeting.

'Hey, it's the Silicon Valley contingent. How's Bill and Melinda?'

It was an ancient joke that had long fallen flat. 'Hi, Matt, great to see you,' I said, turning towards the front door. 'Sorry, but we've just arrived and I really need to get the girls in the house – it's cold, and they're tired and hungry after the flight.'

'Hello, love, you're early. And where's Hazel?' my mother called out by way of greeting, her brow furrowing a little. 'I thought you said she was coming with you?'

Matt lived in Galway, where he worked in advertising – probably because he fancied himself as a bit of a Don Draper – and Hazel was his long-suffering girlfriend.

'She'll be along,' he answered, his voice thick with ambiguity as he engulfed our mother in a huge bear hug. 'Hey, yourself.'

'Whoops, be careful. Don't crush your niece,' she chided.

'Sure we have a spare, don't we?' he guffawed. He looked down at my daughter and grinned. 'So which one is it?'

'Katie,' I answered tersely. 'And she's not an "it".'

'Calm down, sis. I'm only messing.' He turned his baby-blue eyes on me – and that devilish puppy-dog look that charmed pretty much every woman on the planet.

Apart from his sisters, obviously.

'So, when *is* Hazel coming then?' I pressed. I got along well with his girlfriend, though I still couldn't for the life of me understand how she put up with my head wreck of a brother.

'Oh, a work thing came up – she's going to pop down in a day or two. There was, I don't know . . . some last-minute contract or something that needed to get done. Court stuff.' He rolled his eyes. Whatever his girlfriend had going on wasn't necessarily on his radar.

I tilted my head in contemplation while Matt and the others chatted. He'd been dating Hazel for about a year – and I'd be lying if I said I didn't like her. In fact, I loved her, and I truly hoped that my brother would do his best not to mess it up this time. Relationships were never his strong suit – or more likely, knowing my roguish brother, *fidelity* wasn't.

'Anyway,' he added now, nudging Nate, 'you know what women are like. Always changing their pretty little heads at the last minute.'

'Didn't you say the girls were hungry, Joanna?' Mum said, shooting me a conspiratorial glance. 'Better get them inside.'

As always, she knew exactly when to intervene.

Chapter 2

'Nice houses round here . . .' the taxi driver commented as the car wound along the road. Romy glanced down at the MyTaxi app; his name was Farhad and he spoke with a subtle accent. 'Like from *Home Alone*, yes?' He had lived in Ireland for ten years now – even though it was very different from Delhi, he said.

She had to smile. Her dad's outdoor light displays and mum's indoor festive decor put the very best of Christmas movies to shame and, growing up, her parents always went out of their way to make this time of year wondrous and magical.

'Well, we're not quite the McCallisters, but it was a lovely place to grow up,' she replied. 'But just so you know, the entrance sneaks up on you a bit. It's coming up about twenty yards on the left.'

She pulled her phone out of her bag and clicked on to the selfie lens, checking her reflection. Not too bad, all things considered . . .

Almost a day's travel to get here. But on her minuscule publishing assistant salary she couldn't afford a plane ticket from London at this time of year – Christmas fares were a form of daylight robbery – and she wasn't going to ask her parents for the money. It would just make them worry more than they already did.

And she really didn't want to tell them that she had travelled by bus to and from the ports on either side, for the same reason.

'GPS is telling me to turn here? Is this correct?' he asked, snapping Romy back to reality.

'Yup.' Catching a long-awaited first glimpse of her childhood home, she smiled.

'*Very* nice house,' he commented, and again she felt a bit self-conscious; the house was like something out of a vintage Christmas card and the upmarket area spoke for itself.

Yet, he had picked *her* up at a bus stop.

A moment later, she got out and grabbed her suitcase out of the boot of the Honda before providing Farhad with a final thank you. Then on the app gave him a good rating and a tiny tip. It had been just a short trip and she couldn't afford much – but 'twas the season, after all, and he was a nice guy.

Romy noticed two cars already in the driveway – one evidently a rental, plus the instantly recognisable Beetle – and realised that her siblings and extended family were already here.

Despite her tiredness, her heart lifted. She couldn't wait to see everyone, and of course there were two brand-new members of the clan that she hadn't yet met . . .

Unlike the rest of the family, she didn't make her nieces' acquaintance after their birth and it had been absolutely killing her. But airfare to San Francisco would have been truly insane – and even though Joanna had wanted to arrange a ticket at the time, Romy didn't want handouts. It just wasn't her style.

Besides, she didn't want to run the risk of taking time off from the promising admin role she was in that looked like it might turn to something higher up in editorial . . . until it didn't.

So what else was new . . .

Anyway, she wasn't going to focus on or even *think* about depressing work stuff now.

Hefting up her suitcase to keep it off the slippery path, Romy looked up at the house and sighed happily.

The sky was just turning dusky with the last of the low winter sun and the multicoloured string lights decorating the roofline twinkled happily. Then, as if on cue, her dad's 'famous' giant illuminated reindeer sprang to life on the lawn.

Being surrounded by these reminders of her youth made her happy and nostalgic all at once, as great memories of seasons past, and more carefree times, flooded back in a rush.

I really needed this.

Picking up the suitcase, she began the trudge up the stone steps to the front door, to be immediately welcomed by one of her mother's home-made holly-berry wreaths surrounding the old brass knocker, the arched door frame bordered by a thick festive garland of fresh pine, twinkling lights and red velvet bows.

For as long as Romy could remember, this house had been her salvation – a place of love and laughter in which she could truly cocoon and escape from the rest of the world.

And this year would be no different.

She reached a gloved hand out to turn the heavy brass doorknob, but before she could even grasp it, the door flew wide open and she was met with the tantalising scent of cinnamon and nutmeg, mixed with tangy smokiness from the open fire blazing in the living room to her left.

'Love, you're here!' her mum exclaimed, with delight in her eyes.

Then her brother, Matt, appeared alongside her mother like an excited puppy, snatching her suitcase, and all at once, Romy was consumed. Wrapped in her mum's arms, it was as if a million greetings and questions were being thrown her way as she was ushered through the door and into the welcome warmth.

She saw a flash of Joanna's stylishly coiffed blonde hair as her ever glamourous sister turned to introduce a little pink bundle in her arms, and her dad bringing up the rear with an identical, noisier bundle.

Her brother-in-law emerged from the kitchen in the back with a glass of wine and a plate of mince pies, as her beloved dad engulfed her in his strong arms and she looked down on the innocent faces of her nieces for the first time.

It was pure joyous sensory overload.

And right then, Romy didn't have a care in the world.

Chapter 3

All three of you arrived in a flurry today – and I truly could not be happier to have our entire clan together again under the same roof.

How lucky I am to be a mother to such interesting personalities; each so unique unto yourselves.

My darling Joanna, so driven, ambitious and focused – and now you're a mother, too. I am beyond excited to spend this first Christmas with my granddaughters. And I have no doubt that I'll continue to be amazed by whatever it is you've set your mind to next – you've always been the girl with the next big idea up her sleeve.

You're probably already lining up your goals for next year, and I wouldn't doubt it if you were single-handedly running that Silicon Valley company of yours by the end of it. Though I must admit, as ever I remain a little at a loss as to what exactly it is you do.

Then Matt, my dear, sweet boy . . . no, that's not right – man. Now you are a man who is going in the right direction – and are trying your best every day. I know you have always been competitive with Joanna, but I think you should set your own goals now.

Your big sister has played by a different set of rules her whole life. And also well aware that she is not a man – hence the difference in the rules. Whereas you, on the other hand, well, let's be honest here. We both know you have and will continue to have it much easier.

Regardless, I'm confident for your future, even though you are still working out the kinks of life. And thankfully, there is Hazel now too. I think you have found your match in her, sweetheart. Do your best to hold on to this one.

While of course you've always loved your fun, I can already see that she's been good for you, helping you grow into the solid, responsible man you are beneath the immature macho bluster.

And Romy. Oh my baby girl, now I must admit I worry most of all about you – as does your father.

While I know your determination abounds – it's impossible not to be concerned. You know I wasn't sure if moving to London to seek out a career in the big city was the right answer for you . . . and with full transparency, I'm still not sure.

You have always had such a good heart, one that I fear might be taken advantage of all too easily in a cut-throat world.

Bear with me, mo chroi, *I'm your mother and I have a right to worry.*

And while I'm all too sadly aware what the future holds for me, I sorely wish I had a crystal ball to consult as to what it ultimately intends for each of you.

◆ ◆ ◆

'Nate, pass me another sausage roll,' I said, juggling Katie, who was sleeping in one arm while I reached out the other to take the plate from Nate. 'Honestly, I feel like I've been looking forward to these all *year.*' Then, glancing in my mother's direction, I frowned a little. 'Mum, aren't you hungry?'

Her own freshly baked pastry went untouched on her plate – and I'd noticed the same with an earlier serving of her famous breakfast fry of black pudding, rashers, mushrooms and hash browns.

'Ah, don't worry about me. I was just up way too late last night.' She smiled weakly and I found myself once again in assessment mode. She had definitely lost some weight. 'Here, give Katie to me, I can hold her while you eat.'

She quickly got up and took my daughter from my arms, which I had to admit was helpful, and I appraised her frame as she turned away. She wasn't a big woman, had always been tall and lithe, but it was clear that she was smaller under her clothes. But I decided I would hold my tongue – for now.

'So, what's the plan for today?' I enquired of the table. Each member of the family was busy eating and having their own conversations, and all abruptly stopped as my question hung in the air.

'Does there always have to be a plan, Jo?' Matt smirked, rolling his eyes. 'Isn't it enough just to be able to sit back and relax without an agenda?'

Admittedly, my brother was right. It's just . . . I had a hard time when I didn't have a detailed schedule to follow.

'Now now, Matt,' Romy interjected, grinning. 'You know that at ten a.m. it's time for present wrapping, followed by Mass at eleven. After that some lunch, preferably finished by one p.m. so it's time for the twins' nap. Then at two p.m. time to watch a movie – something like *Love Actually*, which is approximately two hours long, because at four the twins will need to be fed and then at five, dinner will be served.' My sister's voice was proper and dripped with authority, and even I had to smile at just how well she mimicked me. 'Upon completion of all activities, we will then fill out surveys in order to determine which were most successful and which need to be discontinued. Formal analytics will then be carried out and correlated with algorithmic forecasting and/or projections, and all will be evaluated before findings sent to upper management.'

She, Matt, and my traitorous husband erupted into laughter, and out of the corner of my eye I even saw Dad snort a laugh.

'Romy,' Mum said, also hiding a grin, 'don't make fun of your sister. Motherhood is a huge adjustment – especially moving from such highly structured days to . . . well, chaos.' She rocked Katie peacefully in her arms. 'And she's right to impose routine. I was much the same with you three.' She looked down and placed a gentle kiss on the baby's forehead.

'You must be so relieved to be going back to work then, sis,' Matt commented, and Romy looked from me to Nate.

'Are you doing company day care or getting a nanny in?' she asked conversationally.

'When *do* you go back to work, hon?' Dad asked, and suddenly I felt the eyes of the room on me.

Nerves flooded into my bloodstream and I looked down at my plate. 'Well . . .' I started.

'I think we're targeting the last week of January,' offered Nate, sending a supportive smile in my direction.

The nerves turned to guilt at the fact that even my own husband didn't know what I was thinking.

'Probably counting down the days, eh, Jo?' Matt chuckled as he took a huge bite of sausage roll, which left a smattering of flaky crumbs across his cheek in the same way it had when he was a two-year-old. 'Can't wait to get back in the office and start cracking that whip – there's that big promotion coming up soon too, isn't there?'

I touched my hand to my own cheek and looked at my brother. 'Napkin. Your face.'

He simply smiled at me and continued chewing. The crumbs stayed put – at least until Dad tossed a napkin in his direction.

'You're in line for another promotion?' Romy asked, wide-eyed, and was I imagining it or was there a hint of envy in her tone?

My sister and I had always been close, despite an eight-year age difference and being complete chalk and cheese. While I was the go-getter in the family, she and Matt had always been more go-with-the-flow.

I squared my shoulders and gave a non-committal shrug. 'Yes, there was chatter about an upwards move before I went on maternity. The new platform is about to go live soon . . .'

A major new product launch was in the offing for the new year, coinciding with when my maternity leave ended. The financial tech start-up I worked at – well, I was actually executive vice president – was growing in leaps and bounds. Truly, the sky was the limit and

I was on board a rocket ship. And because of that – well, probably because of how I was programmed – I had worked literally up until the moment my waters broke. Regrettably, this had been in the middle of a conference call with shareholders and, yes, I had been mortified.

By habit, I liked to keep personal and professional life completely separate, and had stressed about having to leave so abruptly. It was expected that I would be back to oversee the launch of Nano-AI, which had been my first baby for the last few years – a highly anticipated piece of tech that would launch us to the next level.

But now, I wasn't so sure . . .

'And yet the earth continues to spin on its axis without you,' Matt teased. 'So, why the hesitation then?' Despite the joker facade, my brother was, in fact, sharp as a tack and I gulped a little, before realising that everyone was still staring at me. 'I'm sorry – what?'

'Someone's got Mammy Brain,' Romy joked, and instinctively I stuck out my tongue at her.

'It's not that,' I said quietly. 'It's just . . . a different pace being at home. I really want to ensure that the girls get off to a great start in life and—'

'It's a transition,' Nate offered. 'We just want to get through the holidays, and then begin the process of hiring a nanny. FinTech has an amazing campus childcare programme, of course, but we really want the girls to be at home with a dedicated professional.'

I felt a deep sense of almost . . . revulsion as my husband continued to talk about 'The Nanny Plan', as he had taken to calling it. It had even been the title of the PowerPoint he had created. Truth be told, I wasn't the biggest fan of some stranger coming into my house and taking care of my children. Not when I was perfectly capable.

But of course there was also the glaring truth. I couldn't take care of the girls if I had a full-time job – a *very* full-time job, with a path that only went upwards . . . and if the product launch went well, likely straight to VP in the next six months or so.

I had always believed that I could have it all, but lately I'd been thinking that maybe I didn't *want* it all.

Not any more.

Chapter 4

Like every mother, I want nothing but the best for you. All of you.

So I'm grateful for the opportunity to hold each one of you close, see your smiling faces and, yes, as always, try to detect any waves of trouble beneath those bright facades.

Because I know you, all of you. I have worried about you since the moment I knew you existed, when you were all but a small spark of life inside me – and I will keep on worrying about you for the rest of eternity.

It's what mothers do.

Now, don't roll your eyes at that. Everyone knows Irish mammies are more talented than bloodhounds at sniffing out what's really going on behind those smiles.

Though in truth, it's hard to believe there could be anything wrong anywhere in the world when we're all together in this house, with the tree and the lights, mountains of food, and general festive mayhem.

Impossible to imagine the perfection of this time being tarnished.

Which is why I'm especially glad that you didn't seem to notice my own inner turmoil.

Although, OK, Joanna, I saw the look that you gave me when you first got out of the car. Of course you never miss a trick and, yes, I know I'm down a few pounds. It's just my appetite is a bit off. I was warned about that, of course, but I really wasn't sure what smells or tastes would trigger it – or when.

Jo, again, I'm always so awed by you. I always have been, but now that you are a mother too . . . I just want to soak up your interactions with the girls. I am really going to enjoy observing you just now. This is such a special time – and the girls will benefit in the long run from the bonding we all do together.

I also can't wait to soak up spending as much time as possible with you all myself. A mother's need for connection with her children never ends, no matter what age they happen to be.

Matt, I really do hope that Hazel shows. It was a bit of a disappointment to see you arrive solo. I truly hope there isn't trouble in paradise.

And Romy, my sweet, brave baby girl. Yes, you walked in during a flurry of activity – hugs and kisses abound – but I did spot that there was no airline tag on your suitcase. Unlike your sister, who tears these off practically the moment she gets off the plane, you're not one for that kind of detail.

When you were a kid you kept those tags on until I took them off for you.

Honey, I know you're terribly proud of moving to London to make a career for yourself in the literary world. That it was always your dream.

But the city is such an expensive spot, especially on a lower-paying job – and I'm concerned.

You can talk to me and your dad if you're struggling. And you should definitely ask for help if you need to.

There's no shame in that.

OK, enough for now. I hear the twins are awake from their nap and I have few enough opportunities to help out with my only grandchildren.

And I need to make a jump on prepping more food. The other thing about this family is that we are all so very good at eating.

So cross your fingers for me and my appetite over the next day or two.

My legendary festive recipes have always been favourites for good reason.

◆ ◆ ◆

'So how's life in the Big Smoke?' Matt enquired, as he lounged on the couch in the front living room.

Romy looked at him from where she stood by the window, taking her eyes momentarily off the twinkling Christmas tree. 'Shoes off the couch,' she said, in a perfect mimic of their mother.

Begrudgingly, her brother kicked off his Brooks trainers one at a time and wiggled his socked toes as he readjusted his body on the couch.

She crinkled her nose. 'Ugh. I can smell your feet all the way over here.'

'Like roses, I'm sure,' he replied. 'So how goes it in London Town? Find the next J.K. Rowling yet?'

'Not exactly.'

The truth was that after multiple internships and a deluge of lower-paying administrative roles, she was still struggling to work her way up the ladder to editorial, where her heart truly lay. Never mind finding the next 'hot' author – in truth, Romy would give anything to be involved with any authors at all.

She turned her attention back to the tree and reached for a crude home-made clay 'angel' bedecked in green glitter.

'Hey,' she said over her shoulder, 'it's Skeletor. I'd forgotten about him.' She had made this ornament in school and Matt had promptly named it Skeletor. She'd been upset at the time but had to admit now that her brother was right – it absolutely looked more like He-Man's nemesis than the Angel Gabriel.

'A classic,' Matt said. 'So are you going to keep avoiding my question or what?'

Romy sighed. He was as persistent as a Jack Russell terrier when he wanted to be.

She shrugged. 'London is fine.'

'And how's the latest job going?'

She rolled her eyes. 'It's . . . going.'

Sighing, he leaned forward, his expression changed from 'highly annoying older brother' to 'concerned and only slightly annoying older brother'.

'Seriously, why don't you let me help you? I have a couple of publishing connections over there. I know you said you don't want to work on the marketing side, but at least it'd be something to tide you over and maybe a faster way up to editorial?' he offered earnestly. And if Matt was being earnest, it must be obvious that things were bad.

Averting her eyes, she played with a strand of sandy blonde hair that had escaped from her messy topknot.

'I told you, I don't like handouts,' she said simply. To say nothing of the idea that she had no interest in advertising or marketing books; her passion lay purely in the storytelling side, finding great writers and sharing their talent with the world. But even with her Arts and Literature degree, the publishing industry had proved a remarkably difficult one in which to progress through the ranks – that is, if you were lucky enough to secure a position in the holy grail of Editorial. And so far, Romy was struggling to do either.

'It's not a handout. It's simply . . . help. I'm not offering to pay your rent, sis; I'm offering to help you get a head start in obtaining the job of your dreams, so you can pay your rent and have enough left over to maybe have a life. There is a difference.'

Romy swallowed hard. 'Matt, I really appreciate it. I do. You and Joanna have both offered assistance and introductions, and it's not like I'm turning up my nose or anything. I just – well – I just want to do things on my own. I want to work my way up on merit. I want to live my life on *my* terms. Unlike you, a social life is not the be-all and end-all for me. And I definitely don't want anyone thinking of me as the useless little sister of high-achieving Moores who needed to call on connections to get anywhere.'

Now it was Matt's turn to roll his eyes. 'You're placing me in the same category as Joanna? Much obliged.'

Romy couldn't help but smile. Their brother had always been proud of his ability to coast through life, while still managing to nab the proverbial first-place trophy. Overachiever he was most certainly not.

'You know what I mean. It's not like you aren't successful.'

'Not going to argue with that. It's just . . . maybe keep it in mind, OK?' He smiled at her. 'London can be a tough city, and everyone needs an outlet now and again.'

'So everyone keeps reminding me.' Romy poked the errant strand of hair back into the rubber band on top of her head. 'Ah, I'm still just finding my bearings really.'

She tried to ignore the undeniable truth that, following a brief diversion into bookselling directly after uni, she had been in London for almost two years now – working positions that all too often led nowhere. While she'd made some wonderful friends in the business, lower-level industry salaries weren't enough to support much of a social life in – as Matt pointed out – such an expensive city.

And as for dating . . . after going on a string of incredibly frustrating and unproductive dates via OKCupid, Coffee Meets Bagel and Tinder, she had ended up deleting most of them from her phone when she realised the lads she met were more interested in short-term hook-ups than anything meaningful.

Which made the dating scene a little trickier, to say the least . . . especially when lads now seemed to expect everyone to look like fitspo influencer types IRL, whereas Romy had been 'blessed' with her dad's rugby-player frame.

It wasn't as if she was overweight, just big-boned, as her mother always said, but this, coupled with her limited wardrobe budget, meant that she just couldn't compete with the polished, well-heeled InstaHuns.

But this reminded her of something and now she eyed Matt's discarded trainers on the floor. She couldn't remember the last time she'd bought a non-work-related pair of shoes, let alone athletic ones. Probably back at school – for mandatory PE lessons. PE had been anything but mandatory since then. 'Are those Brooks?'

Matt cast a glance down. 'Yeah, latest edition. Why? Are you in the market?'

She shrugged non-committally. 'They expensive?'

'Eh' – Matt made a face – 'one-twenty, one-thirty, something like that?' he said offhandedly, as if dropping a hundred and thirty quid on trainers was no big deal. 'Why? Planning a new diet in the New Year . . . *Operation Transformation* or something? You know those things never work, sis.'

She felt her insides steel.

'Just maybe setting myself a challenge . . .' She let her words hang in the air, wondering if Matt would pick up on anything. She'd intended on mentioning her plan during this stay, just casually, because she guessed it was something the family would baulk at.

'Cool.' He sounded disinterested, though, so Romy decided to steer the conversation in a different direction.

'How about your own New Year's resolutions? With Hazel – maybe even a diamond for Christmas?' she enquired, noticing him briefly tense at her words.

Her brother had settled down a hell of a lot since he started going out with Hazel last year, and seemed to truly adore her, which was why they'd all anticipated that an engagement might even be on the cards.

But since his arrival, he'd been nothing but evasive when pressed about her unexpected non-appearance thus far.

'Not sure,' he replied airily. 'I guess we'll just have to wait and see how it goes, you know?'

A beat of silence passed.

'No, Matt, I don't know. None of us do, because every time we've brought up her name you start to squirm,' she said bluntly. 'What's going on? Did you two break up? Something's wrong, I know that much anyway.'

Matt groaned and put his hands over his eyes, as if blotting out the light of the room could remove him from his sister's inquisition.

'OK, you've got me. The truth is, I actually came down a little earlier so I could have a day or two by myself. It's just, there was a situation . . . at the office Christmas party last week.' He flicked a gaze in her direction, his expression wary. 'I might have had one too many drinks, and well . . . You know how these things go, everyone's going a bit mad on the gargle . . .'

Romy had seen that look on her brother's face countless times when they were kids – whenever he was in trouble. No one could ever accuse Matt of having a poker face.

'No, I don't know how these things go. Please don't tell me you did something stupid . . .'

He grabbed a cushion and placed it over his face, like he always did when they were kids and didn't want to face a lecture. 'Kind of.'

'Matt, just tell me.'

Sighing heavily, he sat up to face her, then ran his hands through his dark hair, making small spikes of it stand on end, and immediately Romy was reminded of the time when, at fourteen, he'd been caught drinking up the woods with a gang of lads.

He wore pretty much the same expression then – one that she always attributed to not being particularly sorry for his actions, more sorry that he got caught.

And she figured he was up to his old womanising tricks again.

'It's not. I mean it's not . . . great. Just not a big deal really. There's this colleague – at work – and . . . um . . . well, something got blown way out of proportion. At the party. Everyone was drinking, and things got a bit out of hand . . . and . . . I kind of decked someone.'

'What?' This time, she truly was caught unawares. Her brother certainly always talked a good game, but she couldn't seriously imagine him getting in a physical fight. 'But why? What happened? And who did you hit?'

'Some guy – from the office – who was being an ass.'

His cheeks reddened and he looked sharply down at the floor. And Romy knew right then that her earlier suspicions were likely correct, and there was more to this than he was prepared to let on.

A lot more.

'The main problem is that he's a superior – my boss, actually,' he added, wincing, and she looked up, horrified. 'And I broke a couple of his teeth. So now they have to do . . . well, they're calling it a disciplinary investigation, but honestly, it wasn't that big of a deal,' he stuttered. 'Just a big misunderstanding, really. I've apologised for the teeth thing, so I'm sure when he calms down he'll retract the complaint. But yeah, in the meantime . . .' He tripped over the rest. 'While all that official stuff happens, I've kind of been put on a leave of absence . . .'

Chapter 5

Romy and I wandered in companionable silence along the wood-land path through the forestry trail close to our house. It was still pretty frosty and wet underfoot, but thankfully I kept a wardrobe full of clothes, as well as shoes (and hiking boots), that I might need during visits home, just in case.

Never knowingly underprepared.

Whereas my little sister could not have been more different, and was currently wearing the same pair of flat Converse she'd arrived in.

'Your feet are going to be drenched in those.'

She reached up and wiped her gloved hand across her nose. Her cheeks were bright pink with the cold. 'Doesn't matter,' she mumbled. 'I'd rather be out here freezing and wet than listening to Matt suck up to Mum and Dad.'

'I hear you.'

'What do you think?' she asked then. 'About all that?'

What did I think? Much like the rest of us, I'd been gob-smacked last night when Matt had told us about his work issue. He'd tried to play it down to my parents – insisting it was just a scuffle that had got out of hand – but the fact that there was going to be an official investigation told, for me, its own story.

'I think there's definitely more to it than what he's told us anyway. More likely he and this guy were squared up in some kind of macho territorial thing over a woman they were chatting up or something – you know what he's like. Either way, it's pretty pathetic. He's a grown man, not a five-year-old.' I shook my head in dismay. 'He should know better.'

Romy was nodding in agreement. 'I thought the same, especially when he's being so weird about Hazel. But then to go on and play the whole "poor little old me" card with Mum and Dad, who of course fall for it hook, line, and sinker – *again*. I don't know how he does it, Jo, but somehow Matt always manages to come up smelling of roses. I mean, seriously . . .' Her voice trailed off but the frustration in her tone was palpable, and I got the sense that this was about more than just our brother.

'I hear you. And put it this way, if he worked for me, there'd be no pussy-footing around with an investigation. Nope, his ass would already be out the door.'

Romy chuckled. 'I want to be like you when I grow up.'

It was an old joke but I hadn't heard it for a while and it felt good.

'Are you OK?' I asked then, putting my arm around her shoulders. 'You seem a bit . . . down this year.'

'Ah, I'm OK. Just wish I had a bit more of that devil-may-care swagger myself sometimes – then I might actually get somewhere in life.'

'No, you don't, that's not who you are.' Growing up, we'd always been close, but time – to say nothing of living on opposite sides of the globe – had taken its toll on our relationship over the years. 'Though I do wish you would let me help out every now and then.' I cast a sideways glance at her, referencing the plane ticket to California I'd offered when the twins were born – as well as other things from time to time. 'I know it's not easy when you're starting out . . .'

I was eight years her senior. When I finished university, it was a different world. She had come of age during a major recession and that alone would have changed the trajectory of her career. I had already been established and was on my way up, but she had stalled on the bottom floor. Not to mention the fact her chosen field was notoriously difficult to break into, whereas mine was arguably more open and dynamic.

She sighed. 'I'm not really just starting out, though, am I?' she replied, her voice heavy, and I immediately regretted my words.

'No, no, of course not. I didn't mean it that way. I'm not blind to how things were different for me either. I shouldn't have said that.'

Romy's experiences would have been different to mine in more ways than one. As a child she had always been on the bigger side, whereas I had inherited my mum's Scandinavian ancestry – tall, with an athletic build and the ability to eat pretty much whatever we liked without worrying about it. Romy was shorter, like our dad; also blonde, but full-figured with curves and boobs that I didn't have, and had sorely envied when we were younger.

To my mind, she was drop-dead gorgeous, but I also knew that she had been picked on for her size in the past. And guys had acted as if she should be grateful that they'd even give her the time of day.

'I so admire you, Jo, you know that. But . . . sometimes it can be hard being the one bringing up the rear all the time, when the others have already crossed the finish line.' She smiled. 'Matt seems to just coast through life no matter what, and you . . . well, where do I even start? You've done so many amazing things in business, found a lovely and successful husband. And now motherhood under your belt too. I'm in awe of you. Everyone is. You're the one who really can do it all.'

Then she sniffed a little and I wasn't sure if she had started to cry or if it was just the cold.

As if reading my mind, she wiped her nose. 'And then there's me. Forget getting to the top of the career ladder; even a decent grip on a rung would be more than enough. No boyfriend. A splurge for me is buying a takeaway of a Friday evening. Once I've covered the rent I can't afford anything else, including a social life. I'm thirty years of age and I've nothing to show for my time on earth. Nothing. I haven't accomplished anything – not a single bloody thing.'

I felt at a loss for words. I had suspected as much about Romy's situation, but had never asked how she felt about it, assuming she'd come to terms with the fact that her choice of career would be challenging unless she happened to be in prime position to discover the next literary superstar.

But I especially hated that she believed I was at one end of the spectrum and she was at the other. Doomed forever to remain in the shadow of the ultimate overachiever.

And for a moment, I felt like spilling my guts to her. To tell her what I was thinking. To let her know that I really *didn't* have everything figured out. And while she and everyone else might think I could do it all, it didn't necessarily mean I wanted to.

I opened my mouth and took a deep breath, steeling myself to make my own inner thoughts public for the first time. To tell my sister things I hadn't even told Nate. Verbalise all of the stuff that I had been withholding even from myself . . . but then, she spoke again.

'So, I've decided that next year, I want to achieve *something*.'

'That's great,' I replied encouragingly, though I'd never been one for New Year's resolutions. For me, resolve was an ongoing state of mind.

'Yes, and I . . . oh!'

Whatever my sister was about to say next was interrupted by someone almost crashing into her from behind, as she stepped sideways to avoid a puddle. 'Sorry,' she apologised, as a jogger trying to pass us on the trail held a hand up in a friendly gesture.

He glanced at us and was about to move on, then stopped.

'Well, hello there, strangers,' the guy greeted us, and I vaguely recognised but couldn't place him.

'Hey, Luke. Really sorry about that – I almost sent you flying into next week.' Romy laughed, and at the mention of the name it immediately clicked into place who he was.

Luke Dooley, an old Gaelic teammate of Matt's and by all accounts a local sporting hero back in the day.

'Not a bother, sure I should have made myself known instead of creeping up behind ye,' he said, grinning. 'Home for Christmas?'

Romy nodded, and I noticed with interest that she was blushing a little beneath his gaze.

'Yep, just out blowing off some cobwebs,' I said, smiling inwardly at her almost schoolgirlish reaction. While he'd been too young for me to notice when we were growing up, it seemed my sister hadn't outgrown the hero-worship thing, and I could see why.

He was also very handsome, probably even more so as an adult. Age had filled out all the gangly youth, giving him a more rugged jawline, and the activewear attire he now sported emphasised his toned chest and athletic legs.

Yep, Luke Dooley was now a bit of a hottie. Though, as he chatted away easily to us, he also seemed refreshingly down to earth.

'Same as meself,' he said with a wink, while continuing to jog on the spot. 'Nothing like a good 10k to get the blood moving. Haven't seen you in yonks, Romy – how's life in London?'

'Great . . . It's great,' she mumbled, though both of us struggled to get a word in as Luke continued to – as my mother would say

– 'talk the hind legs off a donkey'. Though I noticed how his eyes seemed to soften a lot when he addressed my sister.

Interesting . . .

'Right,' he finished eventually, 'better get going before I seize up altogether. Matt home too? Sure maybe I'll catch ye all down in The Shamrock one of the nights for a catch-up?' he added, referring to the village local.

'Definitely,' I replied, for Romy's benefit, and as Luke moved off again, she shot me a glare.

Then once he was at a safe distance, we both dissolved into laughter.

'I'd forgotten how good the views around here were,' I chuckled, before returning to our previous topic of conversation. 'So, what was it you were thinking . . . about the New Year's resolution thing?'

'Actually, I might try to meet up with Luke,' she said thoughtfully. 'The very man for what I have in mind . . .'

I stared at her, surprised, wondering for a second if she was actually planning to ask him out, which would've been a first. Good for her.

But if I'd had a crystal ball and a stacked deck of tarot cards, I still would never have predicted my sister's next words.

'I'm going to train for a marathon next year.'

My mouth dropped open and I turned to look at her, incredulity written on my face. I hastily tried to rearrange my expression – but she simply smiled.

'The Dublin Marathon, Jo. I'm going to do it, I'm going to run it, and I'm going to finish it.'

◆ ◆ ◆

The entire family was looking at Romy like she'd started sprouting carrots out of her ears.

Her dad shifted uncomfortably in his chair while he balanced baby Suzy in his arms. 'Pet, I think it's great to set goals for yourself. That's a sign of character. It's just, well . . . a marathon, love? There are experienced runners who can't even do that.'

'Thanks for the vote of confidence, Dad.' She knew they'd be dubious, but she was especially stung by Joanna's initial reaction.

'I'm not saying you couldn't do it. I'm totally not saying that,' her sister had said earlier in her American twang, while they were out on their walk. 'But maybe you might want to start with, I don't know . . . something shorter, just to see? I have a friend who's a marathoner – but she started with 5k and 10k races – and then worked up to the long-distance stuff after.'

Matt was nodding thoughtfully. 'Like Dad says, it's . . . brave. But in fairness, I don't think anyone in this room would be wrong in saying that you aren't a runner, sis. Sure, you were never even able to run a lap of a pitch in school.'

Hurt, she snapped her head in his direction. 'I'd just like a little support, OK? This is important to me. It's a way for me to feel like I can achieve *something*. I have just felt so . . . stuck in a rut lately and to me this feels like movement – a course correction, the kind of redirection my life needs.'

Joanna suddenly looked contemplative. 'You know, you're right, I totally get it. I understand. There's nothing wrong in wanting to try something new. Start down a new path. Actually, even I've been thinking—'

Romy looked at her hopefully, but whatever her sister was about to say or whatever show of solidarity she was about to reveal, she didn't get to finish the sentence.

Because bloody Matt cut her off.

'It'll be expensive to start,' he smirked. 'I know plenty of running types. They drop serious dough on their gear and you said yourself you haven't a ha'penny. You planning to run twenty-six miles in those ratty oul Converse or . . . ?'

'Matthew. Apologise to your sister,' her dad barked, and his admonishment immediately reducing Matt to the naughty child of old, he muttered a begrudging 'sorry'.

'I know about the expense,' Romy admitted. 'But I was thinking about doing a few hours with Deliveroo or somewhere in the evenings so I could make some extra money to buy that stuff – whatever I need to do it right.'

Her mum smiled. 'Love, you've always been one for hard work and getting stuck in no matter what. I'm proud of you for what you are trying to do. And I know you'll do it too.'

As always, her mother knew exactly the right thing to say and Romy beamed. 'Thanks, Mum.'

'But why not let your dad and I help you with the stuff you need to train, maybe starting with the runners as a Christmas present. How does that sound?'

Automatically, she started to shake her head in refusal, but something in her mother's tone stopped her. She'd wanted support, after all.

'I think that sounds brilliant, thank you.'

'And let me get you a second pair, or a voucher for Lifestyle Sports or somewhere,' Joanna added. 'As a Christmas present, like Mum said. You're going to need two pairs anyway. One for training and then another to run the race. Every runner I know has loads – apparently each pair only has a few hundred miles in them. You burn through serious rubber with the training alone and then there's all that other stuff to stop you chafing and blisters and all that. Let me check in with my friend who ran the San Francisco

Marathon this year – I'll ask her advice about all this stuff, or any other tips and tricks she might have.'

A momentary worry emerged as the enormity of what Romy was about to embark upon settled in. Until she'd actually said it out loud, it didn't feel real.

She had, of course, researched a little and knew that she'd need to quite literally do the groundwork – put in hours of training, as well as how much tarmac she would be pounding – but to have it presented like that in 'a few hundred miles' and with all this talk about chafing . . . well, there was no denying it made her heart flutter with nervous anticipation.

Joanna seemed to read her thoughts. 'Don't worry. Everything's doable once you have a plan of action.'

Romy took a deep breath and swallowed away the doubt. 'Thanks, guys.'

'Yes, you're well able for this, love.' Her mother came and sat next to her, leaning in close, resting her head for a moment on Romy's shoulder. 'And, sweetheart, believe me, I would give anything to see you cross that finish line.'

Chapter 6

After lunch over a lukewarm cup of coffee, I wound down the twins for their afternoon nap.

Balancing my left foot on the bouncy seat Katie was snuggled in, I gazed absently at her twin, who was staring at the PlayMobil animals above her own chair. I felt so far away in my thoughts that I didn't even hear the kitchen door open and my mother enter.

'Earth to Jo,' she said quietly, but I jumped nonetheless.

'Sorry – I didn't mean to startle you. Just thought you might need a warm-up.' Mum held a pot of coffee in her left hand and her own cup in her right. 'And maybe a bit of company?'

I nodded. 'Yeah, that would be lovely.' I retracted my foot from the edge of Katie's chair now that her eyes had grown heavy. 'And . . . she's out.' I looked with satisfaction at both of my sleeping daughters.

Mum gazed at them too, an expression of intense melancholy on her face. 'I think you got lucky with these two, love. They're such good babies.'

I was about to remind her that, no, they'd been little demons in the early days, but, unsettled by her maudlin tone, I looked up. 'You OK?' I enquired, pretty certain that there were tears at the corners of her eyes.

'Of course,' she said reassuringly, patting my arm. 'I suppose I've been thinking lately about how fast time goes. It feels like it was only yesterday that I was sitting here drinking coffee, with *you* in your chair. And look at you now, with your own.' She shook her head, now definitely biting back tears. 'It's like I just . . . blinked.'

The unease that had crept into my chest when I'd first arrived returned full force now and, taken with her melancholy, I searched her face, looking for answers.

'Mum. What's up? Is something bothering you?' I reached out to put my hand on her shoulder.

She placed a protective hand over mine. 'Like I said, I've just been reflecting on the passage of time. The season does that to you, of course. It's pretty much what it's all about, isn't it?' She smiled then. 'And that's not a bad thing either. Just think of all that has happened since last Christmas – remember?'

This time last year I had been in very low spirits – about to give up on the prospect of ever becoming a mother. Nate and I had struggled to get pregnant – and we'd just got through my last round of IVF before making the trek back here for the holidays. We'd already spent a fortune and gone through three previous rounds and we weren't feeling hopeful.

Well, at least, I wasn't.

All my life, I hadn't really thought about having kids. They were this sort of abstract idea that existed in some nebulous form throughout the majority of my adult life. I had spent years popping the pill, while also figuring that at some point I would just have them when I fancied it.

Plus, Nate and I had both been so focused on our careers, pushing and driving forward at breakneck speed, that it wasn't until one day when I was in the OB/GYN's office for my annual check-up that the idea had actually been planted in my head.

'So, have you and Nate taken the idea of a family off the table then?' Dr Amoretti had enquired innocently.

Off the table? Had the idea ever been *on* the table? Not without being dissected and analysed, taking into account all variables and possible outcomes, like any potential project my husband and I embarked upon.

The look of surprise and contemplation must have shown through on my face because before I could reply, she said, 'If you haven't decided one way or the other, then I would say it's likely time, Joanna. Fertility decreases rapidly after age thirty-five. But I'm sure you know that.'

At the time of that appointment I had been thirty-six. Was thirty-six . . . old? Too old?

Of course not, I had thought; I was at the top of my game. I wasn't . . . *old*.

After that, I had rushed home, feeling frantic. Did I want kids? Did Nate want kids? What did that mean for my career if I wanted them? What if I couldn't get pregnant? Were they part of The Plan?

And it was with that question that I had calmed down.

Of *course* they were part of the plan – *now* – and I would be able to get pregnant if Nate and I wanted them. There was nothing in life I hadn't been able to accomplish thus far – and suddenly I just knew, without a doubt, that I wanted children.

Nate was on board but unfortunately my body had other ideas.

After months of trying without results, we consulted with my doctor and a fertility specialist, which is where the IVF came in. While my company had stellar medical benefits, they only covered so much, and when intervention didn't appear to be working and we started spending a lot of our own money, I was frustrated.

I didn't like not getting results. If you invested in something, you needed to achieve an outcome – a return.

And I got results with everything I pursued.

So, to put it mildly, this time last year I had not been merry and bright. I was down in the dumps because we were at the end of the road. If the most recent round of IVF failed, then that was it. *I* had failed.

When you feel like you can do anything, you feel responsible for everything.

But little did I know what was in store. I was already pregnant. The previous round of IVF had worked. And surprise . . . I wasn't just having one baby, but two.

Which for me, as Nate pointed out, was pretty much entirely on brand.

All in.

'And now here we are, twelve months later,' my mother replied, as if reading my thoughts. 'See how much can change in a single year?'

Suddenly, I felt as if everything was teed up right that second. Now was the time. I had my opening. I needed to say something, or I would burst. The idea that I had floated past Nate on the way here. I needed to get this off my chest once and for all.

'I don't want to go back to work,' I blurted.

Mum looked as if she needed a translator. 'What do you . . . ?'

I took a deep breath and sought to calm my racing heart. 'I mean it, Mum. I've decided I don't want to go back to work after maternity leave. I don't want the girls to grow up in day care. I want to stay at home with them – the way you did for us. I don't want to try to do it all, Mum – I don't want to be superwoman. But I want to do this.'

Chapter 7

OK. So I'd sensed some clouds bubbling up – but I didn't expect all this.

The three of you each seem to have arrived with your respective Ghosts of Christmases Past, Present and Future.

Matthew, sometimes I don't know what to do with you – and this worries me when I try to consider the future. I saw that hangdog look on your face when you told us – the one you have used since you were a little boy. The one you wear whenever you hope that someone else will step in to clean up whatever mess you made.

But Mummy can no longer clean up your messes, sweetheart. And neither can your father. You have no business behaving like that. It's definitely not how you were raised.

Which makes me wonder what you're not telling us. Because I also know you well enough to know that there's more to this story.

And it just makes me wonder what other lessons haven't you learned?

In any case, this is going to have to be a race that you run on your own.

And speaking of races . . . Romy, you are also full of surprises. The Dublin Marathon! When you first announced your plans, of course, I would be lying if I didn't say I was worried.

I know things haven't been easy for you lately, and I have to say I was relieved to hear you finally admit that out loud. You might not be asking for help, honey, but we can still provide moral support with our hearts, and our love.

I'm just not entirely sure if you're trying to prove something to the world – or yourself.

Which brings me to your sister, who we already know could run the world. Jo, never in a million years did I expect that you would want to give it all up for babies.

But then again, why wouldn't you? It is possibly the greatest accomplishment of all.

But also the hardest.

So while I admire your passion and commitment to everything you set your mind to, I worry that for once, maybe this time, perhaps while ensconced in the blissful bubble of maternity leave, you haven't really thought things through.

And, my darling Jo, if, for some reason, you also feel that you have something to prove . . .

What is it about life that we are all always so eager and willing to line up for the next race?

When the one we'll never, ever win is that which we run against ourselves.

◆ ◆ ◆

'I'm sorry, you're thinking about doing *what*?' Matt spluttered, incredulity painted all over his face, almost spitting out a mouthful of Mum's famous sherry trifle.

After my mother and I had spoken, she encouraged me not to make any quick decisions and perhaps broach what I was thinking out loud over the course of our stay – without, I noticed, offering any opinion of her own.

But that was Mum to a tee – never overtly opinionated, always preferring us to tease and talk things out before we came to any definitive conclusions.

Whereas I always tended to grab the bull by the horns.

So later, once I was confident the twins were down for the night upstairs, I'd decided to do just that – tease the subject of switching my corporate gears to the domestic, while everyone was gathered in the living room after watching *Elf*.

Maybe it was because that particular movie's theme was heavy on work versus family (albeit in a silly, cheerier way), but probably more that my modus operandi in general was always to throw a big idea out on the table and just see how it flies.

I was genuinely curious to see what everyone thought, and since I'd tentatively flown the notion of staying home with the girls by Nate on the way here, I figured he would appreciate my further attempt at crowdsourcing within the Moore family hive mind.

'It's the optimal choice, isn't it?' I said to the others. 'I really don't want to do the whole working-mother thing when my maternity leave finishes. It's just not feasible to be wholly efficient or effective in both areas, which is why I've been . . . pondering the idea of being a stay-at-home mum. The way that ours was.' I looked fondly at Mum, who wore a small – albeit indecipherable – smile.

Truly, I had no idea if she thought my idea was a good or terrible one.

'Even so, why on earth would you *want* to do it?' Matt reiterated, shaking his head in disbelief. 'I mean, I have no idea what you make – well, I kinda do – and it must be close to mid-six figures. No one walks away from dough like that. Seriously, Jo, just get a nanny, or a wet nurse or a feckin' robot – whatever it takes.'

I gulped, thrown a little by the reminder. In truth, my salary was even closer to seven figures, and with the bonuses and stock options I was set to receive after the new product launch – along with a further increase after my inevitable promotion – I truly *would* be walking away from a lot. But I hadn't expected my little brother to understand anyway.

This was about so much more than money.

'Money isn't everything, though,' said Romy, echoing my line of thinking. 'You should just do what feels right – for all of you, Jo.'

'Says yer one who doesn't have any,' Matt shot back.

'Ah now, please,' Mum said wearily. 'No need for that.'

'Your mother is right.' Dad glared at each of my siblings before turning to me. 'I suppose, love, if you've really thought it through, it's a grand idea. Seems to be coming out of nowhere, though. I mean, we were all only talking about the new project and the promotion . . .'

As a now retired bank manager, my dad had always been deeply fascinated by my job and how much technology had upended the financial industry in just a matter of years. But I couldn't possibly expect him to understand the personal element.

'Actually,' I pointed out quietly, 'you and Nate were talking about all that stuff.' I glanced idly then at my husband, curious to know what his input, which was always rational and surely incoming, would be.

As yet, he had been silent and now, to my horror, I saw that his face wore the look one would have after almost getting hit by a semi-truck and watching their life flash before their eyes. The problem was, I wasn't entirely sure why.

'Honey?' I ventured. 'Remember we talked about this on the way here . . . in the car.' It was now painfully obvious that I hadn't properly sold this idea to the most important person of all. Or worse, had gotten it very, very wrong.

I honestly thought he'd be delighted by the prospect that I was serious, given his own family situation and absent mother, who had little to no interest in him or his brother unless they could improve her social standing at the country club.

He ran a hand through his hair and let out a breath.

'I . . . honestly? I didn't think you were actually serious in the car. It's a noble thing, don't get me wrong. But, Jo, I just can't picture it. I just can't picture *you*, I mean. With everything you have built, everything you've achieved and are about to. I just don't . . . I mean . . .'

Abruptly, he stood up. 'Hell, I really don't even know what you want me to say, since it sounds like you've already made your decision.' He turned on his heel and headed for the door. Just as he was about to exit, he placed a hand on the door frame and took a deep breath, before turning back around to face me. 'You know, you really should have looped me in.'

As Nate left the room, taking all of the oxygen with him, I felt two inches tall.

◆ ◆ ◆

Romy studied her nails. Everyone was silent – and it was . . . awkward.

Finally, her mum spoke up quietly. 'Jo, I think you'd better go and have a chat with him, love.'

And at that same moment, there was an ear-splitting scream through the baby monitor propped on the sideboard, which soon turned into two similar yowls for attention.

'Damn . . .' Joanna was moving towards the door when her mum spoke again.

'Don't worry, just go. Your dad and I will see to the girls.'

Her dad had already jumped to attention and once the others had left the room, Romy and Matt found themselves once again alone.

She stared at the tree, feeling a bit deflated by all the family drama so far.

'So that was quite the announcement . . .' her brother muttered. 'Trouble in paradise too, it looks like.'

'So? That's between her and Nate,' she shot back, annoyed at her brother's once again unhelpful contribution. 'And I'm sure they'll be able to sort it out like adults – unlike some.'

Matt held up his hands in supplication. 'Ah, come on, sis, I don't want to spend Christmas fighting with you – or anyone else for that matter. I feel shit enough about things as it is.' He leaned forward and put his head in his hands, then ran his fingers through his hair, massaging the back of his skull with the same cutesy naughty little boy look he always used when he got into trouble. 'Look, forget I said anything. I just thought that by bringing my crap out into the open, I could maybe get some advice. Same as Jo just now.'

Romy felt herself soften a little then. In fairness, her brother did look utterly miserable. She knew that he liked to play the cheeky chappie thing and loved nothing better than being the life and soul of the party – the ultimate lad's lad – but his anguish just then was real. And he was her brother, after all.

'OK. But don't just brush this under the carpet, thinking it'll go away. You're a big boy now and you need to own your mistakes.'

He grinned at her and held up his fingers. 'Scout's honour.'

The doorbell rang and Romy was about to get up to answer it when they heard her dad utter assurances to her mum through the baby monitor that he would go.

'Hey, did you know we aren't doing the Christmas Eve thing this year?' Matt said then.

'We aren't? Why not, I wonder?' Romy was surprised by this. Her mother usually loved nothing better than to host a small get-together for family, close friends and neighbours, whereupon she served her famous home-made mulled wine and festive favourites.

It was a Moore family tradition and could be fun, but a bit of a pain having to get dressed up and make small talk with Jimmy from next door, or Mary from down the road. So she couldn't say she was upset that it wasn't happening. Though she wondered why.

'Maybe just for this year, they didn't want to upset the twins' routine or something. Or Jo's, more likely.' Matt rolled his eyes.

'True, but I suppose the folks aren't getting any younger either . . .' she contemplated. 'These things take a lot of effort, especially on Mum's part.' She smiled fondly, thinking of how when they were younger, her dad usually disappeared into his tool shed for most of

Christmas Eve, while her mum whirled round the troops, getting her children involved in baking, chopping and all the additional preparations it took to host the annual neighbourly gathering. Before her dad reappeared just in time to open the door, take coats and partake of all the goodies.

Much like when he'd gone to answer the doorbell just now.

Romy could hear voices and activity in the hallway and wondered if one of those guests was in fact calling to wish them festive greetings this evening instead.

Until she heard a voice they both recognised and Matt quickly sat up straight.

'Here you go,' Romy said, raising an eyebrow. 'Party or not, it seems your lovely girlfriend has finally joined the festivities.'

Chapter 8

'I'm – I'm sorry.' I stood in front of my husband in the bedroom that had been mine until I left for university at seventeen. 'Maybe it was stupid of me to think that what we'd talked about in the car was a proper heads-up about this. No, not maybe – it *was* stupid. I'm sorry. We should have discussed it all in more detail.'

I had always made it a rule to accept responsibility for my actions and to be able to take the blame. I had always lived that way, both professionally and personally. And Nate knew it. Because he knew me. Even if he was struggling just then to align with my latest endeavour.

For the first time since I'd come in, he looked up and met my gaze, and I felt myself relax just a little. If there was one thing I knew about my husband, it was that he wasn't petty and he didn't hold grudges. He might have stormed out of the room a few minutes ago because he had been caught unawares, but he was a communicator at heart.

And knowing this made me wonder why I had been so reluctant to speak frankly with him in depth before about my professional change of heart.

He put his phone down on the side table next to the bed and turned to face me full on.

'You caught me off guard down there,' he admitted, leaning forward and knotting his hands in front of him. 'That brief thing in the car . . . that wasn't a heart-to-heart about our family's future. At least, I didn't take it that way. At all.'

'I know that now,' I said, feeling my voice catch in my throat. 'And to be honest, maybe I hadn't quite come to terms with the notion myself. But now, being here at home, and all of us together – I suppose it brought it all into even sharper focus, that it truly is what I want.' I shrugged. 'Honestly? I'm confused about why I'm having these thoughts to begin with. If you'd asked me if I'd ever contemplate being a stay-at-home mother a year ago, I would have probably laughed in your face. But now . . .' My voice trailed off, as I sought to verbalise, truly, what I was trying to get across. 'As you know, my mum was there for me when I was growing up – for all three of us.'

I smiled at the rush of memories that flooded my brain.

'I remember that, no matter what, she was always at my camogie matches and Irish dance competitions. She was always there to cheer Matt on during hurling and soccer. And when Romy was in a school play or anything like that, she was in the front row. She was present, she was engaged in our lives. Sure, Dad did his best, but he did have to work . . .'

A Stanford born and bred tech genius, Nate was executive vice president at his own start-up, so it's not as though we'd be paupers without my salary, but his company was still in its infancy, whereas my career had been more solid.

We lived well; hell, by most people's standards we were stinking rich. We also had some assets and other investments in the form of rental property and stock options that could be liquidated once my income and additional perks were no longer in play.

Nate seemed contemplative. 'San Francisco is literally the most expensive city in the country, Jo,' he continued, and I realised he was struggling with the idea of being the sole breadwinner. Our house in Nob Hill was also one of the most salubrious addresses in the Bay Area.

Not to mention the clothes, the shoes, the extensive travel, expensive restaurants . . . the list went on. We did well, and we also *lived* well. Very, very well.

Now, I already felt guilty about the twins' designer snowsuits. Dropping hundreds of dollars on something that would fit them for a month or so seemed silly and flippant considering what I had been thinking about.

I couldn't spend money like it was going out of style if I wanted to pursue this.

'I'm sorry, I guess I haven't entirely thought this through, not really.' My voice was thick and I felt like a ticking time bomb of emotions, hormones and general angst.

Nate got up from where he sat and came next to me, wrapping me in his arms. I buried my face against his chest and breathed in his scent, instantly finding comfort.

'I'd just be throwing a monkey wrench in everything,' I admitted, my voice muffled against his body.

Vibrations of silent laughter reverberated in his chest.

'Understatement of the year. But we will deal.' He pulled away ever so slightly and looked down at my face, kissing me on the forehead. Then he smiled. 'You know, after so many years of all the superwoman talk – I guess I should be happy that you are indeed a mere mortal like the rest of us.'

But while my husband's voice was light, I could also make out the shadow that crossed his face as he pulled me back in for another embrace.

And I wondered now if maybe the realisation that I wasn't that person had actually disappointed him.

'You should have said you were on the way,' Matt said, still a little taken aback as he welcomed Hazel into the family festivities, though with all the drama thus far, Romy mused, the house had been far from festive.

Though she was pleased to see that Joanna and Nate had, in the meantime, emerged from their confrontation apparently unscathed, each now holding a twin and smiling as they presented their daughters to the latest arrival.

'I didn't know myself until the last minute,' his girlfriend replied easily. 'Things wrapped up faster than I expected so I thought I'd make a break for it, before something else popped up.' Her smiled faded as she now considered Matt's tentative expression. 'I hope that's OK?'

'Of course it is! We're delighted to see you,' confirmed Cathy, enveloping her in a warm embrace, as if to make up for her son's weirdness. 'But I'm sure you're tired after that long drive. You should unpack and get settled,' she suggested, glancing at Matt, intimating that perhaps he and his girlfriend needed to catch up on everything privately.

'Oh, it's grand,' Hazel said, waving a hand. 'To be honest, I'm just delighted to be away from work, out of traffic and keen to get the holiday started.'

'Perfect timing then. I was just about to sort out some party nibbles. And maybe a glass of bubbly to kick off properly?'

'Cathy, you've read my mind as usual,' Hazel chuckled. She threw her dark chestnut hair over her shoulder and turned back to admiring the babies again. 'Honey, your nieces are beyond cute. I can't wait for them to open up their pressies on Christmas Day.'

Nate guffawed and bounced Katie in his arms; she offered Hazel a big, toothless grin. 'I'm not so sure they'll manage that yet,' he joked. 'At least, not this year. Next year, there'll be no stopping them.'

As a group, the family began moving in the direction of the living room, chattering happily among themselves.

Romy, though, hung back a little, the only one who seemed to notice that her mother's smile had quickly faded at the mention of 'next year'.

Chapter 9

The sun is just coming up over the water this Christmas morning – and the house is quiet.

Not a creature is stirring . . .

I've always so loved watching the sunrise from this vantage point. I placed my desk in this particular spot when we first moved here so many years ago, because of this glimpse of the sea on one side and the woods on the other, and have never moved it.

Which means I have lived through pretty much all the seasons of family life watching the sun rise from this spot.

And I find so much comfort in that.

Probably because it's the most natural thing in the world that I now get to appreciate this view before everything sets once and for all.

Everything is ready, every preparation made; and all is set for yet another wonderful family Christmas.

I am going to allow the silence to continue just for a moment longer though, because I know that once today truly begins, it will fly by.

Whereas I like to think that, right now, I am living in a moment frozen in time – in a still life, for just a little while at least.

I don't want today or tomorrow or the next one after that to fly. I have but a few more days with you all in one place and I want it to last.

Savour every moment, every second.

Because I know that today is the very last time I will see the sun rise on this, the most magical of days.

Painful too to recognise that next year, while you will all be gathered together once again under this roof, I will not be here.

I like to think I will be present in spirit, though.

And while I have my own drama, so do you it seems – as has been evident over the past few days.

And that is the worry. How could I possibly unburden my own situation now? Or even contemplate breaking my sorry news to you when you are all trying to navigate through your own concerns?

There I go again, trying to solve your problems or make your lives easier when I know that I don't have this ability – and certainly don't have the time.

I wish I did. Oh, how I wish that. I will never have enough time with all of you. You all have been my whole life.

I am really not ready to go. But I suppose I am going to have to be. As they say, time waits for no man – or woman.

I wonder if I have an obligation to tell you, though, should an appropriate moment present itself? Since it's just a matter of time before you do find out.

I think I'd prefer to wait until you've each returned to your own lives, so you can digest it privately, and your dad thinks so too, but of course he will be fine with whatever I decide.

The problem is, I haven't decided. I suppose I just have to play it by ear.

Life is awfully frustrating sometimes, isn't it? There is no one clear set of directions or ever a single path. But I don't need to tell you all that, do I?

You all have proven there are different choices – different roads – one can take.

If only everything in life came with directions.

After breakfast on Christmas morning, the family all gathered round the tree to unwrap their presents, a glorious pile of wrapping paper and ribbons littering the floor beneath.

Last night, once the twins were fast asleep, the adults had relaxed in the living room in front of the fire for a few drinks and lots of chatter and laughter, a welcome opportunity for calm after the veiled chaos since their arrival.

Romy was glad that her parents had – for whatever reason – decided against the traditional neighbourly Christmas Eve party this year, and it was just the family cosy together, catching up on each other's lives while they stuffed themselves silly with Mum's festive favourites instead of having to share them – or indeed her folks – with everyone else.

The perfect Christmas Eve.

Now, Joanna dangled a new necklace featuring a diamond solitaire in front of Katie, who was thoroughly entranced by the gem. She grabbed at it with a pudgy hand, but Jo pulled the chain up so it was just out of Katie's reach before she clasped it around her neck.

'Someone likes sparkly things – just like her momma,' Romy teased.

'High maintenance in the making, I'd say,' Bill chuckled. 'Good luck with that, Nate.'

'Just what I need,' Nate replied dryly. 'Three women with expensive taste.'

Romy then turned her attention to her brother and Hazel, who were curled up on the couch opposite. It was clear Matt hadn't yet filled her in on his work drama, though knowing her brother's penchant for burying his head in the sand, she guessed he'd just wait until after the festivities. 'I love yours, too, Hazel.'

The other woman glanced at her wrist, where a diamond tennis bracelet had found a home. 'Isn't it gorgeous,' she gushed.

'I think she needs a ring to match, though,' joked Nate, as Matt squirmed in his seat, face flushing, and Romy felt relieved that he wasn't *that* immature at least.

While she wouldn't wish any ill will on his relationship, clearly her brother was nowhere near ready for marriage.

'Mum, need any help with anything?' he piped up, earning him a chorus of laughter from the others.

'Oh, that's funny,' teased Cathy. 'I think that's the first time you've ever voluntarily offered to help in the kitchen.'

'First time for everything,' he quipped, jumping up – then he leaned down and kissed Hazel on top of her head.

'I'll help too,' Romy offered, bouncing lightly up on to her feet, getting used to her brand-new running shoes, which her mother had typically magicked up at the last minute from somewhere. They were great and very comfortable, so much so that she already felt like getting out and hitting the tarmac.

Tomorrow, maybe.

First, there was the small matter of demolishing her mother's Christmas morning sausage pastry wreath, to say nothing of the turkey dinner feast that awaited later. Her mouth watered just thinking about it.

'We'll all help,' Joanna suggested, also rising to her feet. 'Let's test that old "too many cooks" theory.'

'And what did I do to get so lucky this year?' Cathy said, beaming.

Joanna winked. 'Careful now, once you let us behind the curtain, we might end up stealing all your yuletide tips and tricks.'

Chapter 10

So now it's all over I find myself torn between delight that we had such a joyful get-together (despite the drama) and melancholy that such a deeply treasured part of my life is now in the rear-view mirror.

It was so hard to say goodbye to each of you this time, and while I know it will likely not be our last meeting, my heart felt so heavy with the knowledge that it was without doubt our final family Christmas together.

I struggled so much about whether I should tell you while you were here, but in the end instinctively felt that this shouldn't dampen this oh-so-precious time together.

But now that you're all back home safe and sound . . . here it goes: last month I was diagnosed with Stage IV pancreatic cancer – and upon further investigation we found out that it had also spread to my bowel. (I know you noticed my weight loss, Joanna, I saw it on your face when you first arrived.)

Sadly, my prognosis is . . . grim. The likelihood that intervention will be successful is under five per cent. Therefore,

I have chosen not to undergo treatment and I also fully understand what this ultimately means.

But I do not want to live out my remaining time on this earth wandering down some futile path with the hope that I will be within that five per cent, or any sicker than I need to be.

I am not hopeless; I simply want to wring as much happiness as possible out of the time I have left. I am at peace with this, and your father has accepted it too, even as we both recognise the reality associated with the decision.

Saying that, I do not know what the coming year will look like, because I truly don't know how much time I have left.

What I do know is that I love you all. I always have and I always will – no matter if I am in this world or beyond.

I also know that you are all going to be upset by this. Confused, sad, and possibly angry too.

You might think this is unfair, and while of course I also wish I had more time, at the end of the day, life isn't fair.

You can make plans, and hope for the best, but if the universe has something else in store for you, then you simply roll with it.

And that is what I am intending to do.

Just . . . roll with it.

Chapter 11

FEBRUARY

Ten down, two to go . . .

Romy glanced at the bulky device on her wrist as her legs began to feel heavier. It was as if the ground beneath was stealing her energy with every step.

She'd been surprised and delighted when, having sought out Luke Dooley in the local pub on St Stephen's night, and tentatively outlined her intentions about taking up running, he'd given her not only some great advice, but a book entitled *Run Your Ass Off.*

'When you're starting out, it's not about focusing so much on the finish line,' he'd advised Romy over a pint of Guinness, his earnest enthusiasm for the subject lighting a fire beneath her. Or maybe it was the lively twinkle in his green eyes as he spoke. 'Much more important is the fitness journey to the start line – getting there with a body that is physically able to run the race itself.'

'OK, so a fair bit of work to be done for starters then,' she chuckled self-deprecatingly, knowing all too well that she herself was a million miles from the glamour-puss types that usually flocked around him.

And Romy guessed it probably seemed weird to most of those ladies that the village 'catch' had spent the most sociable night of the year chatting in the corner to her, of all people.

It certainly amused Matt no end anyway; he'd teased her mercilessly on the walk home. 'You and Dooley looked *very* cosy in there. Should I be worried that an old mate is making googly eyes at my sister?'

'Will you stop – it wasn't like that . . . we were just chatting. Not every guy has a one-track mind like you, you know.'

Though Romy had to admit she'd secretly enjoyed being the focus of Luke's attention – especially the way he looked at her, making her feel as if she was the only woman in the room.

Stupid, she knew, since he probably made every girl feel that way.

But she definitely couldn't deny the little flutter in her heart when he'd appeared at her doorstep the following morning, an old battered running guide in hand. A bit like the guy with those handwritten signs in *Love Actually*.

Minus the heart-stricken declaration of love, to be fair, but still . . .

Town heart-throb or not, Romy realised that Luke Dooley was a genuine sweetheart and the no-nonsense advice he'd imparted, plus the accessible training wisdom in the guide, had got her off to a great start.

As had the Garmin tracker watch that Jo had couriered over first thing in the New Year, and while she was nowhere near as tech-reliant or savvy as her sister, Romy quickly realised if she didn't have that annoying little taskmaster, she'd have no way of knowing how far she had come.

In more ways than one.

Leaden legs be damned, she was determined to keep on going through Hyde Park until the long-awaited beep on the device signalled she was getting close to her goal. She grinned with self-satisfaction and her legs felt almost magically fresher as she mastered the milestone of her furthest ever distance, as confirmed on the device face.

Eleven miles. *Eleven.* Who would've thought it?

But the remaining distance, plus the climbing heat of the bright London February morning, caused the feeling of energy-sapped legs to return as quickly as it had departed. Her brain continued this mental flip-flop from positive to negative and back again with every few steps, as the emotional and rational sides of her brain argued furiously on the merits of this newfound endeavour.

And the emotional side was still clearly mourning the loss of weekend morning lie-ins.

Who are you kidding? In a race, you wouldn't even be half way.

Incredible; twelve miles is almost a half-marathon. A half-marathon!

But you're so slow, you could end up finishing last . . .

Who cares? As long as you do *finish . . .*

Tell you what, treat yourself to the brunch of the day in Myo's after – you deserve it.

Grand so.

Debate settled, Romy's mouth watered at the thought of poached eggs on sourdough toast with smashed avocado and a side of Irish-style sausages that her favourite cafe served, instead of the spicy English-style chipolatas you seemed to get everywhere else in London.

She focused then on her more toned waistline. While the weight hadn't exactly fallen off, she'd definitely toned up, which had led to a need for a very satisfying wardrobe update too, thanks in part to her brand-new job covering maternity leave for an editor at a highly regarded literary publisher.

An editorial position was pretty much the job of her dreams and, even better, there was a very strong possibility that she'd get taken on full-time in the department once the cover period ended.

Her new colleagues were fun and inspiring and best of all, Romy finally got to spend her days surrounded by the written word.

It seemed that once she'd made the decision to just grab life by the scruff of the neck, things had begun falling into place. Her new-found confidence from following through on the training plan seemed to have shone through in the job interview, hence the new role.

Though the training plan's prediction of increased appetite had been particularly spot on, she mused, feeling her tummy rumble as she ran the final few yards of what felt like the (latest) longest mile of her life.

She gritted her teeth and swung her arms, mentally willing the numbers on the Garmin to change as, step by step, she ground it out. While faster, *much* faster runners streamed by her.

Initially, she'd felt a little out of her depth upon seeing so many others routinely circuiting the park with their easy gait, while she had visions of herself just trudging along like a heifer.

But she had since been struck by the openly supportive spirit that seemed to exist within the running tribe. A knowing smile and fleeting wave as they passed one another seemed to underline an unspoken bond between runners; an acknowledgement of each other's endeavours was apparent, no matter the shape, size, age or, in Romy's case, speed.

Glancing down at her wrist again to see 11.9 miles registered, she wanted to cry with relief, suddenly recalling the collective expressions on her family's faces when she'd made the announcement in December that she was going to run the marathon.

She understood their doubt, certainly, and in truth shared it, having obviously never been the sporty type.

If you could all see me now . . . she thought, elated beyond belief as the device finally beeped, signalling the completion of her longest distance so far.

She felt like crying. So many emotions were new to her – from two minutes ago feeling like she wanted to stop and collapse on the ground, to right now and the sheer badass feeling that she was *unstoppable.*

She pulled out one of the four small bottles tucked into her hydration belt to drain any last fluids from it, knowing a wet tongue was probably the best she could hope for until she got to a shop, the other bottles having been long drained already.

As she limped slowly towards the nearest park exit, her thoughts automatically turned to Cathy, and this time an all too familiar emotion resurfaced. Romy felt a lump in her throat as a potent mixture of dread and despair forced itself upwards.

Her mother would be so proud. She looked forward to their regular phone chats more than ever these days, knowing now that they were finite.

Romy, who had on some level been living in a state of terror about her mother's future in the six weeks since she had told them about her diagnosis, felt herself shakier and more unsteady as time passed.

Of course, her mum always tried to put on a brave face whenever they did those stupid family video calls – the ones she herself felt only served to highlight the fact that they weren't together.

Better than nothing, she knew, but still. She should be there, at home. Not in another city; another country even.

And she had tried to be, and despite the new job had wanted to return home to Ireland altogether, but in the meantime Matt had opted to temporarily transfer from Galway while awaiting the results of his firm's disciplinary investigation.

Cathy had insisted that the last thing she wanted was fuss, and certainly didn't want any of them uprooting their lives for her sake.

The whole situation didn't seem real and what's more, they had all been equally shocked and upset when their mother told them that she was simply going to manage the pain and live out the rest of her time as is, instead of seeking treatment.

Joanna in particular had thrown a fit over that admission and, initially, Romy felt much the same, as if their mum was just giving up and throwing in the towel.

But gradually, she had gotten it. And while her sister vowed to get her in front of some of the foremost medical experts in the world, she had embarked upon a little research of her own and begun to understand that her mother's chances were slim, if not minuscule.

So she developed the understanding that her mother wanted to do it her way. She wasn't giving up – she was just living her life on her own terms and doing what she felt was best.

Romy subscribed to that in her own existence now, too – and she had to respect that her mum and the doctors knew what was best for whatever time she had remaining.

But she couldn't help but curse the timing. For as long as she'd spent trying to eke out a life in London, right when she could have done with some free time and flexibility to spend back home, the job of her dreams had fallen into her lap – its associated responsibility meaning she couldn't exactly take off at the drop of a hat.

It was the one cloud that seemed to loom larger every day, just as so many other aspects of her life seemed to be coming good.

The job and a new-found appreciation of exercise had, as intended, given Romy a sense of purpose in life that for so long had been absent.

While at the same time the pull of home and family tugged in the opposite direction.

Of course, everything still wasn't a bed of roses either, she mused, adjusting her bra strap, a fresh bead of sweat causing her to wince as it stung a newly chafed patch of skin. Another painful shower awaited and she grimaced, remembering her first ten-mile run, when wet weather and an ill-fitting sports bra had left her so badly chafed she'd actually screamed out in pain as soon as the shower water touched her skin.

But running had, if nothing else, given her a new perspective on the world and she was definitely learning the hard way; a steep curve of chafing, blisters and dodgy tummies from energy gels of a warm, gloopy consistency that turned her stomach now even thinking about them.

And in the midst of all the hard lessons, Romy knew she truly was finding something new within herself – a sense of resolve.

For so long she had felt lesser than, the high-achieving shadows in her family causing her to doubt herself. Now her outlook was changing, she could feel it with each and every passing week.

Following a simple plan, building something from the ground up, was changing her world, and her mindset.

Where once there had been fear and doubt, now that famous sports slogan had become Romy's life motto. *Just do it.*

She just wished there was something – anything – she could do to stave off the impending storm.

Chapter 12

'What do you mean, it's . . . gone?' I glanced distractedly at Nate, all the while keeping an eye on Katie, the first of the twins to have recently started rolling onto her front.

Interesting . . . I knew from the parenting gurus that this was a sign she'd soon be ready to crawl, and no doubt her sister wouldn't be far behind. Then the fun would start. Possibly.

Six weeks into my new position as official Bates' Homemaker-in-Chief, so far this domesticity thing had been, well . . . a bit monotonous.

Almost too easy.

To the point where, OK, I might as well admit it, I was starting to get a little antsy. Was this really . . . it?

Course, I also missed adult conversation, stirring debate and all the things that went hand in hand with being in the boardroom. Whereas days with the twins mostly consisted of one-way discussions that went nowhere, and with no discernible or desirable outcome. While they occasionally cooed back at me when they were in the mood or actually awake, they still slept a lot of the time, and when they were up complained and cried until I put them in front of Baby Cartoons, and then not a peep.

I also knew this stuff went hand in hand with their age, but at the same time it was a bit, well . . . mind-numbing, and I was looking forward to cracking on with the more challenging milestone stuff like crawling and standing up and *definitely* weaning them onto solids.

Though, on the other hand, I was also deeply thankful that this brief . . . lull, or whatever it was, with their care had given me the headspace to process what my beloved mother had told us after Christmas, once we were – as she described it – 'safely back home on the other side of the Atlantic so you didn't fuss'.

Fuss? I didn't want to *fuss* – I wanted to hop straight back on the plane and stay home for a while, take care of her, do whatever I could to make things easier, and if I couldn't urge her to seek out adequate medical attention as yet, at least take the opportunity to spend some time with her and persuade her otherwise.

But she didn't want to be persuaded, or indeed stifled. Which was, of course, Mum all over.

I still felt numb every time I thought about it, and while I'd already made the arrangements to fly back soon, there was no denying that my new-found domestic situation made travel considerably more difficult.

I couldn't single-handedly schlep twin babies across the Atlantic and back, to say nothing of the fact that I wouldn't be much use to my mother in any case if I needed to take care of the girls too. If anything, all of us stomping back into the household would make for more messy, noisy upheaval, when what she needed right now was peace.

Though at least it seemed my brother, who had decided to move home temporarily while waiting for his work situation to be sorted, was close to hand to 'help out'.

For the moment, my parents and I had video calls, and once again I thanked the heavens for technological developments in my own (albeit former) field that allowed such miracles to happen.

We Skyped and video-called almost every other day and the last time I'd spoken to her she and my dad seemed upbeat and cheery. Knowing my mother, I wouldn't be at all surprised if she ended up one of the apparently minuscule percentage who beat the odds and conquered this goddamn thing.

But there was no denying that the news had been one hell of a shock to the system, particularly the admission that she had kept the information to herself all throughout our visit home for fear of spoiling the festivities. Which was, of course, entirely on brand.

Though I suspected that this was probably more a case of me and my siblings dropping all our own individual bombs into the mix too.

And I felt desperately guilty about that now; that I had been so focused on my own petty concerns that I had all too easily dismissed my observations about her weight loss and (albeit well-disguised) frailty.

So in that sense I was glad I'd had all this free time on my hands to think, research and seek out new treatments and oncologists specialising in this particular area. If I couldn't be on hand personally to help, then I could do what I did best and seek out any tools available to give my mother a fighting chance.

'Jo, can you focus, please? I'm trying to tell you something important here.'

I jumped a little, having pretty much forgotten that Nate was actually in the room. You'd think that, given all this time on my own, I would've been jumping at this rare opportunity for conversation with my husband, but the truth was I was only half listening.

One thing I had noticed lately was that his tone had taken on an almost patronising air – pretty much, it had to be said, since I'd decided (because there was no pretending that this had been a joint thing) to walk away from FinTech, instead of returning to oversee the grand product launch, the new AI I'd overseen to send the company into the stratosphere and, as intended, trigger a major takeover by one of the giants.

My heart sank whenever I thought about how it had (to put it mildly) turned out to be a bit of a misfire, and my fellow board members had been pretty pissed off at my last-minute decision to 'abandon ship'.

It was also a major setback financially, given that the share options I'd been counting on to supplement this year's loss in salary had taken a spectacular nosedive when the launch went south.

And since I'd already waved goodbye to the job – plus all associated promotion bonuses – my new-found performance graph as a SAHM had unfortunately started well into the red.

'Joanna, like I said, our 401ks, everything. It's . . . gone. I was waiting to see if I could do something to rescue before looping you in, but . . . we're in trouble, hon.'

As his words finally penetrated, my head swivelled back to meet his gaze.

'Looping me in? Very funny. No, seriously – hilarious.'

'Jo . . .' He reached for me then, and one look at his ashen face and grave expression told me that actually no, this wasn't a joke. Or else he had suddenly become a very good actor.

I frowned, and a prickle of unease ran up my spine at the mention of our retirement plan. 'What . . . but how? Where? What did you do, Nate?'

He ran a hand through his hair and looked out of the bay window of our three-storey Victorian, with its direct view down over the Bay to Alcatraz and the Golden Gate Bridge.

'Firstly, I want to assure you that I've already done everything, everything in my power to try to rescue this before I said anything.' He turned to look at me and now his eyes were filled with tears. 'I fucked up, Jo, I know that now. But believe me when I tell you that I made what I thought at the time was a calculated decision.'

'Jesus, Nate, will you just spit it *out*?' I demanded, my ears ringing, even though I knew I had yet to hear the worst. 'What the hell happened?'

'The launch last month . . .'

'At FinTech? What's that got to do with anything?'

He groaned and winced all at once as he turned back to look at me. 'It was a sure thing, you said it yourself. And it was all going so well. Everything was on course, all set to smash that share price out of the park.'

At this, something that felt dangerously close to guilt came hurtling out from the recesses of my mind.

'Well, yes, but we know what happened. And if I had been there it wouldn't have made much of a difference anyway . . .'

I thought I'd done everything right, had gotten every last duck in line before I left the company.

While I kept telling myself that my replacement just didn't have the product experience or market knowledge for such a big launch, thus ensuring that the tech not only fell flat on its face but bombed completely, I couldn't help but question my own part in its failure.

Implosion, even.

What had I missed? And more to the point, what else had I got wrong?

Was my sudden, out-of-the-blue eagerness to swap corporate responsibility for domestic a kind of subconscious manifestation of doubt about the product? Performance anxiety, even?

I couldn't be sure. But now, I was certainly struggling to figure out why I'd been so eager to walk away, when I clearly wasn't cut out for domesticity.

Maternity leave had been, much as my mother had pointed out, a temporary bubble, a breather from the norm – not a fully formed life plan. Whereas I needed ongoing challenge to thrive.

But worse, was I no longer cut out for the corporate world either?

Had I, the great Joanna Bates, lost her edge?

Regardless, I wasn't sure what any of that had to do with this conversation.

'Jo, I had no way of knowing you were going to rip up the game plan at the last minute, or that out of the blue you'd decide not to go back to work without telling me first. Please understand that, OK?'

And then suddenly I did understand. I understood exactly what had happened. As realisation dawned, I started running the calculations in my head and they were . . . not good. My heart thumped like a jackhammer. 'Please don't tell me you invested—'

'I'm sorry, Jo. I did, I put it all – everything – on black.'

The room began to spin. He didn't . . . *couldn't* have . . . 'You mean, you leveraged everything – *all* of it into FinTech stock?'

'I know, I'm sorry, and yes, I should have told you, should have discussed it with you before pulling the trigger. And don't get me wrong, I'm not for one second suggesting that any of this is your fault . . . it's neither of our faults, really, but I just wasn't to know, would never have dreamed in a million years that you would just . . . walk away from the job, and that the launch would backfire so badly.'

I stared at him, unable to believe that my own husband had gambled all of our assets and investments, our children's future, our entire livelihoods. Gambled it all on a product launch, over which I, of all people, would have presided.

And lost.

Because of my decision. My grand decision to pack it all in – my entire life's work – for the nobler option of being there for our children.

Or as a way of hiding from the truth?

That somewhere, deep down, I'd already realised it was going to fail.

'Jo . . . honey? Say something.'

But I couldn't answer, because right then I felt the ground quite literally shift beneath my feet as my head filled with stars, and I dropped to the floor.

Chapter 13

Time . . . I just wish we had more time.

There are so many things that I want you to know. So much I still need to impart before it is lost to the ether.

Like wanting to ensure the traditions we have lovingly created as a family over the years continue when I am gone. Ensure that you are privy to all the little things, so you continue to maintain the family bond formed over the course of so many wonderful years.

Stories that remain in my head, but not yours. Experiences I may have never told you about at all. I want you to know these things. I want you to know everything.

But above all, I want you to remain there for one another.

I know your dad will do his best to keep things going. But he will be hurting too. He and I have spent more of our lives together than we ever have apart, and with my early exit from this life, he is going to have to adjust.

Your father will need to be the one to stand on the porch for me now when the time comes.

So I need you to be there for him, and also for each other, no matter what. I hope that you continue to be not just close as siblings but remain friends and stalwarts for one another.

I also want you to know that I will be watching over you, so, much like a benevolent Santa Claus, I'm going to be aware of good behaviour as well as bad. Ha.

The three of you have achieved so much already and I am so proud of the people you have become.

Yes, there have been times in the past and even recently when you have given me deep and abiding headaches. I would be lying if I said that wasn't the case.

But in the end, you have made me proud far more than not.

The greatest honour of my life has been to be your mother. And my greatest reward is knowing that I will have just a teeny bit of immortality because you will still be of the world, even if I am not there.

I love you all with my whole heart and every fibre of my being.

When I am gone, mourn me a little, but please then move on, knowing that I am still close by, still loving you as much as I do in the flesh.

Guiding you, even.

Remember, they always say it's the little things in life that are important.

Because when you look back, you realise they were the big things.

Chapter 14

APRIL

Romy leaned against a tree in Hyde Park. She stretched her right leg back and pushed forward, lengthening her calf muscle.

After repeating the stretch on the other leg, she stood up straight and rolled her neck, feeling pleased at the several small pops that echoed in her ears.

It was a beautiful, albeit warm, April day – and she had set aside this morning to do a training run of fourteen miles – her longest thus far. Admittedly, she hadn't been overly keen to tackle this today. She'd had a restless night and was feeling more than a little sluggish.

'Why do I do this to myself . . .' she muttered, adjusting her earbuds as a belter from Lizzo came to life in her ears, hoping the anthem would rouse some energy.

She pressed a button on the side of her Garmin to begin tracking her time and miles and shot an envious glance at another runner, who rounded the corner heading east in front of her. The woman was clearly 'in the zone' and having a much better time than she was.

But it wasn't just that Romy was tired and unmotivated today. In truth, she had been enjoying her training programme so far and she saw herself making progress – and better still, she had even lost a stone since she started.

Today was different and she had more on her mind.

Her mother was deeply unwell now. During Romy's most recent trip home, Cathy had tried to smile and joke as always but it was obvious that she was just keeping up a strong facade.

There were cracks in it, too – every now and then she witnessed the ghost of pain that crossed her mother's face and it hurt her heart to try to imagine what she must be feeling. And when they'd said their goodbyes this time before she returned to London, Romy couldn't help but fear that it could be for the very last time.

The dread of it made her choke up, the balanced inhaling and exhaling she had been doing got thrown off, and she felt a sob bubbling up in her throat.

Jumping off the path and into the shade of a tree, she held her chest for a moment and closed her eyes, hoping to calm herself. She felt herself trembling and getting light-headed. For a moment, she wondered if she should sit and put her head in between her knees. Or simply curl up into the foetal position right here and now and bawl her eyes out.

'Are you OK?' a male voice asked, causing her to open her eyes in shock.

A range of emotions ran through her, all confusing. Especially since she hadn't expected to open her eyes to this.

The man in front of her had auburn hair that curled around his ears and sharp blue eyes. He was taller than her by a couple of inches and the set of his jaw and the width of his shoulders instantly reminded her of the actor who starred in a historical time-travel saga set in the Scottish Highlands that she had been bingeing on TV of late. Albeit in a T-shirt and running shorts.

'Yeah – grand, thanks,' she finally spat out, realising he was watching her, concern growing on his face.

'You sure?' he asked cautiously. Clearly he thought she was in the middle of some medical crisis.

Romy put a hand to her forehead and wiped away a sweaty lock of blonde hair. How fitting that she would meet a guy at a time when she was red-faced, dripping in sweat and about to have a nervous breakdown.

And was that an Irish accent too?

She tried to manage a tight smile. 'Seriously, I'm grand. I, ah, just lost my breath for a second. I'm fine, honestly. Thanks for asking. Nice of you to check.'

The man smiled and bobbed his head. 'No worries. Are you in training?' He stood back and started bouncing on the balls of his feet, his clothing betraying him from the get-go as a fellow runner. And she knew that now he was trying to keep his heart rate up.

'Yes,' she admitted. 'For the Dublin Marathon.' She shrugged a little and then added, 'My first.'

'Nice one. And I thought I recognised the accent.' He grinned and nodded in the direction she'd been headed. 'I'm in training myself and have a couple more miles to go, if you fancy tagging along. If you're up to it, that is.'

Before she could overthink it, Romy nodded. Maybe it would help.

Running usually curbed her anxiety when she was thinking a lot about her mum, and maybe some company would further help calm some of the panic she had been feeling since the weekend.

'I'm Damien, by the way. Irish like yourself as you can probably guess, but I've been working and living over here for yonks.'

'Romy. Here just a couple of years.' She rejoined the path alongside him before a sudden burst of worry bloomed in her chest. He was clearly very athletic and his long legs would easily outpace hers.

As if reading her thoughts, he said, 'You set the pace, yeah?'

Feeling a fresh surge of gratitude, she agreed, and they started out.

For a while they ran in silence, and she struggled for something to say while simultaneously trying to contemplate how she was going to run and also hold a conversation with a complete stranger, fellow compatriot or otherwise.

She hadn't tried this feat with anyone yet, and now she worried that this might have been a bad idea.

She chuckled lightly. 'Maybe we could slow it down just a bit. I'm a bit of a newbie.'

'Grand. And sure everyone has to start somewhere, Romy,' he said, and she stole a glance at him out of the corner of her eye. She liked the way he said her name.

'If you'd have told me a year ago that I'd be training for a marathon, I would have called you cracked.' She smiled, trying to push away the thought that a year ago there would have been several things she never believed would be happening just now.

Like a job she loved and a sense that finally she was figuring out her place in the world.

Or time with her precious mother that was slowly but surely running out. She gulped afresh and tried to concentrate on the task in hand.

'Are you enjoying the training?' he asked. 'I've run a few myself. Frankfurt, New York – and Dublin too, obviously. It's one of the better ones, to be fair. Incredible support.'

'Not at the start and I've got the scars to prove it,' she said between puffs of air, purposely deciding not to fill him in on the sore nipples or blackened toenails. Though of course he would've had his own fair share of war wounds, but still.

They passed a few more moments in companionable silence, until Romy spoke again. 'I suppose it's been a welcome distraction too,' she admitted. 'My mum is . . . unwell at the moment, and it's just been an awful time.'

Damien was silent for a bit and then said, 'Sorry to hear that. Do you get to see her much or . . . ?'

Romy winced, once again painfully cognisant of the physical distance. 'No, my family's back home – in Dublin. I started a new job in January, so I haven't been able to get over as much as I'd like. We video-call a lot and all that too, but of course it's not the same.'

Again he was silent, and undeterred by the fact that she had just met this guy, she felt the need to talk, not just to fill the void, but because it was a bit of relief to unload.

'I was going to move home altogether, but she wouldn't hear of it. Plus my brother moved home from Galway and he also insisted I should just stay on since he was there. But it's been horrible. Especially knowing that it's going to happen . . . You think you can prepare . . . but you can't. Every day you just worry and wonder, is today the day?' She wiped her forehead and willed herself not to cry. 'Anyway, I suppose this . . . running, I mean, helps relieve some of the stress a bit.'

Damien made a sound of agreement in his throat. 'I can imagine,' he said. 'Of course it's going to be hard. Sorry.'

Weirdly, she felt her heart flutter a little at his words of sympathy, the vibration flushing through her. But then the fluttering continued.

Oh wait, that's not my heart – it's my phone.

She glanced at her left arm where the device was held in a protective Velcro case. Looking at the screen, she saw her dad's number flash across it and immediately a shock of alarm coursed through her body.

'Oh Christ . . . can you hold on a second?'

Without waiting for an answer, Romy jumped from the path and tapped her earbuds urgently to connect the call. Damien followed in her wake and stood with her a little way off, watching her face go through myriad emotions.

'Dad? I'm here,' she gasped by way of introduction as she tried to catch her breath. 'Is she OK?'

On the other end of the line, though, her dad was breathing heavily and when he replied his voice was thick. He had been crying, that much she knew, and she also sensed that in that moment, he was alone.

All at once her heart dropped into her stomach and, with sweeping premonition, Romy knew what he was going to say.

Chapter 15

I glanced down at the hastily scribbled grocery list, while trying to navigate the double-seater shopping cart that awkwardly ferried both of my daughters.

Suzy shifted in her seat and pounded on the handlebar in front of her, and I shot her a look and said a silent prayer.

'Just a little while longer, sweetheart,' I muttered as I took a brief step away from the cart to grab a bottle of ketchup and place it in the basket. Ticking yet another item off, I looked over at her sister. For the moment, she was happy enough, but I knew how quickly both of them could 'turn'.

So much for this motherhood thing being a walk in the park. These days I was well and truly eating my words. In a matter of weeks, they had turned into little demons altogether, especially since they'd started teething too. One minute they were happy as Larry; the next, one was having a meltdown while the other figured out how to remove her nappy and smear its contents on the wall the second my back was turned.

And speaking of nappies . . . Suzy had suddenly gone red in the face.

'Oh come *on*. Seriously?' I groaned, beginning to push the cart faster.

I was only halfway through the shopping and now I was kicking myself for not placing an order online. But I needed a change of scenery. And I needed to get out of the goddamn house, where the walls seemed to close in on me with each passing day.

Especially since the world as I knew it had imploded in a series of sharp, devastating explosions. And speaking of explosions . . . now Suzy let out a whine and turned her blue eyes up at me, resembling a sorrowful puppy.

'I know you don't want to sit in it,' I grumbled. 'I wouldn't either.' She didn't look impressed with my comment and her expression settled into a frown. I knew what that meant. 'I'm hurrying, baby, Momma's hurrying, OK?'

Feeling my stress levels begin to rise even more, I reached for the baby food and began dumping jar after jar into the cart, not even paying attention to the labels – ultimately, if one of them didn't like yams or green beans or whatever, it was likely that the other one would. Or I'd just end up eating it because I had little time or inclination to make my own lunch.

A sudden buzz in my pocket alerted me to my phone, but whatever it was would have to wait. For poor Suzy's sake I needed to get this over with ASAP.

Putting my hands back on the handle, I pushed the cart forward, and accidentally jerked Katie in her seat. Her head lolled forward and her mouth bumped against the protective bar in front of her. She pulled her head up and looked at me indignantly before opening her mouth to emit a blood-curdling howl.

'Oh *fuuuuck*,' I moaned. 'Momma didn't mean to, honey, I'm so sorry.' I reached forward and pulled her as gently as possible from her seat and hugged her close, massaging her mouth. Poor thing's gums were extra sensitive at the moment as it was.

I bounced her a little, trying to calm her down, but as always, this only made her scream louder. Then once again I felt the buzz of my phone in my pocket.

'Jesus Christ,' I muttered under my breath. 'When it rains it pours.'

As if on cue, Suzy – apparently unimpressed that her sister had my attention, and having also decided that yes, she definitely was over sitting in a poop-filled nappy – took it upon herself to join in with the chorus, and an angry shriek came from her mouth just as big crocodile tears spilled from her eyes.

And the phone buzzed in my pocket once again.

'For Chrissake, where's the fire?' I spat, realising I was now earning the stares of fellow shoppers. A couple of women looked at me with understanding and pity – but others, not so much.

A hipster-looking dude passing by was clearly inconvenienced. He shot me an annoyed look while muttering, well within my hearing, 'Control your demons, lady.'

'I'm sorry, are you talking to me?'

He sniffed the air and rolled his eyes. 'Disgusting,' he added, before moving on down the aisle.

I took a deep breath, trying to calm my anxiety and rediscover some Zen.

What would Mum do? I asked the universe, before quickly recognising my error. She would know how to calm them down, of course, but I wished I hadn't summoned up her image in an attempt to make myself feel better.

I recalled the night before when we were all on a family video call together. She looked well enough and seemed in very good spirits, but it was hard to deny her frailty. And difficult to talk properly with so many of us chatting and wittering over each other all at once.

Frustrating too, because I couldn't wait to tell her that I was 'this close' to getting her enrolled in a new form of treatment that was being trialled here with spectacular results, and which I was confident would allow her to kick this thing's ass. No better woman than my mother, I knew, to smash it stone dead in any case. Either way, I'd vowed to ensure she had the best possible help.

The medical bills would be expensive, sure, and while Nate and I obviously weren't as strong on the financial side, I would do whatever it took to ensure she got the absolute best treatment and care. I'd already lined up some part-time consulting work while caring for the girls to ensure we could lay our hands on some much-needed cash. Again, to borrow a line from a favourite movie, no expense would be spared.

She and Dad would need to come to California and stay here while it was all happening, but our house was plenty big enough for everyone, and I relished the opportunity of having Mum under my roof and being able to take care of *her* for a change, like she'd done for me all my life.

As things were, I felt so useless and frustrated because I couldn't be with her personally; hell, I wasn't even in the same time zone, let alone had the opportunity to spend any actual time with her since she'd broken the news.

It was killing me not to be able to put my arms around her and hold her close and I was counting down the days till I could fly home next month, when Nate could finally schedule some work leave to be with the girls.

Whereupon I could break the happy news about my medical research, and the mountains I'd moved to get her into the programme.

And in all honesty, I was counting down those days for more reasons than one.

Nothing else seemed to be working. Since Nate had dropped his bombshell, life in general was out of control. I mean, I was yelling at strangers and starting fights in grocery stores. Our marriage was struggling and personally, I was losing it. And it was that thought, and this desperate feeling of helplessness – about *everything* – that was pushing me over the edge.

All my life, I'd had it together – had always made everything gel. I was on point, forever on my game. I handled everything that needed to be handled. I had been a star – unstoppable.

The FinTech failure and resulting fallout had shattered my confidence, my self-belief, in ways I still couldn't comprehend.

All compounded by the idea that I had burned bridges in my own career, and the company had since gone completely bust – an indirect result of that disastrous product launch and subsequent nosediving share price.

Par for the course in the business, I knew, but I felt terrible (not to mention guilty) for everyone concerned.

For my part, I knew if I wanted to return I could always get another position elsewhere – tech was the ultimate merry-go-round industry – but I couldn't just abandon the twins for the sake of a few extra zeros in our bank account.

Not to mention face the prospect of going back to the long hours and high-octane stress that came with such a dynamic field.

As things were, I could barely get to grips with a simple bout of real-life grocery shopping with a couple of babies, let alone manage a team.

But I knew one thing for sure: I was going to move heaven and earth to make my mother well again. I was going to fix this – that was my latest project, my number-one goal. Everything else could wait.

Speaking of which . . . that phone again! It just wouldn't stop.

'OK, seriously, whoever's calling – you win,' I muttered, reaching into my pocket and extracting the iPhone.

Glancing at the screen, I realised to my trepidation that I had a couple of missed calls from Dad, plus multiple unread texts.

My vision blurred and a shiver of foreboding raced down my back.

Gooseflesh erupted on my skin, even though I had been sweating profusely while trying to manage the dumpster fire that was today.

With shaking hands, I opened up a text from Nate. And then another from Matt. And another, and another.

All from my family.

◆ ◆ ◆

Across the Atlantic, the phone rang once before he answered.

'Dad,' I cried urgently, my voice several octaves higher than how it sounded normally. 'What's happening?' The words sounded strangled and I had that vision of Mum on our video call just the night before, though already it felt as if it had been years.

I was just overreacting, I reassured myself. She looked good; she was laughing and chatty. She was *fine*.

Wasn't she?

'We're at the hospital – they've admitted her. She . . . collapsed at home this morning, in her study . . . She is very weak, Jo. I told her not to get out of bed, but you know your mother . . .' His voice broke. 'I called the ambulance – I honestly thought that was the end. She didn't seem to be . . . breathing.' He sniffled hard and I felt my heart breaking for my poor dad, while my own anxiety rocketed so high I was finding it difficult to breathe.

'OK.' I exhaled and made my voice sound calm. 'And how is she now?'

'She ended up coming round when we were en route, but only for a couple of minutes. She is in a lot of pain, Jo. Everything is haywire and . . .' His voice trailed off and I heard him sob outright. 'Love, the doctor said she might not have much time . . .'

What? No, no, no. What was he talking about? This couldn't be happening. Not now. I spoke to her just last night. She was *fine!*

Seemingly on autopilot, I tucked the phone in between my ear and shoulder and white-knuckled my grocery cart, pushing it towards the exit.

Determination and focus flooded through my veins even as I struggled to see through my watery vision. No, this was just an overreaction; a precaution, even. They were probably just admitting her to keep an eye on her. But of course poor Dad would be distraught.

'Don't worry. I'm on my way. I'm booking flights right now, and will be on the first possible one out of here. I'm going to be there with you to talk to the doctors and find out what's happening. I'm coming to help, Dad, OK?' I said, injecting steel into my voice even though my heartbeat skittered anxiously, as I made mental lists of what needed to happen. 'Is Matt with you?' I enquired as I passed through the open grocery store doors, wondering what help my brother was being through all of this.

Not a lot, by the sound of things.

'Ma'am, excuse me, ma'am?' someone called out from behind me. 'You haven't paid for those.'

I stopped in my tracks. 'Oh Goddammit,' I cursed. 'Dad, sorry, hold on a sec.' I turned my cart around and shrugged apologetically to the manager. 'So sorry,' I called. 'Family emergency. Not thinking.' I wrenched the nappy bag out of the basket and hoisted out my daughters, one in each arm.

Suzy cried in outrage as I accidentally twisted her ankle. 'Oh, hon, I'm sorry,' I said, trying to free her, all the while under the judgemental gaze of the store security guy.

Finally, when I had both girls and my stuff secured, I turned and called over my shoulder to the full cart I had left behind me. 'Sorry again.'

'Is everything OK there, Joanna?' my dad finally asked, hearing the commotion on my end of the line.

'Of course . . .' I wasn't going to heap any more concern on his already overburdened shoulders. 'So . . . is anyone with you?'

'Yes, Matt's here now, and Romy's on her way back too. I also phoned Nate when I couldn't get you.'

My eyes widened at the mention of my younger sister coming home, and I recalled the text messages from Nate a moment before. Though Romy coming too didn't necessarily mean anything. She probably felt the same as I did, wanting to be there for our father to reassure him that everything would be OK.

Assuring Dad one more time that I too would be there as soon as I could, I disconnected so as to wrangle my wriggling, screeching daughters out of the empty shopping cart I'd purloined to ferry them back to the car.

All too soon, Suzy was screaming in protest at being manhandled into the SUV – and of course to remind me of her dirty nappy.

Fuuuck . . .

Could I get away with leaving her in it, just for a little while, until we got home? But no, I couldn't do that, the poor thing was already sore and uncomfortable from all the bashing around.

No self-respecting mother would even consider . . .

'Ma'am, excuse me? Is this yours?' I turned towards the voice in horror to see that while I was dithering over whether I should tend to one child, the other had rolled away in the shopping cart, right into the path of an approaching (but thankfully slow-moving) car.

The woman behind the wheel of that car was now staring at me through her rolled-down window with a look that could only be described as disgust.

'Oh my God, thank you, I'm so sorry.'

As if on cue, Katie bawled at the stranger, and again a still unbuckled Suzy joined her twin in their now typical caterwaul.

My ears buzzed and my head swam at the sheer stress of it all, and I felt like collapsing onto the ground and joining them.

'Thank you again,' I managed to the disdainful driver, hurriedly grabbing the cart and wheeling it back to the car, whereupon I scooped out Katie and fastened her into her car seat.

Then, trying to gain some semblance of composure, I whipped Suzy back out and proceeded to change her, albeit haphazardly. She was mad as hell at that point anyway, so what the hell . . .

'Right, all done,' I grunted, my voice compassionless, as I finally buckled her back in and then got into the front seat, trying to ignore my dizzying brain, and just let adrenaline take over.

I put my AirPods into my ears and pushed the button to ignite the SUV's ignition. Then remembering I had an ally, albeit a technological one, I employed Siri to call the airline as, hands still shaking, I somehow navigated the car out of the parking lot and back onto the highway.

As I waited to connect with the airline, my other line beeped. It was Nate. I switched over, hoping to keep this brief so I could crack on with booking a ticket on the next flight back to Ireland.

And also so I didn't betray how frazzled I was.

'Hey,' I answered shortly, willing the twins to stay silent for once. But by then I think they were worn out. Finally.

'I've been trying to reach you,' he said, his voice tense.

'I know, I just talked to Dad. I need to fly home, so just finish whatever it is you're doing and come back to watch the girls.'

It didn't even sound like a request coming from my lips, but a direct order. It was strange how in charge and businesslike I sounded right then. As if I had flipped a switch from Meltdown Mom back to Corporate Joanna.

'What do you think I'm doing?' he snapped back. 'Like I don't have the critical thinking skills needed to know that we have to fly to Ireland.'

'We? Hardly. No need for us all to go.'

'What? Jo, of course there is. Don't you think the girls should be there for their grandmother's . . .'

Their grandmother's *what*? What was he trying to insinuate?

There was silence on the other end as he failed to finish what he was about to say, and I cracked my neck, feeling the stress and tension roll off of me in waves.

At that moment, of course, Suzy erupted with a fresh scream of her own and once again her twin joined in.

It was the Last Straw.

'Can't both of you just *shut the hell up* for once?' I shrieked, guessing that I had probably just burst one of Nate's eardrums.

'Jeez, Jo, what the hell . . . ? They're just babies – they don't know any better. They sense that you're tense and upset and are just mirroring,' he muttered.

'Oh, well, thank you very much, Dr Spock, I had no idea.'

Another silence on the other end of the line, and I felt immediately guilty. I didn't need to be doing this to Nate. Yes, we were struggling since the rug had been pulled from under us financially (or in reality, since my husband had gambled everything), but this wasn't the time. He had insisted he could rebuild, get us back to where we were financially, but it was a mountain to climb.

It also meant that he now spent pretty much every waking hour working, and putting even more distance between us. While I spent *my* waking hours not being a hands-on mother and domestic goddess, but focused on a far more important project, saving my mother.

One that this time, wouldn't – *couldn't* – fail.

I flat out refused to allow it.

Suddenly, I felt as if I was drowning. The enormity of the situation was hitting me – I truly hadn't expected to receive this call today – hadn't expected to be told that things were perhaps worse than I'd imagined.

No, it's not that bad, probably just an overreaction. She's fine.

I took a deep breath and tried to calm down – I knew I was close to losing it, to shutting down altogether, and I needed to get back on track.

'Look, I'm sorry,' I said softly to Nate then. 'I just . . . I was having a bit of a . . . situation in the store when everyone was trying to call me, and then I almost took off with a full cart without paying and Suzy had a poopy nappy for at least twenty minutes and the two of them just keep screaming and screaming, and now my mother—'

This wasn't supposed to be how today went. I was grocery shopping so I could make a nice dinner for Nate and me, so afterwards we might relax in front of the TV and drink some wine and take some time for just us – something we hadn't done in what felt like months.

But none of that was going to happen. Not now.

'OK, but I need you to calm down, please. I know you're stressed but I don't want you getting into an accident. Please, just take a deep breath.'

Realising he was completely right, I tried to centre myself and felt thankful that the ramp leading to our house was the next exit. I was not fit to be driving right now.

With my silence, he asked, 'Jo, are you still there?'

Tears had somehow begun running down my cheeks, but I mumbled, 'Yes, I'm fine.'

'I'm on my way home now, OK? Just take it easy the rest of the way.'

I wiped my nose again, on my sleeve, and realised that I still had the airline on hold.

'The flight!' I gasped. 'I need to sort my ticket.'

'I can do it,' Nate offered.

'Could you?' I sobbed in relief, feeling utterly helpless just then. 'Whatever you can get – in coach, obviously.'

His voice was terse again. 'Obviously. But we're coming too, Jo.'

I didn't think that was necessary or indeed a good idea, but I could hardly blame him for wanting to be supportive.

'OK, just keep in mind that we'll all need to be together, so ask them to switch stuff round if needs be.'

The journey would be bad enough given the stressful circumstances, but my headache deepened as I tried to imagine the pure hell it would be if Nate failed to take into account that ferrying a couple of antsy babies on our laps all the way across the Atlantic in tightly packed non-reclining seats would be very different from the first time, when all the extra legroom, plus the massively accommodating Aer Lingus hostesses at our beck and call, made it a breeze. Notwithstanding the fact that these two were no longer quite so angelic either.

'Actually, maybe you should just let me sort the flights altogether,' I muttered darkly.

'Fine,' he sighed, sounding pissed off, evidently sensing I didn't trust him to do anything properly.

But how the hell could I? He was little enough help with the girls as it was, let alone having any true idea of what their needs would be for a last-minute twelve-hour journey through multiple time zones. Hell, I wasn't entirely sure myself . . .

'If you get home before us, maybe just make a start on the packing, even?' I suggested then.

'OK, but what sort of stuff should I include for the girls to wear to, well . . .'

And my anger emerged with renewed vigour. 'And why would anyone give a damn what they're wearing?'

Another deep sigh came from the other end of the phone.

Our relationship was a minefield. No matter where he stepped, something was going to be set off.

'You don't need to bite my head off, Joanna. I didn't know if there was maybe some kind of dress code for these things or something.'

What things? Just what was he trying to imply? She was *fine*.

'Oh, just forget it!' I shook my head, unable to believe that we were even having this conversation. This whole thing was crazy. *Surreal.* 'Look, why don't you just take care of yourself and I will take care of everything else, like always. You just pack your own suitcase if you can manage even that much. OK?'

Before he could respond, I disconnected the call and was happy to find I was still on hold with the airline.

I raised my chin and swallowed hard, making mental check-lists of everything that would need to happen between now and flying back to Ireland so last-minute, as well as beginning to prepare myself to stand at the helm of what would happen once we got there. At the end of the day, I was the eldest in the family, the planner, the organiser – the one who, supposedly, could do it all.

But right then, it felt like that Joanna was from another life.

Chapter 16

Sitting in one of a row of chairs set up in the (now ironically named) living room of our family home, I stared at the open casket in front of me and tried to assess how I felt.

Numb. Blank. Exhausted. In shock that this was even happening. That things had been much, much worse than I'd allowed myself to believe. That I had been in denial.

But most of all, crippled with guilt that I had failed her.

Now my mother – or at least the physical element of her – lay peacefully in front of me. Mourners, mostly friends and neighbours from the community, milled around the room talking quietly with each other as they waited to pay their respects.

While many stopped here and there to offer their condolences, I was tired of accepting. I was tired of being stoic, I was tired of being nice to people. I was just . . . tired.

I stared at her lifeless form, half wondering if I concentrated hard enough would she open her eyes and sit up. Smile, open her arms and embrace me, allowing me to cry happy tears, and this would all be one bad joke. She would say that she had just been resting. That none of this was real. That I was right not to worry.

That she was *fine.*

Squinting my eyes, I swallowed hard, determined not to cry. I didn't deserve it.

She looked like herself but at the same time she didn't. The lip colour they had chosen was way too garish, and in real life she would have never worn that blush shade on her cheeks.

I felt a sudden surge of irrational anger and wanted to scream. I had told the funeral director that her make-up should be natural. But he couldn't even guarantee that had been done right. And dammit, I'd supplied enough pictures. For a moment, I thought about getting up and voicing my displeasure. I needed someone to blame right now and the guy seemed like an easy target.

Actually, who was I kidding? I had been blaming everyone for everything for days. My husband. My children. My siblings. The only person who had escaped my ire was my dad.

But mostly myself.

However, a tiny voice inside me that sounded suspiciously like my mother's chided, *Joanna, it's not necessary to blame anyone. The make-up is fine. Just relax. It's just a shell. Everything is fine.*

Relax? I questioned. How can I relax? You're not here. You'll never be here again. I didn't get to save you, didn't get to hold your hand and tell you all the things I should have told you, how much I loved you and how I wasn't ready for you to leave us – all the things that needed to be said.

Instead, I was too busy planning how to *fix* the situation to even notice that you were slipping away right in front of my eyes.

Until it was too late.

I didn't even get to see you before . . .

And now I don't know what to do. I don't know what I am doing. I don't know what to do next. And while you think everything's OK right now, I certainly am not.

Not by a long shot. Mum, I'm unravelling.

Tears threatened again then and I raised my chin, fighting them back.

No way. I had no right to cry.

Folding my hands once again in my lap, I tried to make sense of who I had become since that phone call in the supermarket.

Everything seemed like a blur.

Right now I was literally the worst version of myself – someone I almost didn't recognise.

Angry. Resentful. Bitter. Impatient.

At least Mum hadn't seen that version of me, I reminded myself. Thankfully, she had only seen the Joanna she knew. Then I squirmed a little in my seat, realising the truth.

That this angry, resentful person hadn't just appeared in the funeral parlour. That person had been around for a little while now. She had been taking up space for the last couple of months if I was being honest.

I didn't like it, either. And more to the point, I no longer recognised myself.

I returned my attention to the casket. My mum had been an incredible mother, an incredible human being. She dripped kindness, had been composed under pressure, elegant and graceful no matter what life had thrown at her. She had always made it look so easy. And I didn't know how she had done that.

Because I was utterly useless. At everything. And there was no instruction manual to look up.

How on earth *did* you do it? I pondered. Why did I think it could be the same for me? And why was everything suddenly turning out to be so hard? Motherhood, marriage . . . life.

I thought of Nate. We had always been so easy together – life had always been so easy. But now everything required immense effort, which made me wonder just how strong or otherwise our relationship truly was in the first place, if the fact that we no longer had so much money had turned everything to shit.

Though I couldn't exactly ignore my own role in basically pulling the rug from beneath everything we had built, either.

I had been so sure that domesticity would be a breeze for me – I mean, being a leader of a multinational tech corporation was surely more challenging than feeding babies and changing nappies, wasn't it?

Now I knew I had made a momentous mistake – not just in not confiding my intentions (or nascent uncertainties about the project) to Nate earlier, in enough time to stop the oncoming train wreck that was our financial worries, but a mistake full stop.

Why *had* I wanted to stay home, anyway? Was I just hiding from reality – afraid to confront the truth about myself, that I *didn't* have all the answers?

I truly hated going down this rabbit hole, too . . . the place where all I did was doubt myself.

Closing my eyes and taking a deep breath, I pictured myself once again in my former office. Looking out over the Northern California vista through my floor-to-ceiling glass windows had always calmed me when I was feeling stressed, and I summoned the Palo Alto view now from memory, hoping to channel the feelings of calm that had been eluding me these last few months since walking away.

Or in truth, since Mum had revealed her diagnosis.

However, my efforts were derailed because just then I heard my name being spoken aloud – and the voice that kept repeating it was insistent to the point of being annoying.

'Earth to Joanna,' my husband whispered. 'Where is the baby stuff? Suzy is hungry, and Katie will be too.'

I opened my eyes and snapped my head in his direction, trying to keep my cool, trying to remember he was supposed to be my ally and the man I loved, but instantly irritated that I could not even have a few minutes of peace at my own mother's funeral.

'Where do you think it is?' I said, sharper than I meant to. 'Where their stuff always is – in the nappy bag in the kitchen. The.

Very. Place. You. Have. Been. Camping. Out. With. My. Brother. All. Day.'

I breathed heavily through my nose as if I had smelled something rotten and fixed him with a nasty glare – something I noticed he was returning in full force after he glanced around to see who might be listening or watching.

'You know, of course I realise you are stressed and upset right now, but our daughters need something, and unlike you I don't know everything about everything.' His face tightened as he leaned closer, whispering harshly, 'I am trying my best, Jo. I really am. Especially now. I don't know how to do anything right with you. And I'm getting tired of it.'

I raised my eyebrows at him, challenging him to please continue.

'Are we seriously going to do this *now*?' I snapped, realising my voice had risen an octave or two – and also that I didn't care who was watching. 'For the record, I don't care if you're tired of it. Quite frankly, *I'm* tired of being the one who does everything. I am sick of being the one who has to fix everything – for everyone.'

Including you.

The unspoken words hung in the air.

Some of the colour drained out of Nate's face and he shook his head.

'Right,' he sighed, resignation seeping into his tone. 'I don't want to fight with you, honestly. I just wanted to find out where our daughters' stuff was. We all know to leave you alone.'

He was backing down from the fight I was instigating. And I don't know why somehow that annoyed me even more.

I plopped back down in my seat and turned my attention once more back to the casket, effectively dismissing him. 'Well, now you know where it is, so maybe you can do something productive – for once. And just leave me be.'

Nate turned on his heel, his face hard and eyes like slits as he departed. 'Gladly.'

And I was once again alone, simmering in my loss, guilt and out-and-out failure.

◆ ◆ ◆

Romy felt as if she had been hit by a train.

She felt . . . broken.

She's really gone, she thought, realising the words still didn't feel real.

But she knew they were. She knew she was awake and not dreaming some horrible nightmare.

The past couple of days had been surreal – first the frantic dash home to the hospital to say goodbye, then all the sitting downstairs for hours next to her mother's casket with her dad and siblings, greeting people she hadn't seen in years, accepting condolences from people whose faces all started to blend together.

And through it all she had felt terribly alone. Even though her family was right there next to her, shoulder to shoulder.

The only real sense of support she'd felt had been from a text she'd received from that nice guy Damien she had met in the park when she got the call. But she couldn't even expend the energy to unpack any reason for his kindness. There was too much else to ponder.

Upon her arrival at the hospital a few days before, she, Matt and their dad had embraced and cried collectively when Cathy passed peacefully away. Then Joanna had arrived from California and they'd come back here, supposedly to all grieve together as a family.

But something had changed.

It was as if whatever small bit of Cathy that was still with them when they held each other in devastation at her loss had changed the entire dynamic once her essence was gone.

Since that time, Romy had been plagued by a real sense of family unease.

Matt, who had always been a natural confidant, even when they digressed into bickering, had been distant. It was like he was there, but he wasn't.

Romy knew he was having his own struggles – and that he had given up a lot to move home and be nearby for their mother in her final months. It was an easy decision, he'd insisted, given his work suspension, but she wasn't sure where that left him now.

She hadn't had the opportunity to talk to her brother about anything other than what related to their mum. Pretty much all family interaction over the last couple of months had revolved around her illness – and now there was this huge, almost surreal void.

Because what was the point in anything else without Cathy anyway? Everything had changed.

Romy pondered this as she pulled on a pair of black yoga pants and a running T-shirt. Shoving her feet into her old Converse, she pulled her hair out of the chignon she had plaited that morning and brushed it out before the mirror, as if in a trance.

She had felt terrible for Jo that she hadn't made it back in time before their mother passed away, and had done her best to help with the funeral director and all related administration on their dad's behalf. She had told her sister multiple times to please let her know what needed to be done and she would do it. But even that seemed like the wrong thing to say, and had earned her nothing but a dramatic eye roll.

In the end Romy had stopped offering, but nonetheless stood at the ready – eager to be her sister's second in command if she or

Matt needed assistance, anything that might help take the load off for any of them.

Their dad especially.

She had been shocked to see him in the flesh upon her arrival at the hospital. He looked as if he had folded in on himself, and at first glance she was worried that he was sick too.

But no, what ailed him was grief.

He had been so stoic all through Cathy's illness, as ever her rock. But now it was like he was a robot operating on autopilot, and she felt suddenly afraid about what would happen next – who would take care of him now?

Who would make sure that her dad, who she knew had never even needed to boil an egg, ate three square meals per day? How would he manage this big old house without her mum's skilled hand?

Feeling called to action, Romy realised that *this* was where she could expend her energy just now. She could slip into that role and try her utmost to make sure her dad was tended to, that the dishwasher was unloaded, that there was food out in case he or anyone else was hungry (and indeed, a steady stream of casseroles and other dishes had been arriving the last two days from her mother's many friends), that the housework was attended to, the plants were watered, that the family could function and their home run like clockwork, the way it was supposed to.

Taking a deep breath, she moved towards the door, steeled with a sense of purpose. Maybe if the rhythms of the house could be brought into tune, then maybe, just maybe, they would all band together and some semblance of family harmony might once again kick in.

She headed downstairs to the kitchen, as ever the heart of the house, already beginning to make a mental checklist of all the more menial little tasks that would've been neglected recently.

However, as she neared the door she heard multiple voices, some muffled, some raised – Joanna's, Nate's, and the girls babbling in the background.

Something, a piece of crockery it sounded like, clattered abruptly against the granite countertop and she heard her sister bark a command. 'Oh, for goodness' sake, that is not where that goes. Here, just give it to me, I'll do it.'

Romy's stomach automatically clenched with anxiety as she wondered what type of snake pit she might be walking into, and turning into the doorway of the kitchen she took in the scene before her.

One of her nieces was sitting on the floor with a spilled bowl of baby food in front of her. Her tiny hand banged the spoon on the ground happily, as if she had just discovered a new talent for drumming, while bits of green gloop flew about like soggy confetti.

Her sister was in her mother's arms, crying, as she tugged a mass of Joanna's blonde hair with a hand covered in something orange and sticky.

Jo was currently consumed with shooting daggers at her husband, who, it seemed, was trying to do what Romy had originally set out to accomplish – unload the dishwasher.

Nate looked frazzled as he wearily turned his eyes between his irritable wife and his baby daughters, who were innocently turning the kitchen into more of a disaster zone than it already was.

And then there was her dad. Her poor broken father was sitting at the kitchen table with a cup of tea in front of him, an open bottle of Jameson alongside it, and she wondered if he was self-medicating to deal not only with his grief, but all this chaos too.

Romy cleared her throat. 'Hey, is there – is there anything I can help with?' she offered, hating how meek she sounded.

Joanna's head turned abruptly over her shoulder in a rotation reminiscent of a scene from *The Exorcist.*

'Yes. Take over unloading the dishwasher – at least you know where things are *supposed* to go,' she ordered. 'Nate, sort Suzy.'

Neither statement was a request, Romy noted, inching forward to relieve her brother-in-law. 'Sure.'

'I'll have her sorted in a minute and then I'll clean up the mess the other one's made on the floor,' her sister grunted. 'Dad, are you hungry?'

Nate sniffed. 'Of course you will.'

Outside of the time last Christmas when Joanna announced her intention to become a stay-at-home mum, Romy had never witnessed a bad word between her sister and brother-in-law. They had always seemed so in tune with one other; even their bickering was good-natured, and they were so effortlessly at ease in each other's company.

She didn't think it had been a facade, either; their marriage was one that she had admired and hoped to emulate someday. But now all that seemed to have vanished.

And she was shocked by the transformation.

The tension between them was palpable, and Romy wondered if all this bad feeling was new, given the stress of the current circumstances, or if there was something deeper that had been festering.

But there was no way for her to speak to her sister about it. Especially not now.

'Dad,' Joanna said, turning to her father, her voice terse. 'I was asking you if you are hungry.'

He didn't respond – he just kept peering into his teacup, as if it held the universe's secrets.

'Dad?' Joanna raised her voice a little.

Romy, who was awkwardly straining to put away a serving bowl on a shelf a touch too high for her, instinctively flinched at her sister's impatient tone, and somehow the dish fell from her grasp and shattered on the floor.

'Oh!' she cried out, watching helplessly while it all happened as if in slow motion.

Nate grabbed little Suzy just in time and pulled her into his arms, unscathed, while Joanna moved to shield Katie from the broken shards, as well as the noise.

And in that moment, Bill finally came to attention. 'Mum loved that. We got it as a wedding present . . .' he mumbled helplessly.

Romy stood open-mouthed with dismay, her hands shaking. 'Oh God – Dad, I'm so sorry. It was an accident. I just . . . got a fright, and the shelf was a bit too high . . .'

Joanna, seemingly oblivious to the fact it was her outburst that had startled Romy in the first place, fixed her steely gaze on her sister.

'Jesus Christ, must you always be so goddamn *useless?* That was Mum's and you broke it. That dish has been used at every family gathering forever – and now it's broken – just *gone* – forever. And Mum loved it. I honestly cannot believe you. I cannot believe this family . . .' She turned on her heel and closed the space between her and her father, abruptly shoving Katie at him. 'So obviously now I need to sort *that* out too.'

Bill, evidently confused at the sudden appearance of his granddaughter in his arms, struggled to hold her, and the child, equally upset by this change in caretaker, screamed her displeasure.

'Dad, you're going to drop her . . .'

'Jo . . .' Romy cried, horrified by all this tension. 'Please don't speak to him like that. I know you're upset, but seriously . . . you're losing the run of yourself.'

Her sister stopped short and put a hand on her hip. 'Huh. Speaking of running, maybe if *you'd* got up off that arse of yours and done a bit more exercise, it might not have happened in the first place.'

As she stared at her sister, who'd now flushed bright red, Romy's world seemed to stop.

Up off that arse of yours . . . What was she trying to say?

'I . . . I didn't mean . . .' her sister began, but Nate started to speak at the very same moment, cutting her off.

'For Christ's sake, Joanna,' he snapped, edging his wife out of the way and scooping Katie up. 'It's OK, Bill, I've got her,' he said kindly, before turning in Romy's direction. 'Seriously, don't mind her. Of course it was an accident – you didn't do anything wrong.'

Still shaking a little, she could do nothing other than nod and, with that, Matt appeared in the doorway with Hazel trailing behind him.

He looked from one face to the other before demanding, 'What in the *hell* is going on in here . . .'

Chapter 17

Oh God, what had I just said?

I opened and closed my mouth – and then did it again. I couldn't seem to find my voice. Which was crazy, considering what had erupted from my throat just moments before.

Useless. If you'd got up off that arse of yours . . .

As soon as the words were out of my mouth, I choked on them. Because my little sister's face just . . . crumpled.

What was I thinking? Or worse, *who* had I become?

'I asked what's going on,' Matt repeated, his voice low. 'Why all the shouting in here?'

My gaze frantically shifted from my siblings to my husband, and then to my father.

Disgust and hurt was painted plain on all of their faces – even my dad's, who had just seemed to wake up from the stupor he had been existing in over the last few days.

'Yeah, Joanna,' Nate sniped, 'why don't you fill your brother in on what's going on?' I opened my mouth once again, this time to defend myself, but he was still talking. 'Matt, it seems that no one in this house can do the job of Her Royal Highness. We are all stupid and incapable compared to you, right, sweetheart?' The scorn dripping from my husband's words was palpable, and I got the clearest realisation ever that we were now well and truly a million miles from a partnership. Maybe even finished as a couple. He despised me.

And he was right.

I felt attacked – now they were *all* ganging up on me. Even though I was just as wounded as the rest of them. I was grieving, too.

But it didn't matter. Even though I was the one who'd got everything done, dealt with the hospital stuff and the funeral director, made sure Dad was OK and visitors were taken care of . . . pretty much *everything* was taken care of, right until the moment they lowered my mother's coffin into the ground . . . oh God.

A fresh tsunami of grief hit, quickly followed by repeated waves of guilt, despair and more anger.

How could she be gone? How – when just a couple of days ago I'd spoken to her and she looked so happy and relaxed and *alive.*

So much so that I was already making plans for when she beat this, once she conquered it. Because *of course* she'd conquer it. My brain wouldn't allow any other possibility. My mother could do anything.

The room began to spin.

I should have been there.

'Honestly, Jo, you have some nerve . . .'

My brother's words suddenly filtered into my brain and I snapped back into action. 'Oh, fuck off, Matt. Nothing happening in this kitchen is any of your business,' I spat at him. 'All you've been doing since I got home is lurking in your room or moping around feeling sorry for yourself. You've been absolutely no help. But that's par for the course, isn't it?'

He took a step into the kitchen – red in the face, like he was about to explode.

'Par for the course? Par for the course?' he bellowed, rounding on me. 'Mum just fucking *died*, and you swan in from America all high and mighty, and pointing the finger? Carrying on like you are suffering worse than the rest of us? Where the fuck were you for the last three months, Jo? Where were you while I was here, watching it all happen right in front of my eyes?'

Where were you . . .

Hazel tugged at his elbow, trying to calm him, but Matt jerked his arm away. 'Watching it all and there was nothing, not a single thing I could do to stop it, or make it easier for her . . . How dare you accuse me of feeling sorry for myself when *you* are the fucking martyr here, though I never realised it before now. I always just thought that you were controlling, but your superiority complex goes much further than that, doesn't it?' His voice was ice cold as he turned to face my husband and shook his head. 'Honestly, I can't figure out how you ever put up with her.'

Nate was nodding in agreement, like he too was coming to the same realisation and wondering why the hell he hadn't checked out of our marriage yet. I looked at my daughters in his arms – they were both shockingly quiet, weirdly so.

As if they too were drawing the same silent conclusion.

The reality of what Matt was saying, along with the strain of the last few months, compounded with every other emotion that flooded through my being right then – grief, frustration, denial . . .

But mostly soul-crushing guilt that yet again I had failed – miserably – at the most important hurdle. And that there was no coming back from that, no second chance. No way of turning back the clock.

'Lads, please, ye need to calm down. Can you imagine how upset your poor mam would be to hear this?' Dad pleaded wearily. 'You especially, Joanna.' His voice was firm and I don't think I had heard him use that tone with me since I was a teenager.

'Yes, cop yourself on,' reiterated Matt. 'This is neither the time nor the place. Grow up, Joanna.'

All this naked hostility threatened to overwhelm me – I felt like a caged animal.

Which was probably why, in the very next moment, I lashed out like one.

'Grow up? *You* telling *me* to grow up?' I rounded on Matt, furious. Beside him, Hazel looked like she wanted to melt into the floor – and something that had been hiding in the recesses of my brain automatically jumped out. 'You're one to talk for someone kicked out of their job after a schoolyard brawl.'

'Joanna . . .' His jaw was clenched.

'What . . . ?' his girlfriend piped up, frowning. 'What do you mean? He left work to be closer to Cathy . . .' But when Matt didn't immediately move to contradict her, she seemed to realise she'd got the wrong end of the stick. Or, worse, had been given it. 'Schoolyard brawl . . . Matt, what's she talking about?'

'Jo . . .' my brother warned again, the wind instantly dropping out of his sails as the colour drained from his face, and I knew he was desperately trying to figure out a way to make me stop talking.

'You mean, you didn't tell her about your macho pissing contest over God knows what – or more to the point, *who*?' I added meanly, feigning innocence about Hazel's cluelessness – though the excuse he'd given her was also news to me. 'I don't know which is worse, lying to us all about what really happened or using our – *my* – mother as a smokescreen for your sneakiness. But nothing new there either, I suppose.'

At this, I heard Romy suck in a sharp breath and Dad looked at the floor.

'Seriously, what is she talking about?' Hazel pleaded. 'Lying about what?'

Now Nate was also looking at the floor, shaking his head in disgust, and for a brief second I regretted opening this particular

Pandora's box. It wasn't my transgression, nor was it my place to force a discussion about it between him and his girlfriend.

But to hell with it, he was the one who'd lashed out at me.

'Matt,' she insisted again, willing him to meet her gaze. 'You told me that you voluntarily took the leave of absence to come home because of Cathy. Nothing about any . . . brawl.' Her voice grew sharper with each word. 'What am I missing here?'

My brother and I locked eyes then, and I knew I had just sent his carefully constructed house of cards tumbling to the ground.

He hadn't told Hazel a word about last Christmas, hadn't given her any indication that his leave of absence was far from the result of wanting to be a dutiful son, but because of his own shitty behaviour.

It was cowardly and despicable and, what's worse, he'd used our mother's illness to cover it up.

At that moment I despised him, and was only too happy that he'd been forced into a corner. Hazel might not know anything, but there was no way he was going to be able to skirt around telling her now.

That his return home had nothing whatsoever to do with being a dutiful son. And everything to do with being a duplicitous ass.

I knew I could also put Hazel out of her misery, could flat out call him out on the real reason for the fight, upon which he still refused to elaborate, and which I was pretty sure meant he'd been up to his old man-about-town tricks again.

It would serve him right – given the accusations he'd just levelled at me.

Where were you . . .

But as angry as I felt, something stopped me. Because I figured Matt and I had uttered enough home truths.

And that the powder keg that was now this family had well and truly exploded.

Chapter 18

THIS CHRISTMAS

Welcome Home.

Romy stood shuddering outside the Arrivals terminal at Dublin airport and winced as a fresh burst of sleety rain hit her in the face.

She pulled the lapels of her coat tightly around her and scanned the drivers in the cars rolling past – none containing her brother. Checking her text messages, she scrolled to her most recent exchange with Matt, reaffirming to herself that, yes, he did indeed know what time she'd landed. Then she hastily pressed the Call button on his details, hoping against hope that he was somewhere nearby. It was *freezing*.

He answered on the second ring.

'What's up?' he enquired absently by way of greeting.

'What's *up*?' Romy gasped, eyes widening. 'Definitely not my plane anyway. It landed an hour ago – I'm outside Arrivals. I texted you when we hit the tarmac and I'm still waiting.' She knew her clipped sentences made her sound grumpy and impatient. But then again, she was.

To say nothing of edgy and emotional too.

Wheeling her suitcase through the sliding customs doors into a festive, twinkling arrivals hall with a sea of smiling faces – all lined up and waving Welcome Home signs to incoming passengers, amid excited tearful family reunions – made her emotional at the best of times.

And when she'd come through this time, for one brief idiotic moment there'd been a side of her that almost expected to see both her parents waiting with a sign of their own, proclaiming that this entire year had all been a practical joke, a bad dream even. That she'd see her mum there with her arms out, ready and waiting for Romy to move into her warm embrace.

But of course that hadn't happened, could never have happened, and feeling stupid afresh, she swallowed back another lump in her throat.

'Oh,' her brother answered now. 'Yeah, I got tied up. You're going to have to cab it back.'

She breathed out heavily through her nose, her frustration soaring. 'Seriously? How long would you have made me stand here before you even bothered your arse to let me know? It's wet, freezing and the airport is manic.'

'Sorry, Your Highness. Like I said, I was busy. Dad needed help with something.'

'Even so, you could have at least let me know to make other arrangements instead of just leaving me abandoned in the freezing cold . . .'

A pause ensued and she could picture in her mind her brother shrugging, 'I just did.'

And with that Matt hung up, leaving Romy staring at her phone in disbelief.

◆ ◆ ◆

Some thirty minutes later, she reached the top of the taxi queue and hefted her suitcase into the boot of the next available car, now feeling thoroughly cheesed off.

If she was being honest, there was a brief moment there where she almost threw in the towel, trudged back into the terminal and caught a flight back to London. But regardless of how annoyed she happened to be with Matt, Romy couldn't do that to her dad.

Not on their first family Christmas without Mum.

It was bad enough (though not all that terrible, for her personally) that Joanna might not even bother coming this year. And maybe that would be the right decision.

Regardless, this Christmas would be a nightmare and there was little point in anyone trying to pretend otherwise. Having multiple family members absent might even lessen the heartache and shift the focus from the more important 'missing one'.

'Home from the big smoke for the festivities?' the driver piped up conversationally.

Turning her attention back to the here and now, she nodded, suddenly flooded with a dizzying sense of déjà vu as she recalled her taxi ride home for Christmas this time last year.

'Yes,' she said dully.

'I'm sure Mam and Dad will be delighted,' he continued in his thick Dublin accent. 'I love this time of the year – all the returning Irish from all corners of the globe, coming back to the oul sod.'

'No. My mum, ah . . . she's no longer with us,' she clarified slowly, the words sounding surprisingly normal on her tongue, considering the accompanying inner anguish.

In the rear-view mirror, she saw his face blanch and then he glanced back at her over his shoulder.

'Ah, Jaysus, pet, I'm so sorry. I'm a feckin' gobshite, don't mind me.'

She shook her head and looked down at her hands. 'No, it's fine. You couldn't have known. It's just – it's still . . . a bit new, I suppose. And this'll be our first . . . our first . . .'

Do not break down. Do not *cry*, she willed herself silently, unable to finish the sentence.

'Ah, sorry again, love. That first one without them is never easy.'

She mumbled her assent and once again turned her attention out of the window. She didn't want any more small talk. What Romy really wanted just then was time to organise her thoughts in preparation for her arrival.

Despite her best intentions, she hadn't been back all that much since the funeral, and in the interim her father had become so withdrawn, completely lost in his grief.

And she had felt powerless to help him.

'I bet your dad will appreciate having you home all the same. You have other family coming in too?'

Romy took a deep breath. He just wasn't getting the hint.

'Not as far as I know,' she said truthfully. 'My sister lives in California and probably won't make it back this year. Or so I hear. My brother already lives at home with my dad. Well, he does now – he used to live in Galway but . . .' She trailed off, wondering why she was offering all of this detail.

He smiled kindly, albeit awkwardly, and much to Romy's relief, finally decided to give up and just leave her alone with her thoughts as they sped down the motorway and onwards to the address she'd given him.

Forty minutes later, the taxi eventually pulled into the driveway of her childhood home.

Romy remained in her seat as she gazed out of the window, as if setting eyes on the two-storey Georgian farmhouse for the very first time. It felt like her heart was stuck in her throat.

Winter gloom and bare trees notwithstanding, it just didn't look like the same house that she had grown up in any more – and certainly didn't resemble the happy home that had hosted so many wonderful family gatherings, Christmas or otherwise.

There were no festive lights or decorations. That was the first standout. Either her dad and Matt hadn't gotten around to putting anything up yet – or they had no intention of doing so at all. Only the bare clematis creeper hung like a spindly shroud across the double-fronted white rendered facade.

But there was more too, more beyond mere aesthetics. Romy couldn't identify it exactly, but it sent an actual chill down her spine.

It was as if the house itself knew that a different era had been ushered in these days.

'So?' the driver ventured from the front seat. 'This the right spot, yeah?'

He sounded tentative, obviously surprised that she hadn't made any great show of finding her wallet, or any move at all to get out.

'Yes, sorry. This is the right place. And sorry too for . . . well, you know, for earlier. It's a little while since I've been back and . . .' she mumbled quietly, while beginning to gather her things, unsure why she felt the need to apologise (and she could almost picture Jo rolling her eyes at the very notion), given he was the one who'd presumed, but she couldn't help it. He seemed like a nice enough guy, so she hated to make him feel in any way ill at ease.

'No bother at all. I'm sure it's nice to be home. Course, the great thing about family is you can all seek comfort in one another now,' he said kindly, 'especially at this time of year.'

Feeling humbled by his well-intentioned but deeply ironic assessment, Romy again thanked the driver before exiting the car.

A moment later, she was alone on the driveway, staring up at the place that for her had always stood waiting as a beacon of warmth and comfort, no matter the season.

Low afternoon winter sun shone weakly through the bare trees surrounding the plot, and Romy scanned the darkened sash windows upstairs and down, looking for signs of life – any sign at all indicating that there was indeed someone inside.

Tentatively, she took a step forward, allowing her feet to carry her up the gravelled driveway to the granite steps of the porch.

As she approached the front door, this year bleakly absent of her mother's trademark home-made holly-berry wreath and twinkling fresh pine garland surrounding the arch, she couldn't help but recall her homecoming this time last year, when this same door had been happily thrown open amid a chorus of welcoming voices from inside.

Whereas today it remained firmly shut, not even a flicker of light or sound from within, and again Romy had the instinctive sense that she had got it wrong, that she shouldn't have made the journey back this year.

No one was waiting to welcome her with open arms like before, and without Mum, home was different – not just this year, but forever.

Trying to quell her rising unease, she reached out a tentative hand, grasping the brass doorknob and checking if it would turn. It did, without hesitation, and thus was unlocked.

She pushed the door open and it creaked on its hinges, a sound she had rarely heard in this house before. Everything had always been kept in tip-top shape – her dad a whiz with the WD-40.

As the dim entryway came into view she waited, holding her breath, ready to be proved wrong, hoping for an interior door to open somewhere and her whole family to jump out and embrace her in a chorus of cheers – as if this entire year had just been one long nightmare.

But again, going through to the living room, she was met with nothing but darkness and almost eerie silence.

No overhead or lower-level lighting, but also not a single festive decoration in sight, no welcoming glow from a twinkling tinsel-bedecked tree by the window, nor any tantalising cinnamon smells wafting through from the kitchen.

Even the air in here smelled stale, like the space had been shut away from fresh air and sunlight for too long.

It was as if the season had purposely neglected to bestow its magic on the house this year, and Romy felt her shoulders sag like she had just been met with some invisible force, zapping her of what little energy she had summoned up for this year's homecoming.

Suddenly, she wished in earnest that she really had just stayed in London.

She might have been all alone for Christmas there, but surely that would've been better than feeling like she'd just stepped into a tomb.

Chapter 19

'Dammit! Why will this not WORK?!'

No matter how hard I tried to fit the sheet onto the cot mattress, the elastic kept snapping back on me, crumpling the rest in the middle like a lumpy, half-eaten marshmallow.

Could this day get any worse?

As if on cue, from behind I heard the distinctive sound of flesh on flesh followed by a blood-curdling wail.

'Mama! Mama!' Suzy yelped, while her sister offered a series of innocent gurgles. I turned to see what was causing the commotion, only to find that one toddler had the other in a pretty solid half nelson and seemed very happy about it.

Her twin, however, did not.

'Katie, no,' I scolded, jumping forward to remove her hand from her sister's tiny neck. 'Bad girl, you're going to hurt poor Suzy.'

I was sweating. Between wrestling with the sheet and my offspring, I had in fact sweated clear through the simple white T-shirt I was wearing. I put a hand up to my armpit and felt the perspiration, and in that sticky moment I felt like joining my daughters in their cries.

'Oh God . . .' I moaned. 'Surely it's time for your nap.'

However, when I checked my watch, I found that it wasn't even close.

'How is it only ten goddamn thirty in the morning?' I muttered under my breath. I had been up with the sun (and these two), yet felt like I hadn't accomplished a single thing.

And as for sweating through my shirt, what was the big deal? It's not like I had showered yet today. When was the last time I'd showered *before* lunch?

'Not like you have anywhere to go, Joanna,' I murmured, morosely reflecting on days past, where I had jam-packed work schedules, lunch appointments, nights out with friends, outings to chic restaurants with Nate and a phone that buzzed non-stop with opportunity.

All I did now was wipe noses and change nappies – and when it came to connecting with other people . . . to be honest, I felt lucky if I could get a text message from my own husband that I hadn't initiated myself.

I had a hard time recognising my life these days. This wasn't how I had pictured things. The vision I had this time last year was definitely too idealistic for sure, but I could never have conceived that I'd end up creating my own prison.

In more ways than one.

I opened up my messages and typed a feigned cheery message to Nate, *Hope your morning has started better than mine! xx.* Recently, he'd been travelling more – a lot more – and right now he was up in Seattle on a work trip.

I might have thrown a hand grenade into our marriage last year, but the one he'd lobbed in after had devastated a lot more than just our finances.

I stared at the screen, offering a silent prayer that he would respond quickly. Or at all. Provide some reassurance that he actually gave a shit.

But my phone stayed silent.

Turning my attention back to the girls, I was relieved to see that they had finally figured out how to self-soothe and had since drifted off. Watching them both sleep, I contemplated for a moment going back to wrestling with the errant fitted sheet. But no, that could wait.

More important just then was for me to get a few minutes of quiet or even connect with . . . someone. I really needed someone to talk to besides the twins, who obviously had a limited vocabulary and usually preferred yowling over idle conversation.

I tiptoed to the door and cast a backward glance over my shoulder to where my daughters lay collapsed on the carpet, idly wondering if my mother ever did something like this with me or the others when she was at her wits' end.

And just as soon I answered myself. Not a hope in hell.

Mum wasn't a mess like I am. Mum was so much better at this . . . at everything.

I closed my eyes, summoning her face and smile – which, much to my despair, seemed to be getting harder and harder with the passage of time.

What I wouldn't give right now to go downstairs and call her on the phone, ask her what she did when she felt as if she was ready to burst. What I wouldn't give to ask her what I should do about Matt and Romy – or my dad.

And be able to get a reply.

Christ, I'd never gone this long without seeing or talking to them. And I missed them. Losing her was one thing, but I didn't expect her passing would also leave me bereft of an entire family – especially when I also seemed to be losing my husband.

How had that happened?

But a small voice in my head chided me, *Ah Joanna, don't play the victim. You know why . . .*

I began padding down the hallway and put a hand on my heart to calm myself. These feelings – of self-doubt – were starting to appear too often.

I looked around at the messy kitchen and sighed, feeling well and truly overwhelmed. The oatmeal that Suzy had thrown against the wall earlier that morning had now dried and hardened. I would need a spackling knife to remove it – I'd be lucky to get it off without messing up the paint.

And I just didn't have the energy.

So instead I went to the table and sat down in front of a cold cup of coffee, taking a sip. Once again turning my attention to my phone – just about my only link to the outside world – I tried to ignore the growing sense of unease when I saw I had no incoming text messages, no notifications at *all*.

Then pulling up Instagram, I began mindlessly scrolling – a new habit that I wasn't proud of.

In my former life, I hadn't had time for or any interest in Insta-stalking; and while I had a personal account, I certainly didn't spend time on it watching other people. Instead, I had beautifully curated pictures of my own day-to-day life and family, allowing small snippets that offered a tantalising glance into my fun-filled, glamorous world.

Unlike many, I had no need to project a perfect life because I goddamn *had* a perfect life.

Not any more.

Soon, my eyes were drawn to a series of vibrant pictures that had been posted a couple of hours ago by a former colleague, Cecilia, who was in the C-suite at a hot company that was quickly overtaking Airbnb and VRBO.

She was apparently on vacation in the Seychelles right now, somewhere I had always wanted to visit, and while her pictures were amazing, what attracted my attention was the fact that my husband had commented on the post. All of five minutes ago, which meant that he had seen my text, but chosen to ignore it.

'Looks amazing C!' Nate had written. 'What I would give to be there now.'

And Cecilia had already responded. 'Miss you guys. It's been too long. Wish you all were here. But hey, there's plenty of room at the villa. Hop on a plane!'

Nate had responded with a series of roll-on-the-ground laughing emojis, stating, 'That ship has well and truly sailed . . . #anotherlife', before adding a poop emoji as a form of punctuation.

Did he mean that trips to exotic locales were out these days because we were more likely to be considering Disneyland? Or did he mean that we couldn't hang with our former crew now that *he* was the sole breadwinner?

Or, I considered, unsure how I even felt about the notion, could it mean that our ship – our marriage – quite literally had sailed?

Pushing my phone aside before I went down a wormhole from which there'd be no escape, I knew I had to focus my mind on elsewhere, get a grip and take control.

I needed to achieve *something*.

Course, these days, the extent of my dominion ended right here in my kitchen – the aftermath of Oatmeal Wars. Deciding to get it over with, I crossed to the sink, turned the water on and grabbed a sponge in order to start on my task and maybe refocus my mindset.

As the water warmed, I turned my eyes to the calendar and, zeroing in on the December date, felt myself suddenly freeze again and my hands go numb.

Eight months since *Mum* . . .

How I desperately wished I could talk to her again, or talk to anyone at this point. As it was, no one had even contacted me about Christmas this year.

I think maybe that hurt the most.

Gulping, I hung my head as my thoughts came out in a whisper. 'Everything's a mess, Mum. Everything you and Dad built. Romy and Matt won't talk to me. I'm useless at this motherhood stuff, my marriage is teetering on the edge of an abyss, my friends' lives have gone on without me,' I said hoarsely. 'In just a year, my whole world has upended. Everything was fine, was *perfect* . . . and I have no idea how to change it.'

Yes, you do, said a small voice – a painfully familiar voice in the back of my head.

I sniffed. I had so sorely felt her absence in recent months – and no matter how much I tried to summon her words or channel her advice, she had been mysteriously silent until now.

Go home for Christmas and make things right. Do your thing, Jo. Fix it.

I closed my eyes and pictured her face, trying to recall what it had felt like the last time she'd pulled me close for a hug. I so desperately craved her solace and, finding the memory, a sense of comfort automatically enveloped me.

Eventually, my breathing became more even as I considered the thought, steeling myself for what I knew deep down was the right option – the only option.

Go home. Fix it . . .

Chapter 20

'Anyone here?' Romy tentatively called out from where she had rooted herself in the hallway after the taxi dropped her off.

She let out the breath she didn't realise she had been holding and listened intently, scanning for a sign of activity.

Still nothing. The house was so quiet and dark – and the eerie stillness now enveloped her. She breathed in, trying to seek out at least the familiar scent of home – her mother's perfume, with its top notes of lavender and sage – but she couldn't find it.

In the short while since Romy had last been here, every last trace of her mother seemed to have disappeared.

She debated backing out of the door and calling Matt from out front in the driveway, just to make sure he or her dad were home. For some reason, she just couldn't escape the feeling that she was an interloper – an intruder even – in this place. But just as she was about to make her exit, she chastised herself out loud, breaking the silence.

'Stop it. This is *home*.'

Romy shook her head, as if trying to clear the cobwebs and distance herself from wayward ghosts, and marched boldly forth, dropping her bag on the ground with a meaningful thump.

'Hello,' she bellowed louder, trying to inject some cheer into her voice. 'Where is everyone?'

She moved through the ground floor, poking her head into every room, leaving the kitchen for last.

Summoning her courage, she stepped inside, only to find the room dark like everywhere else. Her mind drifted to the last time she had stood right here, immediately after the burial service.

The day the entire Moore family had imploded.

She took a deep breath and exhaled, trying to expel the bad energy that seemed to rise inside of her like a swelling pit of lava every time she thought of that day.

And how, since then, all her grand and laughably misguided life plans had gone out the window.

Romy turned on her heel and left the kitchen, deciding then to try the rarely used spare room – the one her mother used to jokingly refer to as 'Bill's dumping ground', but the rest of them referred to as the den – encouraged by some light coming from the far end of the hallway.

'It's me. Anyone here?' Going inside, she found her dad and brother sitting on opposite couches, staring at the TV where *Die Hard* was on.

Neither initially looked in her direction or moved to greet her, and she willed her feigned energy not to pop like a balloon. She already knew that her dad was dreading Christmas this year. Not just because of the sibling rift, but especially because there was no Cathy.

He'd told Romy not to worry about coming back for it this year altogether, and to just enjoy herself in London. In fact, this had been a familiar refrain every time she'd talked to him since the funeral.

'I'm trying to get used to life without your mum,' he had told her when she'd offered to stay on for a little while afterwards in April, or even move back home to help stave off his loneliness.

But her ever stalwart dad insisted that he'd prefer to be left alone to just get on with it, and that he could call on Matt if needs be. Now, both men cut a sorry tale on the tatty old furniture that her dad was supposed to have thrown away decades ago, and they looked like they hadn't gone outside in days. She cleared her throat and looked at the TV. 'Ah, a Christmas classic.'

Matt looked up. 'I thought you always made out that this one *wasn't* a Christmas movie.'

'Well, people can always change their minds, can't they?'

Her dad turned in her direction then, noticing her presence for the first time. A look of surprise came to his face. 'Love! I didn't know you were arriving today.'

He hoisted himself up off the grotty old couch and Romy shot a glance at Matt, wondering why her brother hadn't made him aware of her imminent arrival.

But what was even more concerning was her dad's gaunt appearance.

His cheeks were even more hollowed in than the last time she saw him and his sweatshirt hung across his shoulders, appearing one or two sizes too big.

He looked feeble, weary and so *old*, and Romy all at once couldn't help but wonder if he was trying to meet his wife in the grave. Shaking away the thought lest it turn out to be a bad omen, she crossed the space between them and wrapped him in her embrace.

'How are you? Sorry, I thought Matt would've told you.'

She looked over her father's shoulder, wondering if her brother would offer up a reason, but he merely shrugged disinterestedly.

'Ah, he probably did tell me,' he said. 'But I forgot. These days I forget a lot of things.'

She frowned, concerned about this new development, and wondering now if there was something really wrong with her dad, or maybe the bigger issues he'd had to deal with that year had made him overlook other, smaller stuff, like dates, times and – she looked around the untidy room, littered with used teacups and biscuit packets – basic necessities.

'Are you OK, though?' she asked, feeling all at once protective and worried afresh. 'You're not . . . sick or anything?'

'Not at all, sure I'm grand. And I'm delighted to see you, even though I told you not to trouble yourself coming, really.' He touched the crease between her eyebrows and smiled wistfully. 'You know, you look more and more like your old mum every day. You really are her spitting image.'

And now Romy couldn't escape the idea that her being here wasn't cheering her dad up at all, but making him even more mindful of what he had lost.

◆ ◆ ◆

'Everyone finished with the chow mein?' she asked a little while later as she, Matt and their dad sat glumly around the kitchen table, eating a takeaway.

Far from festive, and a million miles from the seasonal feasts her mother usually had ready for their annual homecomings, Romy had ordered a family deal from the local takeaway upon discovering that there was barely any food in the house either, making it impossible for her to throw something together for the three of them.

'I've had enough anyway,' Matt muttered at the carton of greasy flaccid spring rolls he'd been eating out of, and pushed it away.

'Dad? Are you finished?'

Her father nodded in the affirmative and, glancing at his almost untouched dinner plate, she frowned. He hadn't eaten much either.

A world apart from last year, she thought morosely, summoning up the aroma of her mother's mouth-watering cooking and stocked cupboards full of festive offerings at the ready, with the promise of unlimited holiday goodies throughout the stay.

'I'll clean up, love,' her dad stated, standing up and taking a few dirty plates to the sink.

Matt rose and left the kitchen without offering any such assistance, having barely made eye contact since Romy arrived, let alone conversation.

So much for being the dutiful, caregiver son.

She opened her mouth to protest, but then shut it in silence, for her dad's sake unwilling to make a fuss. While he was making an attempt at normal conversation, Matt had a definite chip on his shoulder; she could feel the hostility coming off him in waves.

What the hell was up with him?

Especially when ultimately it was he and Joanna who were at war, each still refusing to speak to the other since the bust-up in April, while Romy had been caught in the crossfire.

She herself hadn't seen or heard a peep from her sister since the funeral almost eight months ago. Which hurt. A lot.

Mum would never have allowed such ill will between them to carry on for so long, but then again, if Mum was still around, none of it would have ever happened in the first place, would it?

In the ensuing time, she and Matt had been in touch a bit, via Romy checking in on her dad to make sure he was OK, although much to her frustration, there wasn't really much she could do for him day to day.

And she felt so guilty about that, even though Matt insisted that all was fine and he was coping as best he could, considering. Her brother had packed in the job and his life in Galway altogether and come home, apparently to keep a closer eye on their dad.

His and Hazel's break-up in the wake of Joanna's outburst had likely sped up that particular process. Despite his promises, he hadn't told his girlfriend a thing about the work incident and when it all came out, Hazel too suspected that such evasiveness could only mean that he'd been cheating on her.

Regardless, the happy-go-lucky Matt they'd all known had since become bitter and morose.

Though Romy really couldn't fault him for being there for their dad when he was all alone in the world, ensuring he remembered to take his medication and got out for his walks, ferrying him to appointments and generally helping him navigate a world without his beloved wife.

It was a lot more than she, or indeed Joanna, could say.

Romy and her dad cleaned up the kitchen in relative silence, both lost in their own thoughts. As they completed their task, he suggested she watch the rest of the movie with them, but Romy demurred.

'I think I'm just going to take a shower and get settled if you don't mind. Travel always makes me feel grubby.'

'No problem, pet. I'm sure you're tired too.' Her dad smiled and plodded wearily back out through the kitchen door.

Alone once again, Romy finished up in the kitchen and headed back out, the house silent and dark around her. Everything felt so unwelcoming and cold – almost hostile – this year, she mused, glancing at the bare and bleakly unadorned staircase up to the bedrooms.

But before she took the stairs, she came to a pause in front of another closed door nearby. She glanced at the handle, knowing that all she had to do was reach out and grasp it and she would gain entry to somewhere her mother's presence surely still existed – her study.

Seeking respite from the sorrow weighing heavily in the house, Romy pushed the door open and crossed the threshold.

She was immediately struck by a whiff of her mother's perfume – the comforting scent she had been searching for since she arrived earlier.

Taking a deep breath, she felt something akin to peace wash over her and turned to close the door behind her, flicking on the lights.

Upon examination, the room felt completely undisturbed, and she wondered suddenly if anyone had even entered here since her mum passed away. Or if she was the first person to go in since her mother had walked out, closing the door for the last time before taking ill a little later, and then onwards to the hospital.

A lump in her throat at the very notion, Romy's eyes glistened as she smiled at the stack of magazines, an eclectic mix of *National Geographic*, *Vanity Fair* and *InStyle*, quietly gathering dust next to the powder-pink chaise longue.

A selection of letters and a notebook sat atop the desk, and a red cashmere sweater was cast over the back of the chair behind it. Romy had a distinct vision of her mother entering the room, flinging on the sweater and settling down to attend to her correspondence.

As the spectre disappeared, she approached the desk, reached out to touch the sweater gently and, following a brief internal debate, picked it up and brought it to her face, drinking in the smell.

'It's almost like you've just stepped out of the room for a minute,' she whispered into the garment, picturing her mother as clearly as if she were close by. 'Oh, Mum, I miss you so much.'

For the first time, though, she didn't cry at her mother's memory or absence. It was as if this room itself was some kind of balm for her soul.

As she spied a framed five-by-seven photograph on the desk, Romy reached out, pulling it closer for inspection. It was a family shot, taken last year in front of the decorated tree. All members of the clan had been smiling; the twin babies in matching green and red dresses, each with a cute bow on their peach-fuzz heads. Pure joy and festivity leaped from the picture, and Romy suddenly had a longing to jump back in time, just to be welcomed once again into that loving environment.

'I don't know what to do, Mum,' she admitted hoarsely. 'Our family is a mess, Dad is so sad, Matt seems so angry, and Joanna isn't even here.' She shuddered at the chasm that existed between this family now – realising that now she was home, thoughts of her sister made her feel more sad than angry. 'I walked in the front door today, and it definitely didn't feel like a homecoming. It's Christmastime but it's not. It doesn't feel like it without you. And I want it to be.'

She sighed, her heart heavy.

'I don't know how you even did it, Mum. Every year, this time was always magical. But not this year, especially not this year. I'm afraid that it will never be the same, that our family will never be the same again. Not without you. And I just don't know how to change that. I don't know how to make things right.'

She studied the photograph again, the gloriously decorated tree the centrepiece to their happy celebration. 'And since you loved this time of year so much, most of all I'm heartbroken that we're letting you down.'

Chapter 21

'I still don't know why we're even doing this . . .' Matt grumbled from the driver's seat, as he and Romy drove to the village centre a mile or so from their house, and onwards to Dooley's Farm.

'Because we need to do *something* – for Dad's sake,' she told him again. 'The house is so cold and dark and . . . miserable, the least we can do is try and make things a bit more . . .'

'Normal?' he finished. 'As if this year could ever be normal.'

'I was going to say cheery.' She looked across at her brother, who currently looked the very opposite of the word, but whatever was going on with him, or indeed any of their personal lives, they didn't need to make things even worse for their dad.

If anything, they owed it to him to lighten the burden of grief he was carrying and try to maybe make the best of this year, instead of wallowing in it.

As she'd studied that framed shot of them all pictured in front of the tree last Christmas, she was wholly sure it was what her mother would have wanted.

Cathy had never been one to sit around and feel sorry for herself, if anything the opposite – she was all about trying to find the bright side. And while it was nigh on impossible to find any positives in what her family was suffering just now, Romy felt she needed to try.

But persuading her brother of that was proving an uphill challenge. 'I still think you're being delusional.'

'Look, I'm not suggesting for a second that we pretend to be all happy-happy this year, or try to forget that everything's gone to hell, but I do think it's important we at least make an effort to go along with some of the basics in the hope of improving things for Dad, OK? Like this.'

As they drove through the entrance gates of the local farm cum horse-riding stables where the Moores had been getting their family tree for as long as she could remember, she gestured to the area of cultivated Douglas firs in a sectioned-off plot further up the hill alongside the main farmland area.

Given that the festive season had long since kicked off, the farmyard and surrounds were considerably quieter than usual for this time of year, with only a handful of vehicles – evidently other last-minute tree seekers like themselves – parked nearby and a few people wandering through the lot.

'Well, just don't expect me to get involved in picking the bloody thing out or any of that happy-clappy shite,' Matt reiterated morosely. 'I'm just here to ferry it home.'

She rolled her eyes, wishing he'd lay off the grouching and negativity, which, as Damien always said back when they trained together, achieved nothing.

'Fine, I'm just going to get the smallest one anyway. But maybe while I pay, you could help load it up at least?'

He was already scrolling through his phone. 'Grand. Just text me when you're ready.'

Thoroughly fed up, Romy got out of the car and headed into the lot, now wishing that she'd taken the time to measure the height of the living room ceiling before coming out, since there was a surprising number of different-sized tree choices here.

But her first instinct was probably right – she should just find someone working here and ask them for the smallest one, rather than worrying too much about it.

She had set off further into the space, trying to find someone to ask, when she heard a familiar voice from nearby.

'Hello there, Romy. How are you keeping?'

She turned and immediately smiled upon seeing Luke Dooley, having briefly forgotten it was his family who owned this place. At six foot, he towered over her more diminutive (at least in height) frame and now she almost had to crane her face up to look at him – as opposed to this time last year when they'd been sitting eye to eye in the pub.

'Luke, hi – the very man. I was just looking for someone to help me, actually.' She smiled shyly. 'Sorry, but I have to admit this is my first time picking out one of these, and I haven't a notion what I'm doing.'

'Bit late in the day for it too . . .' he chuckled, eyes twinkling, but almost immediately his face fell. 'Ah, I'm sorry, Romy – about your mam, I mean. That was stupid of me, I feel terrible. Many's the time a man's mouth broke his nose.'

She smiled at the old Irish saying, which she hadn't heard in an age, and the fact that Luke always came across so wise and earnest beyond his years. It was one of the things that made him so endearing.

'Honestly, it's no problem, but it's just . . . well, yes, it is last-minute. As you can imagine, poor old dad wasn't really thinking about stuff like this.' Despite herself, she felt a lump in her throat at the realisation that normally it would have been her parents here doing something this trivial, yet, for them, so customary as to be almost ceremonial.

'Of course I can, and the first year without them is always the worst.'

His voice was soft and so genuinely sympathetic that Romy remembered his father, Frank, had passed away a couple of years back, which was of course when Luke himself took over the running of the family land and stables.

'It's definitely . . . different,' she said, clearing the unexpected croakiness in her throat, 'but we're trying to make the effort for Dad's sake.'

'How's he doing?' Luke asked. 'I've met himself and Matt up walking the woods a couple of times over the last while. Good of him all the same to come home this year to look after the folks.'

Romy harrumphed a little, not about to admit that Matt's decision was born out of his own cock-up rather than any kind of dutiful saviour complex, but then Luke spoke again.

'I've had plenty of my own runs of doctor's appointments and chemist pick-ups – all the while trying to keep up a brave face while you watch them get worse. Believe me, it's no picnic.'

And all at once she felt guilty, suddenly cognisant of the fact that whatever the reasons for Matt's decision, he had done it and he'd been here, right in the thick of it all throughout her mum's illness, and for the worst of it too.

He'd witnessed the struggles and the pain and the horror up close and had to deal first-hand with both his own and their dad's associated anguish all the way through, right until the end and beyond.

While she and Joanna had been spared so much of that.

So maybe it was no wonder that Matt was morose and miserable, she realised, feeling like an absolute heel for not considering this. And guilty afresh that she'd so easily ducked out of her own responsibilities in this regard.

Maybe her dad wasn't the only one who needed a lift.

'Anyway, I'm really sorry again about your mam,' Luke was saying. 'She was a pure lady and we all loved her around here, as I'm sure you know.'

'Yes, we're all broken-hearted.' Again trying to hold back tears, Romy ran her finger over the pine needles of a nearby spruce.

'But what I will say is it does get better with time,' he continued, again with the gentle assurance of someone who'd been there. 'The first year is definitely a killer, no doubt about that, and sometimes the force of it hits you like a truck. Main thing, I think, though, is to focus your mind as much as possible on pointless things, little distractions, anything at all to help keep the harder stuff at bay.'

She nodded, comforted a little by the notion that it would get better, because at the moment that time felt very far away.

'Anyway, sorry for banging on about it, I'm sure that's the last thing you need,' he said, blushing a little. 'Especially when I'm supposed to be helping. Sorry, my mam always says I'm worse than any woman for nattering on. Ah here, you're not supposed to say stuff like that now either, are you.' His face went an even deeper shade of red. 'Christ, I'm a gobshite, don't mind me.'

Despite herself, Romy had to smile again. The fact that he always seemed so unsure of himself, despite his immense popularity, made her warm to him even more.

'Anyway, you said you needed some help?' Swiftly moving on, Luke pointed to a nearby spruce. 'This is about the size your mam always went for, if that's anything to go by.' Then he looked back to the parking area. 'Have you a way to bring it home, though? I can always pop it on the trailer and nip down to the house with it later if you'd like.'

'Thanks, but no need, it's fine. Matt's waiting out in the car. He, ah . . . needed to take a call.' Lest he think her brother was rude.

But again Luke seemed to instinctively understand. 'I get you. Like I said, the first year is the hardest. I must give him a shout, see if he ever needs anyone to go for a pint with . . . or even a good oul training session. No better way to focus the mind. Oh, and actually' – Luke smiled then – 'I almost forgot. How'd the race go? I was going to do Dublin myself but one of the horses ended up foaling the night before, so duty called.' He groaned. 'You know the feeling, months of training gone to waste. Was the book any help to you in the end?'

Romy's face fell, for more reasons than one. She was embarrassed now that he'd gone out of his way to give her so much advice about running this time last year. Especially when that idea more than anything else had become half-hearted over the last while, and she now truly appreciated why her family had initially been so dubious about her intentions.

She definitely couldn't figure out how she'd managed to kid herself into thinking she had the wherewithal, never mind the ability, to run an entire marathon.

The only good thing to come out of all that nonsense was Damien, whom she'd started seeing since they'd struck up their conversation in Hyde Park that time. He'd checked in on her a few times immediately after the funeral (about the only one who'd bothered to) and they'd met up afterwards for a couple of training runs, but it was very clear very soon, based on his elevated level of commitment and effort, that Romy had been fooling herself to think she could do this.

It just wasn't in her.

And taken with crippling grief in the wake of losing her mother, she had relegated the marathon idea to merely another in her long line of failures. The expensive running stuff that had been so generously gifted last year lay in a crumpled pile in the back of her London wardrobe, much like her grand intentions.

Her family had been dead right in their assessment of her – Joanna especially.

Useless . . .

She swallowed hard. 'It started well, but . . . I suppose I wasn't really up to it this year,' she admitted to Luke, mortified. 'Not with . . . the way things went.'

'I hear you. It's hard to get the motivation at the best of times. But no doubt you'll be back on the road again, when you are up to it. And let me know if Matt or, ah . . . even yourself fancies heading out for a pint or two while you're here?' Then his face closed again. 'Ah, Jaysus, sorry, Romy. I keep putting my foot in it. Oh course ye won't want to be out on the session this year. God, I'm an eejit.'

She shook her head. 'You're not, honestly. Yes, this year will be weird, no point in pretending otherwise. Maybe we will try and make it out some night for a quiet one,' she told him, though it was indeed hard to imagine anyone in her house being in a sociable frame of mind. 'And thanks too, by the way, for coming up in April to pay your respects. Much of it is a blank, but I do remember seeing you and your mother, and we appreciate it.'

Pretty much all of the time surrounding the funeral was a blank, apart from the horrible way things ended, but seeing Luke here today had brought the memory back to her, how so many people in this small community who'd known and loved her mother had gone out of their way to pay their respects.

And now, knowing how much it meant, Romy wished she'd done the same for the Dooley family, and couldn't remember why she hadn't – especially when he'd always been so generous towards her.

'Like I said, it's an all too familiar scenario to each and every family at some point, I suppose,' he said, as if reading her mind. 'Doesn't make it any easier, though. Anyway, let me drop this out for you. You said Matt had the car? Not the Beetle, I hope? Some job trying to drive home with this yoke sticking out in front of your windscreen.'

This time, she burst out laughing. 'No, he's driving Dad's Hyundai. But you're right, imagine!'

Romy paid for the tree, and as she and Luke walked amicably back through the lot to the car, him easily hefting the seven-footer on his shoulders as if it were made of paper, she thought again about what he'd said.

Little distractions . . .

That's how it would be this year, she realised sadly, thanking and bidding a reluctant goodbye to lovely Luke as he helped Matt secure the spruce in the boot of her dad's SUV. Any other time she'd be over the moon at basically being asked out for a drink by him. But she guessed he was just feeling sorry for her and simply aiming to distract her from such a difficult time.

Which was pretty much why she'd decided to get the tree in the first place, Romy mused, although she hadn't properly articulated it to herself until now.

Primarily to brighten up the house a bit and thus her dad, yes, but also in the hope that by focusing on menial stuff like getting the shopping in, preparing food and just going through the motions of all the typical rituals associated with the season, the days might pass faster and easier.

And maybe, just maybe, they could distract themselves somehow, not just from the crippling, all-pervading grief, but from everything else that was missing this year.

Chapter 22

'I thought you weren't coming,' Romy stated, her face neutral.

I couldn't tell how my sister felt about our out-of-the-blue arrival at the house first thing this morning, but she certainly wasn't overjoyed that we had materialised – or should I say that *I* had materialised.

As she proceeded to make herself breakfast, I sat alone at the kitchen table. Nate was upstairs settling the twins for a nap after the long flight, and while Dad was delighted to see the girls, I could tell he was also a little jittery about having us all under the same roof again, given what had happened the last time.

I swallowed hard, willing my sister to say something, anything. Even if she raged at me, it would still be better than her silence.

'So . . . we, uh . . . just flew in this morning,' I mumbled, feeling stupid – I was stating the obvious. I shrugged. 'It's Christmas,' I said, trying to sound light, as if the preceding months hadn't happened and this wasn't the first time we had been in each other's presence since our family had basically blown up.

'Nate and the girls here too?'

I nodded confirmation. 'Yes, of course, he's upstairs with them. They wanted to see you – all of you. So did – do – I. I couldn't imagine not coming home for Christmas.'

Although the truth was it had very much been an impulsive, last-minute decision. Once I'd made up my mind (and persuaded Nate) to come, I'd sent a breezy text to Dad as a heads-up that we were catching a flight.

As Nate had pointed out on the plane ride over, 'At least everyone will be happy to see the girls.'

Exactly. They surely would all want to see Suzy and Katie, if not their mother.

'I suppose that's a bonus, even if it means they also have to deal with us,' I'd quipped from the seat alongside him in a feeble attempt at humour.

Nate gave a short laugh. 'Us? Don't include me in this, Jo. I know *I'm* not blacklisted.'

While an automatic biting response began to formulate in my head, I knew there was no use in starting another fight thirty thousand feet in the air and bringing that extra baggage to Ireland with us too. He and I were already well over our limit in that regard, both literally and figuratively.

Though starting marital therapy had at least helped me remove a portion of the chip that had formed on my shoulder since learning our life's savings had disappeared. While it was easy to place the blame solely on Nate, I had to admit my part in it too. This time last year we'd both made life-changing decisions without properly consulting the other, which, as our therapist had pointed out, wasn't how a partnership should be.

I looked at him. 'You know, when I suggested making this trip, I wasn't entirely sure you'd come along. That you would want to, I mean.' I held my breath, anticipating what he would say next.

A very pregnant pause followed.

'I mean, if we're being truthful here, I thought about it. I thought about telling you that I was going to stay home, in *our* home, for the holidays this year. But I didn't want you to face all this alone.'

'Why not?' I asked.

'Because for one thing, it would be unfair to send you into the lion's den without any backup.' He smiled. 'You know, in good times and in bad, and all that jazz? Plus, they're my family too and this Christmas will be a particularly tough one – for everyone.'

I barked a laugh, unsure if tears would follow next. That was an understatement.

Nate took another sip of his beer. 'But we gotta make the best of it. One thing I do know for sure is that Cathy would want us to. So my advice to you is forget about Christmas pudding this year, and get ready to eat some humble pie instead.' He glanced sideways at me, his meaning clear. 'There's a lot of making up to do.'

Now, in the kitchen, Romy's darkly levelled gaze was reminding me of exactly that.

'Does Matt know you're here?' she asked pointedly, and I had to do all in my power not to look away. I don't think I had ever felt intimidated by my sister until now, and since I'd last seen her, something about her had changed.

Towards me, at least – and I wished that there wasn't so much emotional distance between us now.

'I'm sure Dad has mentioned it,' I replied, though honestly I couldn't be sure.

Romy nodded. 'I wouldn't bank on it. I got in at the weekend, and he's barely spoken to me since,' she said, voluntarily offering up a little information about herself. 'Everything just feels . . . so different.' Her voice sounded tired and sad.

I took a deep breath. While I still had my own beef with my brother, Romy had done nothing to hurt anyone, so I knew that I should now be the one to rebuild bridges between us.

To fix it.

Even though I had rehearsed a hundred different things to say beforehand, my mouth had gone dry now that I was here in front of her. The ball was most definitely in my court.

I took a deep breath, about to enthuse that it was great to see her and that she looked good – although, on second thoughts, wouldn't any mention of her appearance sound hollow, given what I'd said last time we met?

And the truth was, she didn't – look good, I mean. Her eyes were weary and her face sad, and my heart ached at the realisation that neither of us had been able to share our grief and lean on one another like we should have this last while.

The fallout had splintered not only our sisterly relationship, but the family support structure overall. Which I guessed now was part of the reason I had felt so lost and rudderless this last year, and I hated the idea that Romy might have felt the same way.

I noticed then that she was still staring at me, as if waiting for me to say something about all that, and because I couldn't immediately find an appropriate lead-in, I bottled it altogether. 'I know. Though I was surprised to spot the tree set up in the living room. I see it's not decorated or anything yet, but to be honest, I didn't think Dad would . . . well, I didn't know what to expect this year, I suppose.'

'You're not the only one,' Romy said tersely, lifting up her coffee cup and walking out the door, leaving me once again alone in her wake.

Her meaning couldn't have been clearer.

◆ ◆ ◆

Just when she thought she was getting a handle on things . . .

Still shaken by her sister's sudden appearance in the kitchen, which had caught her completely unawares, Romy wandered through the hallway, unsure where to go, and all at once again feeling like a stranger in her own home.

Matt had gone out somewhere and she guessed her dad was pottering about in his tool shed, somewhere he'd always sought refuge from the family chaos when all of them were younger and still living at home. Evidently for him it had once more become a safe retreat from the maelstrom within the family, and especially now since all three warring siblings had returned.

Feeling despondent and guilty that their rift meant her dad should even have to hide away in his own home for fear of things kicking off again, and despite her best efforts over the last day or two with the stupid tree and some grocery shopping, Romy had to admit that this year was shaping up to be disastrous in more ways than one.

Matt was right; she *was* being delusional to think that they could even attempt to make the best of it.

Typical Joanna, too, to just swan home when it suited her and not a word to anyone to forewarn or let them know she was coming. Had she even told their father?

But what stung most of all was that Joanna had sat in the kitchen with not a care in the world just now, as if the hurt she'd caused the last time they'd seen each other hadn't even registered.

Though Romy wasn't entirely sure why she expected Jo to apologise or make amends, and in hindsight realised that this was stupid, because clearly her sister didn't feel that she'd said anything wrong.

To her, she'd merely spoken the truth.

Albeit in a harsh, hurtful and totally inappropriate manner. But it was the truth all the same.

She wondered worriedly what Matt's reaction would be to Jo showing up like this when he returned. With the mood her brother was in these days and the two of them still at loggerheads . . .

Romy's head hurt as she thought about it, and she just hoped that any bad blood between them remained beneath the surface, at least until Christmas was over.

The last thing their father, or indeed anyone, needed at this point was another sibling blow-up. Although to be fair, it wasn't as though anyone in the family was actually expecting a bed of roses this year anyway.

So maybe her admittedly loose idea of having a little backup of her own during this visit was becoming more necessary by the minute?

Seeking refuge once more in her mother's study, Romy slipped through the door, took out her phone and sent a quick text to Damien in London. As far as she knew he was flying in tomorrow and would obviously want to spend time with his own family, who lived in the city, though apparently they weren't that close.

Much like her own these days.

Let me know when you're free. Come here or could meet somewhere halfway. Definitely could do with the distraction!

He knew all about her family situation and they had an arrangement to connect over the break in any case. And since it looked like things were going south here already, Romy needed to feel there was at least someone she could rely on (or even just talk to) during this stay.

There was no rescuing this Christmas.

Not without a miracle.

Chapter 23

I've been doing a lot of reminiscing about all those fond family memories of years gone by. We have had so much fun together, haven't we? But it's also important not to look upon the past with tears in our eyes, or long for yesteryear. Not at all.

Instead, I'm hoping you'll maybe consider carrying on all the little things we loved the most about this time of year.

Like decorating the house and the tree: an important tradition and one your dad always relished – a little too much (stay off the roof this year please, Bill!). Everything's in the attic, fully labelled, all ready and waiting to sparkle.

And food: all the old favourite recipes my mother passed on to me, and which have been in our family for generations. It's never Christmas without a feast!

Family: This obviously isn't something that we ourselves have had to do in a long time, but the first visit to Santa.

The twins'll be just old enough for this to be memorable this year, and oh how I so wish I could see their faces.

Gifts. Not just for ourselves, but if you can, put together a few little Christmas 'boxes' for Paddy the postman, and Jim who delivers the oil, and Maura who reads the electricity meter – I always pop in a few of my mince pies with some whiskey or chocolates for them. It's the thought that counts.

Festivity: This is a time for people, about getting together and reminding one another of how far we've come this year – and most important of all, celebrating!

It'd do my heart good if you continued the Christmas Eve neighbourly get-together, for your dad's sake even.

So anyway, this is just my little 'Grown Up Christmas List' as the song goes, but of course we all know some of the very best traditions of all are the ones that happen organically . . .

◆ ◆ ◆

Suddenly, Romy felt like a different person – a woman on a mission once again.

That miracle she'd longed for had, as if by magic, come about right here in her mother's study.

She'd serendipitously happened across her mum's diary on the desk – a treasure trove of chatty recollections and, more pertinently, her heartfelt hopes for their family this year. As if she'd known in advance that they'd need some direction on this first festive season without her.

Celebrate this Christmas as if I was still here?

Because I will be, in my own way – in all the little festive traditions we have followed over the years, and recipes and rituals that have become our family's staples . . .

Her mother was right (as always) – though of course she wouldn't have known how fractured the family bond had become in the interim.

But once Romy read through the entire diary and her mother's fond memories of all those beloved family times together, it became very clear in her mind what needed to happen, inspired in particular by that reference to her mum's favourite festive song, '*Grown Up Christmas List*'.

So, her mind racing, she went back and read through the entries all over again, this time with a pen in hand.

All she needed now was to get the rest of the family on board, a potentially tricky task that obviously needed some gentle finessing, given the current sibling stand-off.

But, Romy mused, standing up and clutching the single piece of paper as she went downstairs to rejoin the others, at least now she – quite literally – had a plan.

Yes, of course this will be a Christmas like no other.

But that doesn't mean it has to be a terrible one.

Chapter 24

'Where did this come from . . . ?' I ran my finger across the words and my heart leaped into my throat, my vision blurring.

So much so that I jumped up to grab a paper towel to dab my eyes, lest any of my tears find their way to the page and smudge the writing.

'I came across some stuff in her study just now,' Romy said quietly, having presented a single piece of paper to Dad and me in the kitchen.

It was a set of handwritten guidelines – much like the list of chores Mum used to post up beneath a fridge magnet when we were growing up.

'So it's . . . an instruction list of sorts?' I stammered hesitantly, crossing my hands in front of me. 'As if Mum knew we wouldn't have a clue how to do Christmas this year without her . . .' My voice trailed off. 'And I guess maybe, we don't. I mean, look at this place. Look at us.'

Both of my siblings had been openly avoiding me since our arrival, unless the girls or Nate happened to be around, in which case we all kept up a polite pretence.

With the exception of that already failed attempt with Romy earlier, I had so far been unable to get either of them alone.

And while I was still hurting over Matt's accusations, I was prepared to set that aside and let bygones be bygones if he was prepared to meet me halfway. But as it was, my brother didn't want to meet me at all.

Even now, having shown us the list, Romy too still seemed reticent to engage.

'Obviously, Mum wouldn't have known that things had . . . changed so much,' she pointed out diplomatically. 'Anyway, I just thought that maybe we should all read it.'

My heart sank a little then, as my sister filled a coffee mug and again left the room, leaving Dad and I alone to contemplate this new information.

My father bobbed his head. 'These days, I feel like I don't know how to do much at all without your mother,' he admitted, sadness thick in his voice as he glanced back towards the doorway and my sister's freshly retreated form. 'I mean, I haven't even been able to keep our family together. Everything is a mess.'

I bit my lip. His meaning was clear, and I felt deeply uncomfortable that he was trying to take the blame. 'None of this is your fault, Dad,' I said softly. 'I was the cause of most of it.'

He patted my arm affectionately, and the small gesture gave me some comfort. 'Maybe if I hadn't been so . . . out of things after everything, then you wouldn't have had to take so much on your shoulders.'

'No,' I admitted forcefully. 'I should have had better control over myself and my frustrations. But I didn't. I lashed out because I was hurting, without taking into account that everyone else was too.'

It felt good to say the words out loud, to admit what I felt to someone other than Nate or our therapist.

'I'm going to try and make up for it, though. When the time is right. I just haven't had the opportunity.'

Dad put his arm around my shoulders and pulled me close, kissing the top of my head. 'We were all dealing with a lot, love. And it was so hard. It still is. I don't think any of us even realised that it was real – that she was truly gone.'

'I still don't . . .' I felt my jaw wobble.

Taking a sip of his coffee, Dad reached for the list of festive tasks. He smiled and looked closer at the page.

'So what do you reckon about all of this then?'

I smiled sadly. 'Like I said, it seems to be a kind of . . . checklist on how to get through this year in her absence. She knew we'd be lost without her. In more ways than one.' I exhaled. 'She didn't know the half of it, really. But maybe that's a good thing.'

'Of course she would have known we'd find this time of year hard. The first Christmas after . . . losing someone is always the hardest. And so typical of your mother to want to give us a helping hand.'

I glanced in his direction, noticing that his voice had changed a little and he sounded . . . uplifted, almost. He smiled fondly as he read through some of the stuff mentioned.

'I was curious to know why she was so keen to label the decorations last year – she was never so diligent about putting stuff away once Christmas was over.' Then he chuckled. 'And what's this? Ah now, I'm still perfectly capable of putting up the lights on the roof. I only fell off that one time. Am I such an oul fella now, that I need the young bucks to help me?'

I couldn't help but smile, feeling heartened at the sight of my dad shaking off the shackles of his grief, even briefly.

'Jo,' he said then, decisiveness in his voice – as if for the first time in a very long time, he had a purpose. 'I think Romy was right to show us this. But more to the point, maybe we should all think about trying to do this for your mother's sake? Follow her instructions, I mean. All of us, together.'

'But how can we? Maybe on any other year, but look at how everything is between us now. Romy and Matt will barely look at me. You're blaming yourself. And here I am wondering if I should have even come home this year.' I tried to picture us all trying to pretend everything was OK, and attempting to go through the motions of the festive season. It would be excruciating.

'Nonsense. You had every right to come. And of course Mum would want us to be together – and especially to work together,' he answered sagely, and I knew he was right.

If Mum had been around, this entire situation would have killed her, irrespective of her illness. I didn't know if it was even possible for this family to be in the same room with each other right now – let alone work together to make this a somewhat 'normal' Christmas.

Even considering the notion felt like a fool's errand. And yet . . .

'She would,' I agreed reluctantly, looking again at the suggested plan of action.

Plan of Action . . .

I sat up suddenly, realising something. Plans . . . actionable objectives . . . they were *my thing*. Exactly what I'd been missing this whole year.

This stuff was, in reality, right up my street.

Where nothing else this year had made sense, with this I could grab the reins, help carry out Mum's wishes and follow her guidance.

And even if this time of year would never again be the same for our family, with this list at least we had a road map to follow.

Chapter 25

All adults and children were gathered together in the living room, in front of the still bare Christmas tree that Romy had insisted upon getting.

Beneath it, Katie and Suzy were too busy wrestling over the same doll – even though they each had one of their own – to care about what the adults were up to.

'What's all this about?' Matt asked, and Romy mused that the last time her father had requested such a gathering was when they were teenagers – usually to issue a dressing-down over some offence, usually caused by her brother.

Glancing at him now, she suppressed a smile, knowing he was probably doing the same, searching his memory to figure out why they'd been summoned – and wondering if it was because of something he did.

But Romy had a funny feeling she knew exactly what this was about. And already her heart began to lighten.

Once she'd read the diaries and realised what needed to be done, her immediate worry was whether the others could – or would want to – pull this off.

Which is why she'd decided to just put the list out into the ether for them to mull over, instead of coming out and asking them to do anything – potentially facing outright resistance from her warring siblings especially.

'I wanted to talk to you all about . . . well, about this.' Bill looked down at the piece of paper in his hands.

'What is it?' Matt asked.

From across the room, where she sat on a couch with Nate, Joanna answered.

'Romy found a list of suggestions about Christmas. From Mum. And how we can maybe get through this year without her.'

Romy didn't look in her sister's direction, but Joanna's voice was hesitant and far less assured than it had been on her arrival.

Intrigued by the change in her, she stole a glance, and was immediately struck by the distance between her sister and her husband – they were at opposite ends of the sofa.

She tried to remember a time when Joanna and Nate weren't practically sitting in each other's lap in such a circumstance, and realised that she couldn't. She'd never seen them place such physical distance between themselves and she wondered why.

But she was brought back to the situation at hand by her father's words.

'It appears that your mother thought we might all need a helping hand this year – without her.' He looked around the room. 'And I don't suppose I have to tell ye all that maybe she was right.' He shot a meaningful look at each sibling; there was no confusing his intent and Joanna now shifted uncomfortably in her seat, and Matt defensively crossed his arms across his chest.

While Romy remained silent, quietly confident while at the same time eager to hear what the overall verdict might be.

A moment of silence passed, until eventually it was Nate, of all people, who spoke. 'What exactly did Cathy suggest should happen . . . in her absence?'

'Yes, because it's pretty obvious . . .' Matt muttered, 'that Christmas isn't exactly going to be the same this year.'

For the first time, the smile on Bill's face disappeared. 'Son, please let's just . . .'

But Matt cut him off. 'Dad, to be honest, I'm not feeling exactly merry and bright, and I'm sure I'm not the only one. While the idea sounds nice in theory, in fairness a lot of other stuff happened this year, and Mum didn't know the half of it – lucky for her.'

He shot an accusatory glance directly at Joanna, who looked duly chagrined.

Bill exhaled. 'Ah now, come on. Of course it's been a nightmare of a year – for all of us. I know I am partly to blame for some of that too, son. I haven't been myself and I've maybe relied too much on you to keep me going in Mum's absence. I'm sorry for that.' He looked back down and patted the page. 'I suppose I have just felt so . . . unmoored without your mother. From the first moment I met her, she was my compass, my North Star. That's what I've lost, personally. And, well, seeing this, and what she is trying to do, has at least given us something to aim for?' he added, and Romy's heart immediately suffused with emotion.

Dad got it too, he understood. All the more reason for them to give this a try.

'It's just so like your mum to know that we'd struggle this year, that we might all need our hand held in . . . getting back in sync. And even though it must have been hard and would have broken her heart to do so, she still took the time to put her thoughts down on paper because she loved us – still loves us – all so much. And let's not forget, Christmas was her thing, so of course she'd want us to mark that together in her honour. She certainly wouldn't have wanted to see us like this.'

'But things *aren't* the same,' Matt countered. '*We* aren't the same.'

At this, Romy felt fresh tears well up in her eyes.

'Maybe we should just give it a chance, though?' she began hesitantly. 'Make the effort, at least. Of course this year won't be the same without her. But Mum knew that, which is why she left us a few pointers. So for her sake, I'm willing to try.'

'I – I am too,' Joanna sniffled. 'As much as I can, anyway.'

Nate sighed resignedly. 'I suppose you're going to need help with the outside lights and stuff, then, Bill?' he chuckled. 'Cathy always did dread you getting up on that roof.'

'Not at all – I'll be grand . . .' he began, but then shook his head. 'Although if she insists, then I suppose I have to play ball too.'

Nate then looked at his brother-in-law. 'Bro, there's no way I can put up all that crazy Christmas stuff myself. I'm gonna need your help. I don't want Cathy coming back to haunt me because your dad ends up in the ER on my watch. You in?'

Looking at each family member before moving on to the next, Matt rolled his eyes, realising he was outnumbered.

'OK then, let's see how far we get.'

Chapter 26

Remember to check the lights before you start putting them up.

This goes for both the outside and the inside strings. Lest I remind you of the Christmas of 1999 and the bulb that just wouldn't work – remember getting everything set up outside, only to discover that one of them – out of . . . oh, two million or so – wouldn't light?

It was like that National Lampoon movie.

My point is, plug in and check everything's working before you go to all the trouble of putting them up.

Next, when hanging baubles and garlands on the tree, make sure to take into account the twins' increased mobility. Last year, we didn't have to worry about them scurrying around beneath our feet – unless if we put them there for pictures – but we knew that they weren't going anywhere without assistance. Little hands . . .

Much like animals – do you remember the time our poor old Lab Ozzie toppled the whole thing over, baubles and all, on Christmas Eve? '97 I think. Regardless, we haven't had any such incidents to worry about in quite some time. Or indeed dogs.

So be mindful, not only for the sake of the tree, but also for opportunities for my granddaughters to get up to mischief.

Oh, another thing. When you're installing the Big Man and his reindeer on the roof, make sure you fix them to the flat part over the dining room. Remember the year Dad got overly ambitious (or lazy, more like) and placed them on the slanted bit near the chimney?

I'm still laughing as I remember that blasted thing coming loose and hurtling like a rocket into next door's garage. Thank God it was just the window we had to pay for . . .

Finally, Bill, please, please, stay off that roof! I already know what you're thinking: you'll chance it anyway. But no one wants to be anywhere near A & E at this time of year.

Instead, grab a drink, sit back and watch the boys get in a tizzy and make a spectacle of themselves.

It's entertaining, believe me . . .

◆ ◆ ◆

The following day, I ascended the ladder to the attic and flipped on the light to illuminate the space.

I hadn't been near it in ages and had a sudden flashback of crawling up here as a teenager to fulfil the same task we were about to embark on now: taking out the tree decorations.

Thankfully, the twins were now safely ensconced in their travel crib sound asleep, though I had the baby monitor speaker clipped on the waist of my jeans, just in case.

The men were outside in the cold, sorting the exterior stuff; Nate and Matt were hopefully following my orders and keeping Dad off the roof. And, more importantly, getting along OK.

While I was certain that what happened after the funeral hadn't caused any bad blood between my brother and husband, I still wasn't sure how Matt felt about our clan being here at all.

'Can you see everything?' Romy asked, calling up to me from below the ladder.

I took a look around and assessed the situation. I knew that the majority of baubles, tinsel and other festive flotsam had always been kept up here.

'Yep, I can see it all,' I called back down.

My sister and I were also still tiptoeing around each other, so I was relieved to at least have something to do in order to keep my mind off the almost palpable awkwardness.

'I'm going to lower a few boxes to you, OK?' I told her, aspiring to make this a team thing.

'Yup,' she replied, her voice clipped.

We spent the next few minutes in silence as I grabbed an ornament box and lowered it to the ground, only releasing it when I knew she had a solid grip. We did this repeatedly until I was out of boxes.

'Seems that's it – for the attic at least,' I observed as I lowered myself down the ladder and then folded it back into the trap that closed into the ceiling. 'So let's just move these into the living room.'

Romy mumbled something in agreement, but she was already wrangling some boxes, testing to see how much weight she could manage on her own. When she deemed her load sufficient, she took off, leaving me to my own devices.

'Holy hell, I'm sweating already,' I babbled nervously, more for something to break the silence.

She ignored my comment, even though I saw beads of sweat on her forehead as well.

'I suppose we should just start hanging up stuff while they do their thing outside?' she commented, not meeting my eyes. 'Get most of it out of the way.'

I swallowed hard and nodded my agreement. 'Whatever you think.' Despite her initial enthusiasm for Dad's sake, it seemed as if she was treating this as a bit of a chore.

Or being with me, more likely.

'Don't forget about testing the lights first,' she reminded me, once I'd untangled the first string and was about to wind them round the tree branches.

I groaned. 'I kinda wish she had suggested one of those pre-lit artificial trees. So much easier, without all this hassle. You just flick a switch and hey presto, you're done.'

Romy looked at me. 'Except that's the very last thing she would have wanted. Too impersonal. And cold.'

Like you.

The accusation seemed to hang heavily in the air, but I decided to ignore it. And my sister was right. Mum would never have opted for an artificial tree, let alone a pre-lit one. When it came to Christmas, or indeed anything, she was a pure traditionalist.

Squatting down on the ground and crossing my legs beneath me, I began the arduous process of unwinding and detangling several strands of lights.

Again, Romy and I worked in silence – and it was deafening.

Clearing my throat, I decided to make a stab at conversation.

'So, how did the marathon go in October?' I ventured. I had been curious about how the race had gone for her – and had even thought about looking her name up on the tracker app, but then something else had cropped up and I'd forgotten all about it.

Anyway, I suppose I was also a bit reluctant to check up on her; it felt a bit like spying. No doubt now if she wanted me to be privy to the information, she would tell me herself.

Another shrug. 'It didn't,' she said, dispassionate.

I frowned and unplugged another strand of lights, placing it in the 'checked' pile I had been assembling. 'What do you mean?'

'I mean,' she replied tersely, 'that it didn't go, because I didn't run it. It was a stupid idea to begin with.' Her voice was undeniably bitter. 'I didn't train enough and anyway, I just wasn't up to it.'

My heart sank and I sorely hoped that anything I'd said or done in the heat of the moment hadn't contributed to her reluctance to see the training through.

'I very much doubt that you weren't up to it.' Reflecting on her giddy enthusiasm and determination this time last year when she'd confided her plans to me, I felt doubly awful. She had really wanted this. 'But you'd been training so well, hadn't you? What happened?' I asked, my voice softening, worried now that I already knew the answer.

She sighed. 'Maybe I thought I could do it, but training was . . . tough. Tougher than I thought. And then, when Mum told us what was going on . . .' She paused and looked up at the ceiling, her expression wistful. 'For a while it set me back and I was about to pack it in altogether, until she urged me to keep going. And I suppose that having a plan and sticking to it helped get me out of my own head for a bit. Plus I got that chance at promotion, and I even met someone . . .' She inhaled and then stopped short, as if forgetting herself. 'Another runner who was helping me along.' She smiled then and my heart lightened just a little bit at the ghost of happiness on her face. She hadn't revealed any of this when we had last seen each other.

But then again, I hadn't really been open to conversation about her love life, had I?

'So what happened?' I asked, genuinely curious. 'With the race, and the . . . guy?'

She pursed her lips. 'Well, you know what happened. Mum died. And then the job prospect went south too, and I just didn't have it in me to keep going with the training plan. It was just too hard. You were right . . .'

'Oh, Romy . . .' Now I felt like hell. 'I so hope you know I didn't mean anything I said back then – it was pure heat of the moment stuff. I was just so stressed out at the time, we all were, and . . .'

'Either way, you were still right. I'm not a doer, Joanna. I'm not . . . like you.'

If only she knew.

'And the guy?' I asked quietly then, hoping my mean and idiotic off-the-cuff remark hadn't ultimately been responsible for undermining her confidence to the point that she'd given up on love too. That would kill me.

She kept her eyes firmly cast down. 'His name is . . . Damien. He's nice – Irish and living in London too.' She glanced up, and our eyes met squarely for the first time. 'At first, I wasn't sure if he was just helping me out with the training, or whatever, but after . . . everything in April, he really helped me through a lot.'

'That's brilliant.' I was heartened to find that my sister had found someone to help her through her grief, as well as the aftermath of our family falling out.

Unlike my own situation.

I plugged in another string of lights – and they remained dark. I unplugged them, jiggled them a little and then plugged them back in. Nothing. So I placed these in the reject pile.

'Well, it's still early days, but . . .' she continued, then she paused for a moment as if forgetting herself, before her voice became defensive yet again. 'Actually, I invited him, Damien – here. For Christmas . . .'

Straight away, I heard the challenge in her voice. She seemed to be baiting me, waiting for me to say that her decision to bring a complete stranger home this year, given all that was going on, seemed like a poor idea.

And as much as I wanted to do just that, I didn't – *couldn't* – take the bait. Not after everything she'd just revealed or the fact that she was confiding in me at all. And especially since none of us knew what to expect about how this year would go, or whether the three of us would even be talking to one another, let alone be under the same roof again.

But talk about throwing a spanner in the works . . .

'Ah, I see. And when is . . . Damien arriving?' I asked, lowering my eyes and keeping my face neutral.

'We haven't arranged anything yet,' she responded, raising her chin in defiance.

'Have you told Dad?' I asked, still keeping my voice perfectly level.

She shook her head. 'I was going to – once I knew what was happening.' She seemed determined to stare me down, to get a rise out of me, and I was equally determined not to go there.

'Well,' I said, 'I'm looking forward to meeting him.'

We carried on for another moment or two without saying another word, then my sister spoke again, as if needing to justify what she'd just revealed.

'Damien . . . gets me – he understands what I've been going through, with Mum and everything. Things are . . . tricky with his family, too.'

'I see,' I continued cautiously. 'Well, I can completely understand that, how it's important to have someone who gets what you're going through when your world has been upended. I've felt that way myself too.'

'But you have Nate, though . . .' Romy stared then, as if she could see right through me. 'Don't you?'

Instinctively, I felt *my* walls go up and my heart began to race. Should I talk to her about this, confide in my sister about what had been happening, had gone wrong in my life over the past year? Now that lines of communication seemed to have reopened, it felt like the perfect moment for a heart-to-heart.

But just then, a loud bang came from the roof, quickly followed by a shout from the guys outside.

'Oh God, what was that?' I exclaimed, looking up at the ceiling, a chill running through me as I automatically thought of Mum's warning about keeping Dad off the roof.

My sister was already on her feet and moving to the front door.

Chapter 27

Romy burst from the house to determine what the source of the noise from the roof had been – praying that an ill-fated trip to the Accident & Emergency Department wasn't on the cards on top of everything else.

'What's happened?' she exclaimed, rounding the front corner of the property, Joanna hurrying along behind her.

And at once, the problem presented itself.

'Oh my God, Nate!' her sister yelled in shock, the blood draining from her face.

In front of them was a toppled ladder, resting on its side in the snow-covered grass. Above their heads was Nate, dangling precariously from the second-storey gutter, and below him were Matt and Bill, the latter with his arms extended, looking up at his son-in-law as he confidently offered, 'Now just drop and I'll break your fall.'

'Dad! Are you serious?' Joanna yelled. 'Nate, do *not* let go. We'll get the ladder over. OK? Matt, don't just stand there – get the ladder. '

'Relax, it's not that much of a drop. Fifteen feet, maybe. Twenty, tops?' Matt called up to his brother-in-law, and Romy realised that her brother was laughing.

'Matt! This is nothing to joke about. God, you are such an ass,' Joanna scolded, frantic, as Romy went to help her right the ladder. 'How the hell did this even happen?'

'Babe,' Nate called out, also with laughter in his voice. 'Seriously, it's fine. I'm going to go for it.' He looked down at his in-laws. 'You ready . . . ?'

'Don't you *dare*,' Joanna stuttered, evidently realising just how awkward a fully extended ladder actually was to manoeuvre – but her words of warning came too late, because a second later her husband let go and dropped the short distance to the ground, landing squarely on top of Matt.

The two men then collapsed backwards onto the snow, both laughing uproariously.

Joanna paused and then let out her breath, their obvious hilarity making it unlikely either was hurt. And despite herself, she joined in with the cacophony – while Romy allowed herself to relax and chuckle a little too.

She couldn't remember the last time she'd smiled like this, that any of them had in one another's company this year.

'You should have seen your face when the ladder fell. Fair play to your stuntman skills is all I can say,' Matt quipped.

'Dude,' chuckled Nate, 'I thought you had the ladder. You said you had it. I had no idea you had the upper body strength of a poodle. Remind me next time, OK?'

'So much for no one getting hurt putting up the outside decorations,' Romy observed wryly.

'I believe the exact instruction was that *I* was to avoid a trip to the hospital,' her dad put in, and goodness, it did her heart good to hear the mirth in his voice and see that old twinkle in his eye. 'Nothing about anyone else.'

Joanna stood over her husband with her hands on her hips. 'Need some help?'

'I suppose,' Nate said, eyes sparkling. And when his wife reached out to haul him up, instead he pulled her forward and she tumbled onto the snowy ground. Joanna sputtered, indignant, as she tried to clear damp from her clothes, and she looked ready to issue a sharp rebuke, but then seemed to think better of it. Having evidently decided on another approach, she grabbed a handful of snow and launched it at her husband, returning the favour.

Before Romy knew it, all five of them had regressed into a good old-fashioned snowball fight (albeit a wet and slushy one), the outdoor decorations and their collective unease temporarily forgotten.

It was already working . . .

Soon the family were all thoroughly soaked through their clothes, not to mention winded, and Bill signalled for a break.

'What? Throwing in the towel already, old man?' Nate chided, trying in vain to grab another handful of snow to replenish his arsenal. 'Especially when this is more of a snowball "scatter" than a fight. Try growing up in Michigan.'

'Yeah, but you're in Ireland now, bud,' Bill joked. 'World Snow-Scatter Champions.'

'Pathetic.' Nate feigned a knuckle crack. 'Whaddya reckon, honey, help me take this tough-talking grandad down?' Then he grinned as his father-in-law turned away. 'Yeah, you better run . . .'

But Romy saw that her dad hadn't in fact given up, but had become distracted by the appearance of a car at the gate.

At this, they all turned their attention to the driveway, and when the approaching car – evidently a taxi – neared the house, her eyes widened as, through the rear passenger window, she caught a glimpse of the new arrival.

Chapter 28

Remember that time when Romy was maybe four or five, and she wanted us all to go carolling on Christmas Eve?

We'd already got into our pyjamas and to be honest, your dad and myself were looking forward to you lot getting off to bed so we could do the Santa thing and then cosy up for a little glass or two.

But of course, she was insistent we go, so we all put coats on over our PJs and off we went. And it was lovely and all fun and games until Joanna caught a chill and ended up spending Christmas Day in bed, miserable, poor thing.

So that was the end of the Christmas Eve carolling jaunts, which we switched out for the infinitely safer and more sensible neighbourly get-together.

Or that time I put the turkey in the oven but completely forgot to switch it on? The result of perhaps more than a little glass or two of mulled wine at one of those very get-togethers the night before . . .

Poor Jo found this horrifying (though, to be fair, even the tiniest little mishap is a disaster when you're a teenager), and was completely convinced that Christmas was ruined. Until your dad skedaddled off to the drive-through and brought back practically everything on the McDonald's menu – even though he'd never eat a bite of it himself.

Anyway, I suppose my point is, as you all begin to navigate your way through a Christmas like no other, just remember: embrace the difference.

We don't or shouldn't have to be creatures of habit.

If you have the opportunity to change things up or introduce something (or even someone) new to the mix, then do!

I just want you all to feel OK about getting through this first season without me and instead of mourning my absence, maybe just embrace the change and welcome the unexpected.

Remember, life in general is way too short to do anything but . . .

Romy headed to the car with mixed emotions; on the one hand excited, yet at the same time a little ill at ease because this unexpected arrival had caught her completely off guard.

'Surprise!' Damien got out of the car, a rucksack in his hands, and her heart gave a little flip at the playful smirk that appeared as he looked at her, and the cute little dimple on his cheek that always left her weak at the knees.

A bit more of a heads-up in relation to his arrival would've been nice, though. When they were last in touch, he'd told her he'd pop over once he'd finished catching up with his own relations.

And especially given his very existence would be complete news to *her* family, Joanna excepted.

'I thought you were going to let me know before coming?' Romy said, mostly for everyone else's benefit.

Damien slung his bag over his shoulder and pulled her close. 'Thought I'd surprise you – that's OK, isn't it?' He affectionately brushed an errant lock of hair out of her eyes before noticing the moisture on his fingers. 'Oh, you're all wet.'

'We were just having a . . . never mind. Anyway, yes, it is a lovely surprise – I just thought we were going to meet somewhere first,' she sang, trying make her voice sound light, while inwardly trying to figure out how she was going to explain the appearance of this complete stranger at the family home. 'I just . . . hadn't actually told everyone about you yet,' she muttered, a little under her breath.

'Well, no time like the present, I s'pose.' He shrugged, looking past her and taking in the rest of her family, standing confused beneath the stone steps to the front door. 'Hello all,' he greeted with a grin.

Romy turned slightly on her heel, to be met with her family's questioning faces, and locked eyes with Joanna, who raised her eyebrows and bit her lip – a glance of support she recognised, but one that also suggested she had no idea what to do or say.

'So, everyone, this is Damien. Damien Kelly. He's a friend of mine from London—'

'Come on, babe, I think everyone gets that we're a little more than friends,' he commented smoothly, and while she wasn't exactly a teenager, Romy still caught the look of discomfort on her dad's face.

'Yes, so yes . . . Damien and I have been seeing each other for a little while – in London. And well, since he was coming home too, I thought it would be nice to . . . invite him here over the Christmas period.' She looked at the ground and clasped her hands, twisting them in circles in front of her. 'I was going to mention it, obviously, but with everything else, I just didn't get the opportunity. But anyway, now he's . . . here.'

She grimaced then, realising that it sounded as if she was asking for permission. Of course it was fine for her to bring someone home for Christmas; after all, Joanna and Matt had been doing this with their respective other halves for years.

But this year is different, surely, a voice inside her piped up, and Romy ignored it.

Quickly she turned to him and said, 'Of course that's fine too. Plans change.' She shrugged her shoulders, and then threw her arms around Damien's neck, embracing him more enthusiastically lest he feel unwelcome. Then she turned back to her family, wearing a purposeful smile.

'Well, welcome, Damien – very nice to meet you,' Joanna greeted with a smile, though Romy immediately recognised her sister's fake Corporate Game Face. But she was grateful at least that she'd made the effort.

'Sorry, yes, this is my dad, Bill, my brother, Matt, sister, Joanna, and brother-in-law, Nate.' Romy duly pointed to each family member one by one, who between them uttered stilted hellos and confused handshakes. 'Pretty much my entire family, except of course for my baby nieces, who are inside sleeping.'

He winked. 'Can't wait to meet them.'

Feeling a little stupid at the idiotic notion of introducing him to toddlers, she flushed.

'Well, we were actually just in the process of putting up the decorations.' She smiled, attempting to change the subject, and keen for some faint signal of acceptance from her family that this was OK.

And this time her brother obliged. 'Albeit unsuccessfully,' Matt grimaced.

Damien looked up at the house, as if noticing it for the first time.

'Wow.' He turned to her dad. 'Bill, your daughter is a princess but she neglected to tell me she actually lived in a palace.'

Flushing uncomfortably at the comment, which she knew was well intentioned but sounded a bit cheesy in front of her family, Romy gave another uneasy laugh. 'He's such a joker,' she trilled. 'Anyway, time to get back inside. It's freezing out and you're right, I am all wet. I need to change.'

With that, the pair breezed past the remaining Moore family, all of whom were somewhat bamboozled by this sudden new arrival in the snow.

Especially in light of their own recent thaw.

Chapter 29

After Romy and Damien went inside, I noticed immediately that some of the initial awkwardness and tension between us had subsided a little, as if we suddenly had reason to band together against this unpredictable outside force.

'You knew about this guy then?' Matt asked me quietly, his tone wary but non-confrontational.

'She literally just mentioned him in passing earlier. Said she'd invited him over for Christmas,' I responded. 'Though I get the sense that his appearance was as much a surprise to her as it is to us.'

Dad nodded. 'A good surprise, I hope.'

Me too. And while I couldn't really say I'd immediately warmed to the guy, I was glad for my sister's sake that he was here to support her if she needed it.

'Should we just finish putting up the outside stuff then?' I decided I would rather brave the cold than have to go inside the house and face additional awkward small talk with the new visitor, who was, after all, a stranger.

'Joanna,' Nate pointed out, 'you're not exactly dressed for it.' He eyed my ballet shoes and I recalled him pulling me playfully into the snow just now, and kind of wished it was just the two of us still.

'I'll go and put some boots and a coat on.' However, the words were just out of my mouth when an all too familiar yowl of impatience erupted from the monitor speaker still attached to the waistband of my now wet jeans. 'Weird, for a minute there, I'd almost forgotten we had kids,' I joked, but Nate looked distinctly unimpressed.

'Sure we're almost finished out here anyway, love. No more accidents, I promise.' Dad smiled at me and then glanced upwards, as if sending up a silent reassurance to Mum too.

I turned on my heel to go and get the girls up, thankful at least that I had the distraction.

Leaving the others outside to finish their work, and heartened afresh by the fact that Mum's first task had ensured we were now actually managing civil conversation, I slipped off my wet shoes in the hallway and padded barefoot up the stairs.

However, on the way, I passed Romy's bedroom door on the landing and heard voices emanating from within.

So was Damien also going to share a room with her? I didn't think my sister was an innocent nor indeed a child, but I also knew that she definitely wasn't one to rush into things. So it felt a little surprising to me that she might already be that familiar with this guy.

But then I reminded myself that Romy's new relationship felt that way to me because I'd only literally just heard about it and, of course, lots of things had changed in the year gone by, hadn't they?

Still, against my better judgement, I slowed my pace a little to see if I could make out their voices.

'You really should have texted beforehand . . .' I heard her say, but her voice wasn't reproachful . . . more . . . submissive?

His shrug was communicated all the way through the door. 'I didn't think it would be a problem. Like I said, I thought it would be a nice surprise. You said yourself you needed backup.'

Immediately, I felt defensive and a little hurt that Romy felt she needed to call in reinforcements. 'Well, I was just a little . . . caught unawares. It's just things are still a bit . . . delicate. Yes, everything's still weird with my mum gone, but at the same time they're still my family.'

'So would you rather I just go then?'

'No, no, of course not. I'm glad you're here. Like I said, I needed the distraction.'

'Good, I can certainly be distracting. Come here,' he purred, and my face flushed, now feeling uncomfortable for spying.

Unfortunately, at that moment one of the girls decided to announce their increasing impatience with my dilly-dallying, and I jumped to attention as an angry cry erupted from the baby monitor.

Shit . . .

Even though I tried to act casually, as if I was just passing down the hall, the door flew open. My guilt at overhearing their exchange was likely written all over my face.

'What do you want?' my sister demanded, and I did my best not to look over her shoulder at Damien, who was lying idly on her bed.

'Nothing. The girls just woke up . . .' I stammered by way of an explanation before resuming my journey down the hall.

I felt sweat break out under my arms in embarrassment as I heard him chuckle, 'Seems we were about to have an audience . . .'

I didn't hear Romy's response, though, because she slammed the door loudly behind me.

I sighed as I went to attend to my increasingly impatient offspring, now kicking myself for intruding on their privacy.

What little tentative progress I thought I had made with my sister had just vanished like a plume of smoke.

This was going to be a long Christmas.

Chapter 30

I'm sure I don't have to tell you that the festive season always truly kicks off with the tree.

When your dad and I first got married, it was something we didn't even think about at first because, obviously, we had always celebrated in our own families' houses.

On our first Christmas as husband and wife, tree farms like Dooley's didn't exist, so we went up to the woods to cut down our own (illegal, of course, but that never stopped your father), but when we got there we realised we didn't bring an axe, because we didn't have one.

So, following a quick detour to the builders providers, not only did your father cut down the very first Moore family Christmas tree, but that day was also the beginning of his burgeoning tool collection.

Course, once we got the tree home we realised that we had misjudged the height of the living room, and at least three feet of it was squashed into the ceiling. So the two of us had to head back outside, dragging the offending spruce behind us, in order to 'trim' it down. (This also warranted another trip to the builders providers – your dad needed a saw this time.)

Eventually, we got the tree back inside and were able to get it to stand up properly in the bucket . . . and then we collapsed on the couch, too worn out to properly decorate it.

Later that evening, with some of the inexpensive decorations I'd picked up in town, we finally decorated the tree and dressed it in lights and a mishmash of different-coloured tinsel, and it was simply . . . beautiful.

I still remember it today, even though ye'd all fall around the place laughing at the state of it.

Even so, I doubt your first proper family tree is something you could ever forget.

Of course, over the years, the number of trees we had, as well as our decorations collection, grew and grew – much like our family.

And when we moved into this house we had room for so much more and so, yes, maybe I went overboard, but digging out all those little bits and bobs we'd gathered over the years is always a joy.

Remember how we would open each box and it always felt like a surprise? As if we had forgotten what we had from one year to the next.

And how we would take hot chocolate breaks and put on Christmas songs in the background.

This is one job that really needs to be savoured.

Have fun, take it slow, just enjoy the experience. Allow the wonder of it all to wash over you once again because that, after all, is part of the magic.

◆ ◆ ◆

'Hand me that box to your left, Matt,' Joanna ordered from her spot on the living room floor, beneath the tree. 'With the glass baubles? Watch out for Katie, though, she's right behind you.'

It was later that evening and the family – including newcomer Damien – was assembled in various positions around the tree.

After the others had finished putting everything up outside, Joanna had ordered in several pizzas as dinner, having pointedly sidestepped her blatant eavesdropping outside Romy's bedroom door.

Now, they all rummaged through various boxes she and Joanna had taken down from the attic earlier – all except for Damien, who had taken it upon himself to observe from a distance on the couch, a glass of Bill's good whiskey in hand.

To be honest, Romy felt a little uncomfortable doing this with him there, and while in theory it should be an intimate family experience, in reality it now felt a bit childish and . . . silly even.

'Here you go,' Matt said as he handed Joanna the container she had requested.

'Has anyone seen the box with all the ones we bought on holidays?' Romy enquired, crawling on her knees and inspecting labels on the surrounding pile. Suzy scuttled up next to her aunt and smiled, as if thrilled to see mimicry of her own mode of transport. 'What? Did you come to help me, honey? I didn't know you could read yet. What a smart little nugget you are,' she teased, tickling the toddler and earning a delighted squeal.

From the couch, Damien smiled indulgently. 'Girls and babies . . .'

'Over here, hon,' Bill said, standing up and hoisting a box, giving it to his daughter.

'Thanks,' she said gratefully. 'I think these are my favourite.'

Joanna was now on her feet, passing glass ornaments to Nate, who was hanging them strategically around the tree, ensuring none would be low-hanging fruit, so to speak, for either of the twins' wandering hands.

'Didn't have to worry about this stuff last time,' he commented. 'A lot can happen in a year . . .' he added, before realising the full weight of his words.

For a moment, the family was silent, lost in contemplative reflection, until eventually Bill spoke. 'Indeed.' Her dad's voice was sad.

'Understatement,' Matt commented dully, gazing at the floor.

Keen to lighten the mood, Romy extracted an ornament. 'Aww, look,' she smiled. 'From our first ever London trip.'

They all paused to look at the ornament.

Joanna smiled. 'Remember that afternoon tea at Claridge's that Mum took us to?'

'Do I what? The clotted cream scones.' Romy grinned at the memory. 'I think that was the very thing that made me fall in love with the place and want to move there.'

'And look, the one from Clearwater Beach,' Matt chuckled, holding up a glass orb containing white silica sand. 'That was the time I got into a fight with that dolphin.' He unwrapped the next one, a hot pink flamingo. 'Another one from Florida. Man, that was a great trip, wasn't it? Though it must've been at least fifteen, twenty years ago now . . .'

The siblings looked at one another, each lost in their own recollections of that happy time, until from the couch, Damien spoke again. 'Let me guess, you did the Disney World thing too?'

Romy flushed, and while it was an innocuous comment, she couldn't help but worry that the others might find it a bit patronising. She was probably just being overly sensitive because of the ongoing family tension and, given this, her boyfriend would obviously struggle to read the overall dynamic.

'Where did your family go when you were kids, Damien?' Joanna enquired, evidently sensing the same thing, and Romy felt grateful for it.

'Just as far as my grandparents' house in Bray.'

'Where did you say you are from again, bro?' Nate asked smoothly.

'I didn't,' Damien said, and she was surprised at this rather curt reply, considering her brother-in-law's general affability. But to be fair, maybe Damien didn't like to discuss family matters with strangers?

'He's from Dublin originally too,' she supplied helpfully.

'Ah, so you're not too far from home then,' said Matt.

Damien simply shrugged and took a drink from the whiskey glass. 'Nope. But I don't really talk to my family.'

OK, so it was definitely a bit of a sore topic, and she made a mental note to ensure her family didn't pry too much, or cross any invisible line in their attempts to make Damien feel welcome.

The Moores had (up until recently, at least) always been a naturally sociable clan, and she sometimes had to remind herself that not every family was as easy and open.

And Damien's slight air of mystique and unwillingness to share too much of himself was one of the things that had attracted her to him in the first place. Plus the fact that he sat and listened when she poured her heart out, instead of automatically offering solutions or platitudes.

Now, though, a somewhat uncomfortable silence ensued while the others continued unwrapping and decorating, each seemingly keen to avoid any topic of conversation that would likely result in some kind of elephant in the room.

'Oh look,' exclaimed Joanna then, reaching into a different box she'd just opened. 'It's Skeletor.' She laughed, and held up the ornament – the one that Romy had made during their schooldays.

Now she herself laughed aloud. 'God, the state of it. And remember Mum carrying on like I was Michelangelo?' She took the ornament from her sister and turned to Damien, her voice full of mirth. 'I made this in First Class thinking I was great, and Matt dubbed it Skeletor the moment I brought it home.'

Damien sized up the object she was holding. 'Ha, pretty obvious you just weren't meant for great things, babe,' he chuckled and she laughed, pleased that some of the tension had been broken.

Joanna squared her shoulders as she took Skeletor from her and hung it delicately on a branch. 'Well . . .' her sister said simply, and Romy recognised the undertone in her voice.

OK, so maybe not.

'I agree with Mum, actually. I love this little guy. Maybe it's not Michelangelo, but still it wouldn't be Christmas without it.' Jo took a step back, admiring it on the tree.

Matt approached from behind and looked over Joanna's shoulder.

'Agreed,' he said quietly, before turning back to Romy and Damien. 'It's always been one of my favourites too.'

For her part, Romy returned to the box of travel ornaments, once again feeling awkward.

Bill now crossed the room, gingerly ensuring he didn't step on any boxes – or his grandchildren. Then he went to the tree and gently picked up Skeletor where it hung from the branch, handling it as if it were a piece of delicate glass.

'Me too, pet. It might not be a work of art, but your mother used to say that handmade decorations were always the ones she treasured the most – because they were made with heart.'

Chapter 31

Early the next morning, I extracted myself from the bed as quietly as possible, careful not to disturb Nate so as to allow him just a little bit more shut-eye.

Creeping from our bedroom, I tiptoed down the hall, taking the briefest of pauses in front of the twins' door, happy to find silence on the other side as well.

Weirdly, the Irish air seemed to be working magic on their sleep patterns this time. Or maybe it was just jet lag. Either way, I was glad of it.

Truth be told, though, I hadn't been sleeping well myself, and I should have been, considering how exhausted I felt. But instead of just lying in bed and contemplating the ceiling, I decided to get up and try to make myself useful.

Heading downstairs to the kitchen, I took a brief detour on the way to flip the lights on the newly decorated tree, standing majestically in the living room as always, but perhaps with even a little more twinkle to it this year, as if it had been waiting too long to finally be called to action.

I had a sudden bittersweet memory of the year before, finding my mother sitting quietly in the early morning light on Christmas Eve, enjoying a cup of coffee in front of the tree.

The painful strength of the memory almost took my breath away, and how I wished I could conjure that same scene again and make it a reality. Except this time I would go over, wrap my arms around her and hold her close, instead of briskly zeroing in on all the pointless stuff I'd thought I needed to do at the time, like switch on the coffee machine, or sort the girls' breakfast.

But I was completely oblivious to how rare and precious those moments were about to become. Or that the sand in the hourglass was by then already starting to empty.

I wiped away an errant tear, crippled afresh by the realisation that I didn't treasure every moment with her while I had the chance. And how I wished I'd known at the time that I'd never, ever get the opportunity to do so again.

My heart leaden with sorrow and regret, I took a deep breath and headed into the kitchen to begin the day and enjoy a brief peaceful spell of alone time.

As the coffee percolated, I slipped the Christmas list from beneath the magnet pinning it on the fridge. Looking through some of the items, I considered the food element and went to seek out my mother's old 'recipe books' – though they were really a mishmash of scribbles and notations – which had always been housed in the drawer closest to the cooker.

Gently caressing the well-worn pages that had long been stained and blurred with various ingredients over the years, I grabbed a pad of paper and a pen, filled a cup with fresh coffee, and returned to my seat, ready to make my own list – the supplies needed to replicate some of these recipes I knew so well.

To the point that, right then, I could almost taste some of them in my mouth.

'How did you do all of this stuff on your own every year?' I whispered as I studied the ingredients for her famous mince pies, shortbreads and sausage pastries amid other festive favourites, while contemplating my own baking abilities. Or lack thereof.

'And what the heck is star anise?' I pondered as I read through the hitherto unknown (to me at least) contents of a bouquet garni she used to put together to make mulled wine. I blinked. 'Or pie weights?'

'They're these little balls you put in a pastry base while it's baking, so it doesn't rise and get too puffy. She always had a bag of them somewhere around here.'

I jumped at Romy's unexpected appearance and clasped a hand over my heart, surprised that I was no longer alone, before giving a nervous laugh.

'Feck, don't sneak up on me like that. Need to put sleigh bells on you,' I grinned. 'Good to know on the weights, though – maybe I'll put you in charge of the mince pies.' I paused as I watched my sister pull her long blonde hair up into a messy bun on top of her head. 'Couldn't sleep?' I enquired.

'Damien snores,' she answered with a grimace, spying my coffee and crossing the kitchen to take out her own mug. 'What are you doing up yourself?'

'I couldn't sleep either, so I figured I might as well make a start on sorting some of the ingredients we need for this stuff. Plus, I've noticed since our arrival that there's a distinct lack of food in this house, which is why I ordered pizza last night. I truly wonder what Dad and Matt eat day to day.'

Romy sat down across from me and sipped her coffee. 'Not a lot, by the looks of them, and to be honest, I had the same thought. I wonder how long Matt's going to stay here? With Dad, I mean.'

I looked up at my sister and met her gaze, relieved that we were once again able to enjoy a comfortable chat together, before I realised a hard truth: never mind how long Matt would be here, I had no real idea how long Matt *had* been here, because I hadn't spoken to him since the funeral, or indeed all that much before then either.

Shrugging awkwardly, I turned my attention back to the list. 'What does he tell you?' They'd always been closer, and I was curious to know if they'd talked much since April.

She sipped her coffee. 'These days, I'm lucky to get the bare bones from him. I mean, you know Hazel dumped him after – well . . . everything. Like us, she figured there was more to the story, and that he'd been cheating. Why else would he have hidden it from her in the first place? He hasn't said much else about it to me either, to be honest.'

'I still can't believe he just quit the job altogether though,' I said, giving voice to some of the thoughts I'd had privately in the interim. 'Did something else happen with that whole situation, besides the disciplinary action?' My stomach gurgled loudly – but I wasn't hungry. It was the mere thought of everything that had happened, and mostly concern about any apparent role *I* might have had in my brother's break-up, that was giving me indigestion with a side of heartburn.

'Last I heard there's something coming up in the courts soon.'

I looked up, surprised. 'My God, I had no idea it was *that* bad—'

'Maybe the guy from the party didn't feel putting him on a leave of absence was punishment enough?'

'Wow. That is not good. Must have been a hell of a punch.' My stomach churned again and at Romy's curious glance, I put my hand to my abdomen. 'Indigestion.'

'I think there's some Rennie in the medicine drawer.' She crossed the room and found the cure for what ailed me. She jiggled a couple into her hand and offered them to me, before adding jokily, 'You sure you're not pregnant again?'

Despite myself, I laughed out loud at the very notion. 'Not a chance.' Nate and I hadn't been intimate in . . . well, in truth I didn't want to acknowledge how long.

I returned to my work and moved on to another recipe – classic sherry trifle, with a twist. A true family favourite, with only about a million calories per serving. I ran a hand over the recipe pages, fondly admiring my mother's neat handwriting.

'You know, I love looking at her words. I love knowing that she touched this page so many times over the years as she got this stuff ready for us all. It makes me wish she was here, for so many reasons. I wish the girls would have known her better. They probably won't even remember her.' I paused, biting my lip a little as, yet again, tears threatened. I looked at Romy. 'But most of all, because she was so much *better* at all this stuff than I ever could, or will be.' Of course I didn't just mean cooking, but my sister didn't know that.

'What . . . you mean the whole stay-at-home mom thing hasn't automatically turned you into a domestic goddess too?'

Turning my thoughts briefly to my gourmet kitchen back home, worthy of a professional chef, I felt myself blushing with discomfort. If my kitchen could talk, it would tell me how ashamed it was of me.

'I'm a bit . . . hopeless, to be honest,' I confessed timidly. 'I can barely keep our kitchen clean, let alone prepare anything worth eating. On nights when Nate is home, I rely on a lot of pre-prepared Whole Foods stuff, just so he has something decent. When he isn't, I just eat frozen stuff or takeout. Or sometimes even just cornflakes.' I tried to keep my voice light, but there was no denying the undercurrent – and even to me it sounded sad and miserable.

And when Romy laughed, I knew she truly believed I was just joking, that it didn't even cross her mind that I might not have taken to domesticity like a duck to water, and not only taken to it, but conquered and even improved it.

Much like I had thought I would.

At first.

'So, is Nate . . . away a lot of nights?' she enquired.

'He has to travel a lot more these days, because he's the only breadwinner now. But it's fine.' I knew my voice was defensive but I couldn't help it. I hated that he was away so much. But what could I do? One of us had to bring in the bacon, to say nothing of trying to rebuild everything we had lost. Which, these days, involved significant travel.

Or so he told me.

'So,' I asked, quickly changing the subject. 'Seems like things are going strong with you and Damien?'

Romy's head shot up from the recipe she had been looking through and I knew I had said the wrong thing, because my thoughts – and probably hers – had turned to our uncomfortable encounter in the hall outside her bedroom door the previous afternoon.

I rushed to clarify. 'I mean, him being here for Christmas. Sounds like things are serious.'

Her face softened ever so slightly. 'Kind of,' she said.

Wanting to learn more about the man currently snoring in my sister's bed, I pushed on, recalling what she'd said about how they'd met. 'So he's a runner too – a sporty type?'

She snorted. 'Ha, I wouldn't call myself a runner, Jo. More of a quitter.'

I opened my mouth to encourage her, to tell her that she could always get back into it and of course she wasn't a quitter, but she cut me off. 'Besides, like Damien says, I just didn't want it enough.'

'Pretty sure you wanted it enough this time last year,' I hummed non-committally, recalling the passion and determination in her eyes when she'd confided her plans.

She sighed heavily. 'You don't like him, do you?' she stated, causing me to look up in surprise. Her eyes were boring into my face with an intensity reserved for witnesses testifying under oath. 'Let me guess, he doesn't measure up.'

Opening my mouth to speak, but not really sure what to say to that, or if I even knew enough about the guy to decide, I was saved by the bell – grateful for once at being interrupted by my daughters, who, based on the sudden ruckus coming from the baby monitor, were now very much awake.

'Yikes. Here we go.' I took a quick sip of my coffee and stood up. 'I'll keep going through these, and get everything we need at the shopping centre later. You coming? For the twins' Santa thing, I mean.'

'I'm . . . not sure,' Romy said. 'I'll probably just be doing something with Damien.' But her face and her tone were apologetic, and I got the sense that she truly did want to come, but knew it wasn't something she could expect him to go along with in a hurry. He barely knew us, after all.

I smiled, not wanting to make a big deal and potentially ruin the fragile truce we had going on just now. 'No worries. Anything at all you – or Damien – need for the next few days, just make a note of it and I'll add it to the shopping list.'

Hopefully this time, I mused, remembering previous shopping expeditions, it wouldn't end in disaster.

Chapter 32

All of this writing about Christmases past has allowed me some very pleasant trips down memory lane, which has been a balm for my soul at the minute, as you can imagine.

Even though I am facing a bleak and impossible situation – staring my own mortality in the face – I am not letting it get me down. I am choosing to remain positive, because when all is said and done I have had the most wonderful life, and I will take that thought with me through to the very end.

And I encourage all of you to do the same. There is very little point in wasting days of your life over things you cannot change. No point in being negative, angry, upset or bitter. It's a waste of time and energy. Rather, focus on the positive – and what you have right now – and do the best with it, and with each other.

Which brings me to my next point . . .

Oh, how I wish I would be there when you take the girls to see Santa. I so loved all your first times going to see the man himself.

Joanna, your first visit – I think – gave us a false sense of security, your dad and I, about the whole thing. You were preternaturally calm for a ten-month-old and completely unfazed by it all. You didn't cry, didn't squirm, nor get freaked out . . . you just sat there in this complete stranger's arms like it was the most natural thing in the world.

Of course, we found out otherwise once we removed you from his lap. And while your outward appearance remained neutral and even-keel, the contents of your nappy proved that Santa had quite literally scared the shite out of you.

Whereas, Matt, you were a completely different kettle of fish altogether for your first. You were almost a year old at the time, and that day we went you were a ray of sunshine. You loved all the lights and decorations and festive music. Your eyes were truly as big as saucers as you experienced your first Christmas. My due date was December 26th and while I hoped I might get a Christmas baby, in true Matt fashion you decided to take your time, and came a week and a half late, just after New Year's. You always have known how to make an entrance.

Well, back to my story. You were enjoying the lights and sounds and colours as we wandered through Rathfarnham shopping centre, and didn't mind waiting in the queue.

You even sat and watched as Joanna had her turn with the Big Man first – sure at that point, she was an old pro.

But when it came to your turn, your dad placed you in Santa's arms, carefully balanced on his knee, and when you turned and locked eyes with him, you let out such a blood-curdling scream that it literally bounced off the walls.

The crowd around us went utterly silent and the screaming continued. A quick picture was snapped, and then Dad grabbed you up like a grenade that was about to explode.

Nevertheless, you weren't a fan of the Big Man for a while. And it took some special convincing when you turned four or five to give it another shot – hence the reason why there aren't that many festive pictures of you in that scenario.

And Romy, honey, you were cool as could be for your first time. Giggly and happy and not a care in the world who was holding you – even if it was a twenty-stone oul fella in a red velvet costume.

We put you on his lap and he bounced you a bit, which elicited some happy baby cooing from you, and we snapped multiple pictures – it was idyllic. We were thinking: third time is definitely the charm . . .

Until, that is, you decided you were going to unmask him for the rest of the children who stood in line behind us to see.

You turned so quickly and ripped off that man's fake beard faster than I could move, and then held the furry thing up in your hand like a trophy hunter! Of course, you had no idea what you had done – and you had no idea that you likely traumatised several children (and parents!) who'd witnessed the whole thing.

Oh, such brilliant memories! I hope that you find some time to look through those old photo albums – and please add one of the twins this year, for posterity's sake.

Pretty certain Katie and Suzy will also give the Big Man a run for his money.

What I wouldn't give to be a fly on the wall . . .

That afternoon, in a two-car caravan, the Moore contingent – with the exception of Damien and Romy – headed to nearby Dundrum shopping centre.

Once they arrived at the local retail mecca, Nate and I wrangled the girls out of the rental and into the twin stroller we'd had to lug all the way from California.

As we all trooped through the busy shopping concourse to the outdoor purpose-built Santa Village, I offered a word of warning to Nate, who was pushing the stroller.

'I just need their outfits to stay clean until the pictures, OK? After that, anything goes.' I crossed my fingers and looked up at the sky. 'Wish us luck, Mum.'

I had packed identical red velvet dresses with white fur trim and matching bows that were now planted on top of each blonde head – or rather, on one blonde head. Suzy had already been successful in removing hers, and was now dangling it over the side of the stroller, getting ready to drop it into a puddle of slushy water. 'Suzy, no. Joanna, um, the . . . er . . . head thing.'

I scooted up, quickly catching the bow before it landed on the puddle. 'Not so fast, Little Miss, you will not foil your grandmother's plans.'

'Nothing wrong with your reflexes,' Matt commented, and I was doubly pleased to find that not only had he made the effort to come along today but seemed to have brightened in general since we'd made the decision to go ahead with Mum's suggestions.

It had been a brainwave; not least for getting through the season, but also in helping to break the initial ice between us.

Though I had to admit that Damien's out-of-the-blue arrival had gone a long way towards that too.

Earlier that morning, when I'd come back downstairs from tending to the girls, I'd found my brother in the kitchen, shaking his head in annoyance at the mess the new visitor had left behind upon making breakfast.

But if this guy made Romy happy, then . . .

Now, once through to the Santa Village area, we made our way to the end of a disconcertingly long queue to where the Big Man held court.

'This place is a goddamn madhouse,' Nate commented, taking in the crowd. 'Remind me why we're doing this again?' Course, for him growing up, Santa visits would've been few and far between, if at all, given that my husband's parents were high-flyers who cared little for inconvenient childish nonsense.

'I'm sure it won't take too long,' my dad commented, ever the optimist.

We filed in line behind a harried-looking woman on her own with three young boys, who all looked roughly the same age – maybe five or six. And it was apparent that the three had recently finished what appeared to be chocolate ice cream, because they now wore it on their faces.

I saw Matt stifle a guffaw at my horrified expression as they moved precariously close to the twins, sitting pristinely in their stroller.

'Boys, get back here now. I need to clean your faces. State of ye.' The woman, presumably their mother, flashed an embarrassed smile at us all behind her. 'Sorry, they're a bit excited.'

She continued to struggle, looking in her bag while also trying to get a hold of one of the boys, who seemed determined to escape her grasp. Immediately sympathetic, I grabbed the girls' changing bag and fished out a packet of baby wipes.

'Do you maybe need some of these?' I offered, tapping her gently on the shoulder.

She turned around to face us properly, a grateful smile on her face. 'Oh, thanks a million – you're a lifesaver. I could have sworn I had them with me. But honestly, I would forget my head if it wasn't attached . . .'

She spied the girls, gurgling cheerfully as Matt made funny faces at them, trying to keep them happy and entertained. 'Twins?' she asked then, nodding her head in their direction.

'Yes, almost eighteen months.'

She threw a hand in the direction of her own gang. 'You got lucky, so! This lot – triplets. Mad about them but I have no idea where they came from. Multiples don't run in my family. Thinking you are getting one, but then three show up. Shocked was an understatement.'

I thought back on my experience with IVF, remembering how stressful getting pregnant had been. I couldn't imagine trying for a baby and getting *three* as part of the bargain. Not that I envied the woman in that moment. She looked like she needed a small army to help her wrestle with hers. Or a stiff drink.

Having sufficiently cleaned the faces of her sons, the woman turned back to me and returned the baby wipes.

'Your girls. I love their outfits. And they are so well behaved. Oh, to have well-behaved children!'

I shared a look with Nate, who barked a laugh. 'Don't jinx us.'

'Well, I envy you. Bringing the whole family to this, how brilliant. My ex couldn't even be arsed with stuff like this when we were married. You're blessed to have so many helping hands.'

I felt myself blush at the woman's praise and looked fondly at my dad, who truly was keeping the girls distracted and under control as Matt snapped candid pictures of the scene on his phone.

In truth, we looked like any ordinary happy family, almost to the point that we'd all temporarily forgotten the tension and heartache of recent months. Mumbling my thanks, I was brought back to the moment by Nate.

'Line's moving,' he said. Keeping one hand on the stroller, my husband then slung the other arm around my shoulders, the first time he had done something like that in months. And also for the first time in ages, I didn't flinch. 'That was nice of you to help. Looks like she has her hands full.'

I bit my lip, thinking of my own recent struggles in stores by myself with the twins. 'Maybe because I've been in her shoes.'

Up ahead, Matt and my dad glanced back, giving the thumbs up. We were next in line. I turned my gaze ahead to where the woman and her errant three now stood in front of Santa.

One of the boys had taken off his shirt, and looked ready to do the same thing with his pants, while their mother tried to stuff him back into his clothing. The other two started a fight with each other, with one of the boys landing a firm smack across his brother's face.

Nate snorted a laugh before turning his attention back to me. 'Hey, if you need help, sweetheart, just say so. There isn't any shame in it, you know, asking for assistance. Telling me when you are overwhelmed. I'm not like that woman's ex-husband – but I'm also not a mind reader.'

I was about to respond that I shouldn't *have* to tell him these things when he took me by the hand and moved up the line again. '*And* I know how much you hate interference. Anyway, here we go. Show time.'

Was that it? I wondered suddenly. Was it my 'I've got this' scorched earth mentality that had thus far prevented Nate from offering an occasional helping hand? Sidelined him, even?

There was no more time to think about it, though, as we unfastened the girls from their stroller and straightened their bows and dresses for the big occasion. We approached Santa, who cheerfully crooned a greeting at the twins as Nate put them in his arms.

Turning to take in the face of this complete stranger, my daughters wore expressions of awe and wonder, before looking at each other and breaking into happy grins and snorting with laughter, apparently finding this one of the most amusing things that had ever happened to them in their short lives.

And while the rest of my family held up their phones, snapping pictures and making memories worthy of our family album, I shared a glance with my husband, realising that such picture-perfect family moments – just like old times – were exactly what our family had been missing.

Chapter 33

'Come on, slowcoach, get a move on,' Damien called out over his shoulder as he ran three strides ahead of Romy.

'You carry on. I told you I'd only come if we go at my pace,' she gasped between taking gulps of air.

He'd wanted to blow off the cobwebs and get out of the house, but there was no way she was going to suggest tagging along with the others to see Santa, and (stupidly, it turned out) thought she'd join him on a run instead.

And since he was insistent the woodland trails nearby would be way too messy underfoot, they'd jogged the few miles downhill to the closest recreational park.

While she felt pretty good on the downward elevation, by the time they'd reached their destination it was obvious that she was way out of sync with Damien's pace, to say nothing of out of shape in general.

Since Romy's body and mind had collaborated to scupper her marathon aspirations, it felt like a very long time ago since those earlier training days when she'd started to feel invincible.

She tried to slow her breathing as he bounced on the spot ahead of her, reluctant to slow his tempo to match hers.

'Might as well just walk it altogether,' he commented, weaving from side to side on the path, as alongside them the waters of the

River Dodder seemed to flow faster still, making her feel even more of a snail.

She dropped back yet further as Damien drifted on. While he'd been supportive of her efforts at the beginning, and especially so the day they'd first met, she'd soon realised he was in fact deeply competitive. Though he had little to fear from her.

'Honestly, go ahead,' she insisted, almost relieved to see him shrug his shoulders and quicken his pace as the path led away from the river and took a sharp incline up towards the soccer and Gaelic playing fields.

She had a brief flashback of coming here with her mum and dad when she and her siblings were kids. They used to scamper down this path with effortless ease and abandon. Well, she and Matt did, at least – at that point, a not-so-childish Joanna was considerably less inclined to scamper anywhere.

Her heart rate had drifted with the effort of trying to keep up with Damien, who, despite knowing she wasn't as diligent as he, seemed almost comically oblivious to the disparity in their athletic abilities. Or more likely he just didn't want to make her feel bad about it.

As Romy trudged on the path alongside the river, waiting to get her breath back, she came to one of her favourite spots. Leaving the path, she headed straight to the stepping stones traversing the river, as a thick canopy of trees arched overhead.

Taking a step onto the first stone, she remembered how far a leap it had seemed when she was a kid. As the youngest in the family, she had watched her older siblings leap across without batting an eyelid, while she had remained frozen on the riverbank, terrified by what seemed like the biggest challenge: the water rushing between the stones, waiting to sweep her away with one false move.

'Don't focus on the river, pet – just focus on the next step,' her mother had urged, going ahead of her and making the crossing seem less daunting.

Of course, Cathy always seemed to know exactly how to coax her on, urging her to keep going even when she was terrified.

Romy crossed now to the other bank, looking up- and downstream, the place bursting with childhood memories.

The time Matt had helped a little girl who'd slipped in off the riverbank. Back then, it had seemed like her brother was an out-and-out hero, though looking back now, Romy mused, the girl could just as easily have saved herself by taking a step out of the ankle-deep water. But the mind of a seven-year-old was hungry for excitement, and so the story had grown to be one of a great adventure where her brother had saved someone from being swept away by a raging torrent.

Recrossing the river as her heart rate subsided, Romy felt ready to continue on her route, Cathy's mantra echoing once again in her brain.

Just focus on the next step.

And the thought struck her that so often lately, it seemed she'd been focusing on the steps two or three ahead rather than the one directly in front of her, distracted by the noise all around, instead of just taking one step at a time and pushing through her route.

Feeling a glimpse of that earlier confidence returning, she started to jog the short climb away from the river and back towards the main park area, until turning to see Damien grinning his head off as he fell into pace beside her.

'Still here?' he said, his complexion maddeningly absent of any sign of exertion, unlike her, she guessed, who probably looked like an overripe tomato. 'See how much faster you can run when you're motivated, though? If you'd listened to me before, you'd be zipping around like a finisher now.'

She drew a breath to respond, but couldn't. The disappointment of failing to run this year's race was still raw, especially here in this place.

Ironic that it was in this very park, on one of those childhood family outings, that Romy had first become aware of the Dublin Marathon.

She remembered walking around the playing fields with her siblings, all three carrying home-made signs to support their Uncle John, who was competing in the race. That day, they all stood on the roadside along the length of the western side of the park and watched excitedly, trying to pick him out from the hundreds of athletes streaming by.

The noise and excitement of the crowds had always stayed with her. She remembered thinking at the time that these people were all superhuman. She had scanned all those faces, trying to seek out her uncle, and was troubled by the fact that many seemed to be grimacing, wearing expressions of supreme discomfort.

When she had aired this observation to her dad, he had explained that at this point the race was already seventeen miles in, so yes, they would be struggling. He then went on to describe just how far seventeen miles was, in terms Romy could fathom: from their house to their favourite beach, a long way in the car, never mind on foot.

And she very quickly started to understand the expressions they wore when he told her that they still had another nine miles left to run.

That particular memory had been stirred on numerous occasions since she had decided to give the race a try herself, and now, as she lumbered along a good five or six yards behind Damien, her recent failure was stirred up afresh too.

'Come on, you're trailing way behind, do you need me to put the frighteners on you again?'

'Very funny.' She gazed at the point along the wall where their dad had hoisted each of them in turn up on his shoulders so they could get a better vantage point.

Damien stopped just ahead, and looked out across the road.

'This is my favourite section of the route,' he commented, as if reading her mind. 'There's a lovely downhill sweep into Terenure and then you hit the main street and it's like a St Patrick's Day parade, everybody cheering you on . . . the noise is always unreal,' he added, sounding nostalgic. 'Maybe you'll be up to it next year. I'll help you put the work in properly, come up with a plan that will actually work.'

She nodded, but remained silent, not wanting to dwell on the subject.

'Instead of that lazy-man's nonsense you were following last time – three or four runs a week? Not a chance.'

'It's not the plan that was the problem, though,' Romy muttered, almost to herself.

'Course it was. A book never made an athlete out of anyone. Even the day I met you it was as obvious as the nose on your face. You were way too under-prepared for when the heavy mileage kicked in, babe. The foundation just wasn't there.'

'We're not all natural-born athletes,' she replied tersely, as they strolled back out of the park. She was exhausted and tetchy and really not in the mood for another post-mortem about her ill-fated training plan. She knew he meant well and was only trying to encourage her, but . . .

'Seriously, though, if you really want this, if you really do want to run down this very road next year, I'll get you there. You just need to be willing to work hard and put in the effort, and forget stupid books. Trust me, that's all there is to it.'

Romy bit her tongue. Maybe he was right.

Not for the first time, she reflected on why her body had failed her after she had worked so hard and achieved so little. But was it her body or her mind that had failed her, Romy wondered, as once again her mother's encouraging childhood refrain swam into her brain.

Just focus on the next step.

Chapter 34

When we returned home after our festive outing to the shopping centre, my spirits were buoyed.

Not only had the twins behaved for Santa, they had been downright picture-perfect, and being surrounded by the family with all of us getting along so well had left me feeling light-hearted, optimistic and happy.

Truly happy, for the first time in ages.

Which was probably why right that same evening, and while our little family seemed to be in such good spirits, I'd cajoled Nate into delving head first into perhaps creating a brand-new tradition of our own.

I brushed the hair back from my face and took a deep breath, hoping the twins wouldn't start to grumble at finding themselves strapped into high chairs like they normally did.

If this was going to work, restricting their mobility would be the key to success (as it was with most things these days).

'Just make sure they don't get their hands on this until my say-so. Some of the roof decorations are pretty big,' I instructed.

Nate's head shot up from his phone; he was totally distracted and in another world, and seemed to be taking a second or two to consider the instruction, and what his response should be, before sliding the device into his jeans pocket and nodding unenthusiastically.

I turned the box over to read the step-by-step instructions on the back.

Yes, it would've been nice to actually bake one of those things from scratch like we had seen on *Home & Family*, but . . . baby steps. Maybe when the girls were a little older.

But for our first time (plus given my non-existent baking skills), today's store-bought E-Z Build Gingerbread House kit would have to suffice.

'Sorry . . . what do you need me to do?' he asked, pulling out a chair beside the girls, who were gnawing on some dry sponge biscuits I'd found in Mum's ingredients press, which I knew she used when making sherry trifle. Since this old Irish recipe had always been a huge hit in the family at this time of year, I knew I'd likely have to give it a go at some point too, but for now I was going the all-American route.

'Just keep an eye – once the box is open these two will be all hands.' Yet for all my optimism, I couldn't quite shake the low-level trepidation in my chest. The picture on the front of the box depicted a happy smiling family, swooning over the work-of-art confection they'd just created together.

Although I knew our end result may not be quite as impressive, I was determined it would be close. This, after all, was supposed be 'E-Z'.

I opened the kit and carefully slid out the plastic tray housing individual pieces for the walls and roof. Setting these on the table, I took out two tubes of icing, which I guessed would be used to stick all the pieces together plus decorate the house, once constructed.

I quickly arranged all of the items on the table just like in the picture, so I could correctly itemise and identify everything.

Katie and Suzy both lit up at the sight of the multiple bags of bright-coloured candies to be used for decoration.

Closely studying the pieces, I bit my lip, trying to differentiate walls and roof, but also puzzled by an apparent lack of gingerbread pieces.

'Dammit, did we pick up a dud box?' I wondered out loud, glancing at Katie and at the last minute grabbing the tube of icing she'd picked up.

'No, honey, not yet.' Swiping it back before she started putting it in her mouth, I glanced, irritated, at my husband, who unbelievably had the phone out again.

Katie's head flew back as she contorted herself, resulting in a smack against the back of her chair. Her wide-eyed expression changed from one of shock to pain, and as she took a sharp intake of breath to fuel the imminent roar, I quickly stepped forward to comfort her.

'Nate, seriously?' In one swift motion the phone was back in his pocket, and he was kissing the back of his daughter's head. I bit my tongue, determined not to let his obvious disinterest – or dare I say even boredom – get to me, but this was supposed to be a fun-filled family-memory-making 101. And he couldn't stay off the damn phone even for a couple of seconds.

Katie started to calm, so, swallowing back the urge to challenge him on it, I got back to inventorying.

'OK, what am I missing?' I muttered out loud, wondering why there were only two walls and two roof pieces. '"*E-Z*" *my ass . . .*'

I picked up the box again, trying to figure out how many pieces there should be.

Then I looked up to see Katie still gnawing happily away on the sponge finger and getting obvious enjoyment, as well as relief from the imminent arrival of another new tooth.

'The walls are in one piece, you have to snap them down the line,' Nate mumbled, having solved my dilemma with a single glance. Easier for the all-American boy, I supposed, though from what I knew of Nate's mother, she definitely wouldn't have been the gingerbread-house-making type.

Returning my gaze to the instructions, I finally spotted the diagram showing a pencil under the conjoined wall piece, with arrows showing where pressure needed to be applied to snap the walls into individual pieces.

But my husband was way ahead of me and had already started on the process.

'Aw crap,' he muttered then, looking at the piece in his hand.

I stared at him, incredulous. 'I can't believe . . . Why would you . . . ?'

'Sorry – it just broke at that angle, it must have been cracked already.'

'You and your big clumsy hands . . .'

'Hey, you didn't even know it was supposed to be separated until I told you.'

'Even so, at least I *read* the instructions. It might take longer to figure things out, but at least it will be done right in the end. Look, you were supposed to put something under the line so as to snap it evenly.' I couldn't control my annoyance as I took the pieces from his hands. 'It's useless already.'

'Don't be a drama queen, it can be fixed with the icing. The walls and roof will hold it together anyway.'

Examining the pieces, I resisted the urge to fire the whole lot in the bin. I'd envisioned a more holistic version of the building process, where we'd work together to create something visually stunning.

Instead, I was already resisting the urge to break the other intact wall over my goddamn husband's head.

I'll give him drama queen.

'Having fun, kids?' Matt quipped with genuine merriment in his tone as he wandered into the kitchen.

Great, that's all we needed – spectators.

'Lots.' Nate rolled his eyes. 'Little Miss Project Manager is busting my chops because I got the walls a little wonky.'

'Well, maybe if you weren't acting like some cowboy builder sitting around glued to your phone, the project manager wouldn't have *reason* to bust anything.' I regretted my retaliation immediately once I saw the annoyance in his eyes, but thankfully he let it slide.

In front of Matt, at least. Then he turned away and swiped a bag of candy from Suzy once again.

'Well, Katie isn't complaining anyway,' my brother chuckled. 'She's making light work of that chimney.' I turned in horror to see my other daughter happily gnawing the remainder of what I'd previously thought to be a piece of trifle sponge.

Oh man . . . But the formerly hardened gingerbread chimney piece had been ground down into a fine brown sludge, which was now adorning my daughter's entire lower face, plus her fingers.

'Oh, for . . .' I held back the expletive, but the look I cast Nate was openly accusatory; enough that he didn't wait for any words to follow and instead just stood up, the chair sliding backwards as he turned and headed straight for the door.

'Just. Perfect.' I sighed heavily, attempting to see if there was anything worth salvaging inside the tightly closed gingery fist of my daughter, who was squirming at the notion of relinquishing her prize.

'Mine!' she exclaimed, clearly ready to fight. The picture of the pristine house surrounded by a perfectly contented family taunted me from the box in the corner of the table, while my brother stood leaning against the worktop, laughing in a way I hadn't heard in a long time.

'You're not getting that back, you know . . .'

I threw both hands up in the air. 'Oh, what's the point. Nate's already gone and broken one wall with his ape hands, and now there's no friggin' chimney. Might as well let these two go nuts on it.'

I was totally ready to toss this brand-new Christmas tradition into the garbage.

'Joanna, I don't think building a gingerbread house is supposed to be a military operation. And it can't be that difficult anyway.' Matt moved over to the table to inspect the broken pieces and chewed plastic packets.

'Ooooh, look what Uncle Mattie has!' he cooed enthusiastically to Suzy, deftly exchanging a floppy piece of coloured cardboard packaging for the tube of icing she had once again been exploring. 'Here – get the scissors and nip the end off the nozzle,' he instructed me then, breaking the other slab of gingerbread in the correct places, leaving one good wall and one broken one.

Then he put the two broken pieces flat on the table and pushed them together before re-separating them. 'Don't cut too much off the nozzle, or it'll come out too fast.'

He made another funny face at the girls as they laughed at his antics, then took the piping tube from me and ran a bead of icing along the fractured gingerbread pieces, pushing them together before wiping the excess with his finger and licking it off.

'Oh yum. Who wants some?' He then offered the piping tube to the girls like he was about to shower them in it, and they clapped in delight at the prospect. 'Right, hands flat on the table, facing up like this.' He demonstrated to the girls, who quickly obliged, then he put a little dab of icing on each of their fingers.

'Now wait till I say go.' Both squirmed with delight and anticipation, totally engrossed with what he was doing. 'When I say go, you can have some.' Katie moved her hand to her mouth.

'Little cheater, not yet,' he scolded her playfully, catching her hand and placing it back on the table as the two girls screamed in delight. 'OK, 5 . . . 4 . . . 3 . . . Go!' Matt called out and the twins, caught unawares by the shortened countdown, licked their fingers, both laughing uproariously.

And despite myself, I was smiling too. 'Great, I'll be peeling them off the walls later from all that sugar.'

'It's Christmas, they're *supposed* to be high on sugar,' Matt laughed, tickling the girls, who were now giggling hysterically.

I watched them for a moment, marvelling at how in tune with them he was.

I'd always thought of Matt as harmless and a total messer. Until last year, when all I could focus on was the stupid fight he'd gotten into at his Christmas party. I'd been so exasperated at his immaturity, I had pretty much forgotten the brother I'd known and loved when we were younger, closer and (perhaps more to the point) less worn down by life.

'Pass me the tray,' he instructed now, pointing to the white piece of plastic that had housed the various components of the Not So E-Z Build kit. He flipped it over and placed the piping tube in Suzy's hand before helping her squeeze the tube and guide it along two sides of a narrow channel that formed a rectangular shape.

He then did the same on the opposite side with Katie holding the piping tube. The two girls dipped their fingers in the channel full of icing and scooped a handful each.

'No – don't do that,' I admonished, unable to help myself.

'It's grand, there's loads left.' Matt picked up the wall sections and placed them into the slots before adding some more icing vertically where they joined at each corner.

'There,' he declared, happy with himself that the repaired piece had held.

'And where did you learn to build gingerbread houses?'

'Seriously, sis, you don't have to do in-depth research for everything. Life is too short to read the instructions.' He grinned at me then, and it struck me that it had been a long, long time since we had exchanged smiles of any sort.

And I couldn't help but return it.

'Right!' he exclaimed loudly then, for the girls' benefit. 'Better get this roof on so you two little decorators can go nuts.' As the girls watched their uncle lift and stick the roof sections into place, they seemed absolutely transfixed by the process.

I felt instantly guilty then for my part in making the initial process such hard work. The people on the front of the box were not smiling because the house had turned out perfectly; they were smiling because it was *fun*.

No wonder Nate had bailed.

'OK, you two, I'll squeeze on some icing and then I want you guys to stick on the sweets.' He opened the pack and let them fall onto the table, and their smiles widened with the realisation that 'sweets' meant what they knew as candy.

The harder ones bounced around the table as they fell from the pack and the girls squealed in delight as they tried to catch them, both having some success at first catching them and then storing them in their mouths.

Again, I was about to intervene, but realised the person calling a halt to this fun would be forever known as a proper grinch.

Some of the sweets found their way onto the slightly lopsided house, but way more found their way into my daughters' mouths and stomachs.

Icing was duly squirted and smeared all over the gingerbread 'house', until the end product was a sorrowful-looking, sweet-dripping mess, and about as far away from the image on the box as you could imagine.

The contented smiles, though, were way more comparable.

Chapter 35

I was thinking of that one Christmas – oh, it had to be when Jo was around ten or so, making Matt eight and Romy three – when Joanna and Matt ended up concocting a plan to sneak down to the tree in the middle of the night, after Santa came, to take a peek at their presents and then (sneakily) rewrap them before heading back up to bed until morning.

Joanna, you'd even gone so far as to hoard a bit of Sellotape in your room so you could tape everything up again (wrapping presents is such a lot of work, I don't know why anyone would voluntarily want to do it if they really didn't have to).

But little Romy must have overheard this plan, because she came telling tales and worrying 'what if they catch Santa?'

What if, indeed?

So, your dad and I concocted our own plan.

We laid out all of the presents as normal once you three were in bed. And turned off the lights, making all of the usual noises of going to bed, assuming the two little divils were listening and planning their next move.

What ye didn't know is that Dad had borrowed Uncle Jim's Santa suit. You know, the one he used to pull out at family gatherings where all the kids knew it was him because he was the only one who disappeared when Santa arrived?

Back to my story. Dad put the Santa suit on along with the fake beard and sat down on the sofa in the dark. All the lights were off and he decided to munch on the milk and cookies that had been left out.

After a while he started to doze off and wondered if you two had fallen asleep yourselves, or decided to give up your plan altogether.

But then, at around 2ish, he heard rustling sounds coming down the stairs, making way more noise than anyone with a sneaky plan should. You were whisper-arguing with each other over whether to turn on the flashlight Matt had, or if that would give the game away. In the end, apparently, you decided against it.

So Dad roused himself, took a cookie off the plate, popped it in his mouth, and when you both zeroed in on the haul under the tree, he cleared his throat loudly in the dark and flicked on a lamp next to the chair where he was sitting.

I just wish I had this on video because according to Dad you both screamed in terror and ran off so quickly that you tripped over each other, ending up on the floor tangled up in your pyjamas, and then crawled/scooted out of the room so fast that Dad was shaking with laughter.

And the next morning, when Christmas dawned, your dad and I struggled to keep straight faces as you both crept downstairs as if Santa might still be there waiting in ambush. Both of you were very contrite and quiet that morning, as if expecting coal in your stockings.

Matt, you kept probing, asking if we had slept well and if we had heard any strange noises or anything. I think that you might have suspected we knew the game was up, worried that Santa had woken us to let us know what bold kids ye really were.

Of course, that wasn't the case at all.

It's just that you two had a little snitch for a sister.

Moral of the story – no peeking.

The following morning, while trying to keep the twins occupied with TV cartoons in the living room, I spied through the window the same postman who'd been delivering on this run since I was a kid.

'Is that Paddy?' I asked Dad, as he dangled a sparkling bauble in front of Suzy's face. It seemed to annoy more than entertain her, but I didn't have the heart to tell him.

He nodded. 'Yep, still going strong, believe it or not.'

I remembered Mum's tip about making sure friends and neighbours weren't forgotten, and nipped out to the hallway to grab one of the ready-made gift bags we'd concocted for that purpose.

'I can't believe he hasn't retired yet,' I observed, trying to calculate just how old he would be. 'He must be over sixty-five by now?'

'Sixty-seven,' my dad confirmed. 'Obviously all of the exercise doesn't hurt. Still pretty spry for an oul guy.' He chuckled at his own joke. 'I'll keep an eye on these two if you want to catch him.'

As I opened the front door, Paddy was just about to ring the bell, and he looked up and smiled.

'Well, Joanna, 'tis yourself . . . good morning! You haven't aged a day, pet. How is that even possible?'

I laughed at this, mostly because I felt at least a hundred years older than I did the year before. 'Dad and I were actually just saying the same about you. How's it going, Paddy? I haven't seen you in such a long time.' But then I automatically checked myself, because it wasn't true. I had seen him last at Mum's funeral. 'Actually no, sorry. I remember you came to pay your respects. Sorry, it was a . . . crazy time,' I explained.

Paddy smiled sadly. 'Of course. Ye all had a lot on your plate. Things like that, well, they are never easy. And your mam, she was a pure lady. I miss chatting with her – she always came out for a natter and a bit of gossip. And she was so proud of you three – so proud. Always telling me about what ye were all up to.' He swallowed hard, as if trying to keep his own emotions under control, and I felt an automatic lump come to my throat at the reminder of how beloved my mother was to everyone.

'Thanks, Paddy. It's been a . . . hard year.'

'Course it has. How are you all doing?' He looked over my shoulder to where Romy was making her way downstairs and into the kitchen. My sister waved blearily at the postman but didn't come out to greet him. 'Ah, I see Romy's home from London too. That's good – always important to be together this time of year. And brilliant that Matt is back altogether of course, helping out with your dad too. Lovely of him to put his own life on hold, and a bit of a gent himself, your brother.'

I emitted a half-hearted murmur, thinking sardonically that Paddy didn't know the half of it.

'It's been tough. But we are getting on with it. We've no choice. Everything happened so fast and it really threw us for a loop. It felt like one day she was here, and the next she wasn't. That's what it seemed like anyway.' I paused for a moment, swallowing the lump in my throat, then smiled determinedly. 'But at the same time it feels like, on some level, she is still around, keeping an eye on us.' I wasn't sure why I was confiding all of this to our long-standing postman when I could barely confide in my own husband.

'Course she is. But the first Christmas without them is always the worst.' Paddy hung his head a little then, and I felt terrible for forgetting that he himself had lost his own wife just the year before. 'Never feels the same without them.'

'It really doesn't. But . . .' I handed him my mother's gift. 'She wanted us to give you a little something to show her appreciation.'

The look of surprise and genuine delight on Paddy's face almost brought tears to my eyes again. Such a small gesture, but I could tell it meant the world.

'Oh God bless us and save us . . . would you believe it.' He reached for the bag as if it contained a world of treasure. And I suppose it did.

Suddenly, I understood why my mother had entrusted all these fond little traditions and memories to us. It wasn't a fussy or compulsive thing; Mum was merely ensuring those small touches that made this time of year so special still happened in her absence.

And maybe so that we, her children, wouldn't forget or neglect to do the same for the important people in our own lives.

'Looks like you've something for us too?' I smiled, changing the subject before I broke down altogether, referring to the assortment of cards and letters in Paddy's grasp.

'Indeed and I do.' He handed over the bundle of coloured envelopes, which looked to be Christmas cards, and then put a finger up, as if remembering something. 'Actually, I have another one in the van, which is why I rang the bell in the first place. Hold on.'

I shivered on the doorstep in the early morning chill, keen to get back inside.

'Here you go – registered. Addressed to Matt, but sure you can sign it for me.' He chuckled. 'The man himself is probably still in bed if he has any sense at all on a day like this.' He gestured to the sleet-filled rain.

Paddy handed me the remaining envelope and a stylus so as to capture my signature on his device, and I felt a prickle of foreboding as I spotted the more official-looking piece of mail.

Hastily signing where indicated, I stood immobile as the postman pulled off a delivery receipt and bade us all a happy Christmas, before driving off happily with his unexpected bonus.

I turned the envelope over, glancing at the return address, and stiffened a little, the greetings cards in my other hand forgotten.

It was from a solicitor's firm with an address in Galway. Immediately I surmised that it had to do with the legal issue Matt was facing, which Romy had mentioned was in the courts.

I glanced darkly back into the house, certain the fragile truce and delicate glow of happiness that had recently descended on our family was about to disappear in a puff of smoke.

Chapter 36

When Joanna came back in after meeting the postman, Romy noticed that her sister's face was drawn and pale.

She held in her left hand a bundle of cards and in her right, a single, official-looking envelope.

Joanna deposited the other mail on the kitchen counter but then, apparently oblivious that Romy was even there, moved to the sink, holding the lone envelope and staring at it like it contained a lethal dose of arsenic.

'What's going on?' Romy murmured. 'Are you OK?'

Surprised, Joanna turned around and whipped her hand behind her back, as if trying to hide what she had in her grasp. 'Grand,' she chirped. 'Just . . . going to make a cup of tea . . .'

She turned back to grab the kettle, but not before starting to stuff the now folded envelope into the back pocket of her jeans.

'What's that?'

'Nothing.' Her voice was tense and as her sister tried to avoid her gaze, Romy became even more suspicious.

'What are you hiding, Joanna? What is that? It's not for you, anyway – who would be sending you post at this house?'

'Oh, fine, then,' she responded, pulling the envelope from her pocket. She handed the letter over, biting her lip as if she had been caught stealing. 'Paddy just had me sign for this. It was registered. It's for Matt.'

Romy peered down at the face of the envelope, taking in the official stamp and return address.

'Oh dear,' she said, sighing.

'My thoughts exactly.'

Romy looked at her, furrowing her brow. 'Well, what were you going to do with it, though? You weren't going to open it, surely . . .'

'No. I mean maybe. Look, I don't know. I suppose I just didn't want whatever might be in this to ruin anything. We've all been getting along so well, haven't we? All of us together. And everything's feeling sort of normal even . . .'

'That's not right, though. You've no right to keep it from him. I'm sure it's important.'

'I know, but think about the timing . . .' Joanna babbled. 'I'm not going to hide it forever, obviously . . . I just think maybe I – actually, you and me – *we* should discuss this a little more, think about when might be the best time to give it to him. What if it's bad news? It'll ruin everything, could even ruin Christmas altogether. And what's more' – she looked at the fridge and the Christmas list fastened beneath the magnet – 'all of Mum's carefully laid plans will be for nothing . . .'

'There's no "we", Joanna. I don't want anything to do with this . . . deception.' Romy stood up and looked at her sister, shaking her head in disgust as she walked out. 'Jesus. You've really learned nothing at all, have you?'

◆ ◆ ◆

Later that evening, since it was Nate's turn to settle the girls down for the night, I took the opportunity to get changed into more comfortable PJs for an interlude of relaxation and movie-watching.

And hopefully lots of wine.

As my husband crept quietly back into the bedroom, I couldn't help but laugh when I spotted his appearance. Running down the front of his shirt was a bright-red stain that looked just like blood, though if I had to guess the truth, one of the twins had been using him as target practice with cranberry juice.

'Katie?' I ventured, raising an eyebrow.

'How did you know?' He pulled his T-shirt over his head.

'She has quite the arm. I've been at the receiving end more than once.' I held out a hand for his shirt. 'Give that to me and I'll soak it in Vanish.'

As he handed me the soiled T-shirt, he chuckled, 'Gonna have to enrol her in softball lessons,' and I recalled with a pang this time last year when he'd talked about how he was so sure I'd smash it like some Tiger Mom with the multiple classes and home-cooked meals.

So much for that idea.

He pinched my cheek. 'I'm going to take a quick shower and then I'll see you downstairs.'

I instinctively put my arms around his bare torso, welcoming an old familiar playfulness and closeness. We still had some stuff to figure out, or mostly *I* had, but this time together here in Ireland with my family was already helping us to reconnect a little, I was sure of it.

Kissing me on the head, Nate disrobed the rest of the way and headed into the en suite.

As water from the shower began running, I picked his discarded trousers up off the bed and felt the weight of his phone in the pocket. Taking it out so as to put the trousers with the soiled

T-shirt, I was about to leave it on the dresser when it started vibrating in my hand, indicating an incoming text.

I'm not a snoop and never have been. I've never looked at Nate's phone or emails or anything else – because I never had a reason not to trust him. But since the phone was in my hand, I couldn't help but glance at the message on screen.

Paperwork finalised and everything ready to deploy. Just say the word.

Frowning, I tried to make sense of the admittedly cryptic message, which seemed to be coming from a San Francisco law firm, but not one I recognised.

What paperwork? What's ready to deploy?

I felt goosebumps run up and down my spine as I tried to figure out what paperwork Nate needed drawn up by a lawyer. My mind then immediately drifted to my brother's legal problems – and I wondered if I was about to have my own.

In Family Court.

Yes, it had been a terrible year, nightmarish even, but had it got so bad that Nate wanted to bail, not just on building a gingerbread house with me and the girls, but on our family altogether? How had our marriage and what I'd thought was such a strong partnership disintegrated to this? And in such a short space of time?

So much can happen in a year . . .

I thought about the conversation I'd had with Mum, when I'd confided in her my grand intentions to give the girls a more solid upbringing, just like the one she'd given us, and how laughably now, in hindsight, that decision had triggered the downward spiral that would likely break my family apart.

Did she know back then? I wondered. Had Mum already realised that deep down this wasn't me at all, that I was being idealistic and completely misguided to think that I could even attempt to replicate the kind of mother she had been? That motherhood wasn't just another project to be attacked, another mission to fulfil, it was something that needed to unfold naturally and wholeheartedly, and needed far more consideration than I'd given it?

Or, in truth, that I was simply deflecting. Had subconsciously grasped on to the notion in an attempt to swerve out of the way of the catastrophic professional failure I feared was on the horizon.

Swallowing hard, I registered that the water had since stopped in the bathroom, and I heard Nate leaving the shower.

Also cognisant that I still had the phone in my hand, I quickly threw it on the bed face down, lest he emerge and realise I had seen something I shouldn't have.

I gathered up the clothes, my mind still racing, as I wondered if yet again I had been interpreting things all wrong.

Was I stupid for believing that we were finding our way back together at the moment, when really he was plotting his exit? That truly couldn't be what was happening, could it? At Christmas? He wouldn't do that to me?

Would he?

When he came back out, I tried to act normal, but there was no denying that internally I was all over the place. As I turned to exit the room, I said casually over my shoulder, 'Oh, your phone is on the bed. It was in the pocket of your jeans.'

'Thanks,' he said, picking it up and looking at the screen.

And before I closed the door behind me, I caught the look of satisfaction that flashed on my husband's face as he read the text I wasn't supposed to see.

Chapter 37

After tossing and turning uneasily most of the night for reasons she wasn't quite sure of, Romy decided to abandon the idea of sleep and just get up.

The moment she left her bedroom, she smelled coffee downstairs and knew instinctively that she would find her sister in the kitchen again.

But when she entered, she was surprised to find that Joanna was not alone.

Unbelievably, she and Matt were at the kitchen table, making pastry dough, it looked like. She crossed the room to pour herself a cup of coffee before returning to the table and taking a seat alongside her siblings.

'I couldn't sleep – so I figured I'd get a start on the food preparations,' Joanna said, her voice sounding over-bright, as if she was worried Romy would say something about the letter, which presumably she'd decided to keep hidden. 'And I found this one down in the den playing video games, so I put him to work. Those mince pies aren't going to make themselves.'

Incredibly, Matt did indeed seem to be in the thick of it, toasting bread and chopping carrots and celery, while Joanna worked on the pastry.

Wearing oven mitts, her sister grabbed opposite ends of the sheet of aluminium foil that served as a repository for the pie weights – the little glass balls she had told her about before, which she'd apparently always assumed to be decorative vase filler.

The three siblings settled into companionable conversation, though Romy was conscious of the fact that while they were, as Joanna had pointed out the day before, enjoying a sort of truce, they were also still very much tiptoeing round one another, cautious and careful to avoid touching directly on any personal stuff.

'Morning.' She looked up then, as her boyfriend entered the room, his mouth open in a yawn. He glanced around, sniffing the air. 'What's for breakfast?'

'Every man for himself in this house, mate,' Matt quipped, and Romy was pleased that her brother seemed to be trying to make Damien feel more at home.

Though Damien seemed to interpret it differently. 'Right. So much for looking after your guests . . .'

'Sorry, everyone's a bit preoccupied this morning, as you can probably tell from the chaos,' she said, intervening quickly. 'What do you fancy – some scrambled eggs on toast, maybe?'

'Not too much, though – I need to get a decent run in today after that disaster last time.' He grinned at the others. 'With this one setting the pace, you'd be faster walking.'

'Probably better I just let you at it yourself this time then,' Romy said, casting her eyes down. 'Plenty to keep me busy here anyway.'

She proceeded to make breakfast for him, noticing that the formerly easy-going air had now cooled somewhat, while Matt and Joanna continued with their tasks.

When her sister had finished rolling out the pastry crust and placed it in the dish, she double-checked the recipe instructions.

'So, should I just dump all the filling in now?' Joanna mused uncertainly.

'Yes, then cover it with the strips, like this . . .' Romy began laying out pastry strips on top of the fruity mince in a criss-cross shape, allowing some of the mixture to remain uncovered. 'Then just pop it in the oven for forty-five minutes or so.'

She handed Damien a plate of freshly made scrambled eggs and went to resume her task of preparing the filling for a second tart.

Shutting the oven door, Joanna turned back with satisfaction and smiled. 'You know, you're really good at this. I really had no idea that you spent so much time cooking with Mum. You've barely even looked at these recipes. Who knew my little sister was such a gourmet cook?'

Damien chuckled. 'I'd say it's pretty obvious that Romy loves her grub, no?' he commented. Then, noticing the temperature in the room instantly plummet, despite the warmth of the oven, he added, 'Ah, you know I'm just joking, babes.'

'Not especially funny.' Her sister's hackles were raised and, evidently unaffected, Damien shrugged, picked up his plate and retreated to the living room.

Now Joanna placed her hands on the table and looked down at the recipe book in front of her. 'No one has the right to say stuff like that to you, you know,' she said. 'No one.'

Romy just shrugged. 'He didn't mean anything by it. He just has a weird sense of humour that not everyone gets.'

Matt made a face. 'That's not humour, sis. That's kind of being an asshole. He owes you respect and an apology.'

Seriously?

Romy picked up her coffee cup and raised her gaze to them both. 'You know, coming from you two that really is a bit rich . . .'

And she followed her boyfriend out of the room.

Chapter 38

'Jesus, your family are something else. Ganging up on me like that. Seriously. I didn't come here to be attacked.'

Back upstairs in her bedroom as she got ready to join Damien on another run after all, Romy fidgeted. 'You pretty much came right out and insulted me down there in front of them, though.'

He snorted. 'Like I said, I was only messin'. Anyway, from what you told me, your sister's no angel either.'

She blew out her cheeks, conceding that he had a point, but now sorely wishing she hadn't confided some of the finer details in that regard. 'That's not the same, and you did say—'

He cut her off. 'I never said you were fat either. If that's how you took it, then that's not my problem. So you incorrectly interpreted what I said *and* you're being paranoid. So maybe you should take your issues up with your sister. Especially since *she* hasn't apologised for anything. Has she?'

Romy furrowed her brow and shook her head as Damien turned the tables on her, smoothly transitioning himself away from being the bad guy.

Yes, it was true, Joanna had indeed insulted and undermined her.

But she had also just defended her in there. That was almost as good as an apology. Wasn't it?

Before she could ponder it any further, Damien asked, 'What were you two arguing about anyway in the kitchen yesterday – some letter?'

For a moment, she was a little disoriented and surprised that he'd overheard the exchange between her and Jo after the postman's arrival.

'Nothing. It was just something for my brother . . .'

'The bully?'

'What? He . . . isn't a "bully" . . . I never said anything of the sort,' she gasped, now deeply regretful that she had told Damien anything at *all* about her family situation. 'I said he had got into fisticuffs with someone last year, not that . . .'

'No, you said he'd beat the crap out of a co-worker,' her boyfriend replied flatly, his eyebrows rising slightly, as if he was enjoying turning her own words on her.

'I didn't—' she huffed, before remembering that she had pretty much said something along those lines in a fit of pique about her siblings in general. 'Look, if I said that, it's not what I meant. I suppose that . . . after Mum died, I was angry with Matt – and Joanna. And I'm not defending him either. It's just he's been through a lot this year and was there for my mum when she was sick, and now my dad, too. I'd hate to see him get raked over the coals for . . .'

Damien sniffed, as if detecting a whiff of hypocrisy. 'You know, I'm disappointed in you, Romy.'

'Disappointed . . . Disappointed in me for what? For caring about my family? They need me. Our mother isn't here any more. And this year especially . . . This year we're all just trying to keep it together by trying to honour, for her sake, the things we loved the most about Christmas.'

And that truly was the point of the list, wasn't it? she mused. Of course Damien wouldn't get it; only someone who'd been through the kind of year her family had could possibly understand.

So maybe there was no point in trying to explain to him just how crucial all of this was.

'Sounds to me like your poor oul mam had enough of a job keeping things going with you lot when she was alive,' he continued. 'And now here you are, sucking up to the same people who turned their back on you when you needed them. They're just playing you, babe – I hope you know that. It's so obvious to someone on the outside, like me. And that's why they're all so defensive and jumping down my throat – trying to push you away from me. Because I see the truth and they know it.'

'What do you mean, what truth?' Romy asked, genuinely curious as to his take.

'They're guilt-tripping you, using all this nostalgic bullshit as an excuse to play happy families when it suits them. And your mother – who, to be fair, sounds like a total saint, don't get me wrong – but when you think about it, isn't this whole set of instructions thing a bit . . . weird? Controlling, even? And speaking of . . . Don't even get me started on that sister of yours, who is a Grade A control freak if ever I met one. Too high and mighty to get involved in doing the heavy lifting, though, so she ropes in you and your brother to do all the cooking, and even your dad for babysitting and stuff. And your brother has you feeling all sorry for him because he can't sort his own shit out. When are you going to stop letting this fucked-up family use you, babe?'

She felt her cheeks flame as Damien illustrated their sibling dynamic as he saw it, and felt her defences waning.

Maybe he had a point? After a shaky enough start, they had all started to get on better and taken steps to move past the debacle in April.

And thanks to the list, she believed they truly were making tentative inroads with one another again.

Romy was pretty sure she wasn't being guilt-tripped or railroaded, though. Her family had never played her, wouldn't take her for granted like that.

Would they?

Chapter 39

It must all feel so festive and inviting around the house by now – so much so that I can almost picture it in my mind's eye.

I suppose I have written a lot about our family festivities, but as you know we've always liked to make that circle a little bigger too.

You dad certainly loves a party and I've always been a big believer in the more the merrier – and especially enjoyed opening up our home even more once Nate and Hazel became extended members of our little family . . .

Nothing beats having a full and happy hearth this time of year. It's always one of the most joyful things about Christmas.

And seriously . . . who doesn't love a party?

◆ ◆ ◆

Later that evening, we were all – Romy and Damien excepted – gathered around the kitchen table sampling much of the food we'd made earlier, and discussing preparations for the upcoming Christmas Eve get-together.

Dad seemed especially jazzed up about this, and it struck me just how lonely the house must have been over the last few months, how quiet and bleak – in the first instance for him grappling with his grief, and then with Matt, who also had his own baggage.

Both in the same house, but pretty much alone.

'What do you think . . . nice?' my dad chirruped happily now as he fed Suzy some mince pie filling, which was mostly ending up in her hair and all over her face. But they were both giggling so merrily, I could hardly complain.

And the sound of laughter in this house again was making my heart sing.

'I don't know – whatever about rustling up a few bits and pieces for ourselves, I just can't see how we can possibly make enough to cater for a dozen people or so more. Avoca is brilliant for that kind of festive nibbles stuff, though,' I suggested, hitting on an easier fix. 'I'll give them a call, and see if they'll drop over a couple of platters on the day. What do you think?' I asked Matt.

'Sure, whatever you think is best.' Despite his enthusiasm earlier, now I thought he seemed a bit downbeat and distracted and I wondered if maybe he'd been waiting on whatever was in that letter.

I bit my lip, deciding that maybe Romy was right; I had no business trying to conceal anything from him, particularly for my own selfish ends.

And maybe, depending on the contents, I might even be able to help?

'Great.' Pleased with myself for having come up with two great solutions on the spot, I couldn't help but wish that I could figure out how best to resolve the mystery of my husband's distant behaviour. Although at that very moment, he seemed happy enough, tucking in to a plate of sausage rolls I'd made earlier with Matt's help. 'I'm sure Romy will be fine with that too.'

A voice from behind me asked, 'Fine with what?'

'Ah, there you are. Did you guys have a good run earlier?' I turned in my seat, smiling at my sister as Damien walked in behind her. 'Grab a plate and dig in.' I motioned to the food-laden table. 'There's also some wine open, so help yourselves. We were just discussing the neighbours' party this year, and wanted your input.'

The pair continued to stand in the door and I noticed that they exchanged a surreptitious glance, while Romy shifted from one foot to the other impatiently. 'Actually, we're going to head out tonight for a change, go for something to eat and a few drinks in The Shamrock.'

Good idea. Maybe a trip to the local pub might help Damien feel a bit more festive, since being here with us didn't seem to be cutting it. And in fairness, was probably a bit boring.

If anything, though, he seemed to actively resent our company, which saddened me a little, given Nate and Hazel had slotted into the family so easily.

Though maybe not for much longer. I swallowed hard, reminded again of my husband's behaviour, and that Hazel was sadly now a thing of the past.

Still, I kept the smile on my face and took a sip of red wine.

'Good idea. But before you go, I just wanted to run a couple of ideas by you about Christmas Eve, and see what you thought.' Quickly, I conveyed my thoughts about maybe getting the help of professionals for the traditional get-together.

Romy's face fell. 'Isn't that sort of missing the point?' she said. 'Getting a caterer in?' She sniffed and flipped her hair over her shoulder, clearly irritated by the idea. Then, rolling her eyes, she said, 'For someone who's supposed to be so keen on domesticity, Joanna, you really seem to go out of your way to avoid it. Getting the rest of us to do your dirty work for you, or if that doesn't work, sure just write a cheque to make everything go away.'

Stung, the wine glass froze at my parted lips. I knew exactly what she was insinuating. And it had nothing to do with the catering.

Well, that hurt.

'What are you on about?' Matt asked, seemingly coming to my defence. 'Sure we've all been doing plenty.' He bounced Suzy on his knee while my dad held her sister.

'I think Joanna is right love,' Dad put in. 'Even with Mum's input, this kind of thing is still a lot of work.'

This seemed to annoy Romy even more.

'Oh, I get it – forget Mum's wishes altogether, as long as everyone jumps when Joanna calls the shots. Do it this way, do it that way, put those decorations over there, use this recipe instead of that one, keep important stuff hidden until *I'm* good and ready,' she mimicked, eying me directly then, her eyes hard as flints, and I knew she was referring to Matt's letter. She turned to Damien, who looked like the cat who ate the canary, and his knowing gaze now met mine, all pretence well and truly cast aside. 'Let's go,' my sister said, her tone flat, before turning on her heel.

Her boyfriend brazenly remained in the doorway for a beat, then raised a hand and smirked. 'Have a nice time party-planning.'

And then he was gone too.

So that's how it is, I thought, my eyes narrowing. You didn't need to be a rocket scientist to understand what was going on.

This guy was trying to alienate my little sister from us, her family, by stirring the pot. Clearly he was privy to, if not everything that had gone down between us, enough to know when and how to throw a spanner in the works.

Well, bring it on – blood was thicker than water.

Not to worry, I resolved silently. *I've dealt with more than enough grinches in my time.*

Chapter 40

When Romy awoke the following morning, her head was pounding.

Next to her in the bed, Damien was lying flat on his back with his mouth open, a line of dry spittle forming a path down the side of his face. His lips were stained bluish red, and she recalled with some chagrin all the wine and cocktails they'd imbibed the night before.

Trying to sit up but feeling her head spin, she squeezed her eyes against the light creeping in around the bedroom curtains. Opening one eye tentatively, she reached for her phone on the bedside locker and glanced at the time.

'Holy feck,' she groaned, realising just how long they'd slept in. 'Twelve thirty.' And she felt a pang of panic as she remembered her mother's words when she was a teenager about sleeping the day away. But they'd only got home at one – OK, maybe more like two, now that she checked her taxi history in the app.

And ugh, they had gone on a pub crawl and thus taken more than one taxi – all of which she'd paid for too, apparently.

Oh well, Damien was her guest, and it was Christmas after all.

Getting to her feet, albeit shakily, she surveyed her room then ambled her way into the bathroom. She turned on the light, wincing at the pain it provoked in her head, and turned her attention to her reflection in the mirror.

'Holy feck,' Romy mumbled again, taking into account the mascara that had run down her cheeks, and the sickly green pallor of her skin. Her hair was a mess of knots and she grabbed her brush in an attempt to pull it all back into a more presentable ponytail.

When was the last time she'd gone on the lash like that? she contemplated, coming up short. And how much *did* she drink?

In truth, she really couldn't remember, but was able to get a bit of an idea when her stomach revolted a moment later and she hung her head in the toilet.

Whoever invented that Twelve Pubs of Christmas tradition was a sadist.

'Idiot,' she muttered, returning to the sink to brush her teeth and wash her face.

As she tried to recall the details, she couldn't shake the fact that everything felt very . . . alien. Yes, she had enjoyed herself in a sort of rebellious and defiant way. Almost like being a teenager out to break the rules – but in all reality that had never been her. She followed the rules. She kept an even keel. She didn't like to rock the boat.

Which brought her back to her next memory – before her departure with Damien downstairs. And her unwarranted outburst at Joanna.

While she had felt emboldened at the time – probably because he had been egging her on, convincing her *she* was being taken advantage of by her family – now she wasn't so sure. In fact, she wasn't so sure at all.

And her mind wandered to another fleeting memory.

Damien had created a bit of a scene in The Shamrock Lounge, where they'd gone earlier in the night to grab a bite to eat. He'd ordered beef carpaccio from the bar food menu and Romy had heard him do so with her own ears.

However, when the lounge girl – an old school friend – brought his dish to the table, he'd berated her and basically called her an idiot, insisting that he'd ordered beef tartare.

Romy flushed afresh at the memory. It had been mortifying, especially since Luke Dooley and his lovely mother were at the next table and had overheard everything. *Talk about embarrassing.*

Not only had Damien been in the wrong, but he had been beyond rude in front of her friends too.

In fact, she had been so discomfited at the time that she'd ended up stupidly gabbling an invite to the get-together on Christmas Eve to both parties, in an attempt to make up for the deeply uncomfortable scenario.

She then recalled Cathy's unflinching demand for manners in public places (anywhere, really) and both her parents' insistence that you never treated anyone who was helping you with anything other than respect and kindness.

But thinking back on Damien's behaviour last night, and indeed on previous occasions, she had a feeling that he had never been taught that lesson – or if he had, he had chosen to disregard it.

He certainly wasn't especially respectful of her siblings during this stay, or any of her family in general, though Romy felt she was entirely the one to blame for that, given how she'd painted their fragile sibling relationship ahead of his arrival.

Maybe it was because she'd felt a certain kinship, considering Damien didn't get on with his own family either. They only lived on the other side of the city, barely forty minutes away. But given his out-of-the-blue premature appearance at her home, it seemed he hadn't in fact visited them on this trip, nor planned to.

At Christmastime, too. Was that the kind of future she wanted for her family? To drift apart so much, to the point that the special time of year they'd always shared and found so much solace in eventually meant nothing at all?

Exiting the bathroom, and pulling on a clean sweatshirt over her pyjamas, Romy took one more look at the passed-out figure in her bed, and decided to just let him be.

Chapter 41

'Hand me a few more of those . . .' Matt said, as I tied a red ribbon around the neck of a bag filled with the admittedly pitiful shortbreads I'd tried to knock up the evening before.

I checked through a guest list of the usual crowd – nearby neighbours and friends of my parents who might like to join us for a festive drink and some nibbles, and most importantly a little celebration in Mum's honour.

'Maybe Romy might pop an invite across to Mrs Foster – if she doesn't think we're slave-driving her, that is.'

'To be honest, I get the feeling that opinion's coming from somewhere else . . .' I ventured hesitantly, not wanting to talk out of school, yet curious to know what Matt thought about our sister's choice of partner.

He looked at me. 'Your man's a bit of an ass, isn't he?'

I tried to keep my expression neutral. 'I wasn't sure if it was just me . . .'

'Nope. Didn't like him from the get-go. Hate the way he just lounges around, making himself at home here like he owns the place. He was a bit smug from day one, and very smart with you last night. Especially given what he'd said himself. About Romy.'

'I know. To be honest, I wanted to deck him. But I've been . . .' – I hesitated a little, eyeing him – 'working on controlling my impulse to shoot my mouth off.'

'Good to know.'

'Matt,' I sighed. 'This is long overdue, I know, but I'm so sorry, truly, about . . . everything in April. I could blame grief and the stress of the funeral or whatever, but no matter, I know I acted appallingly.'

His face shuttered a little. 'Yes – you did. But I said some stuff too—'

'I can't quite explain what was going on with me at the time,' I babbled, almost afraid to be interrupted once I'd started. 'I felt like I was supposed to be the one in charge, make sure everything ran smoothly, yet inwardly I was falling apart – my . . . life was falling apart.'

He looked at me curiously. 'How so?'

I took a deep breath, unsure if I wanted to admit this to myself, let alone anyone else, but I owed my brother an explanation.

And I needed to let it out.

'All this year I've felt . . . discombobulated. Like I was missing my head or something. I don't know how to describe it.' I swallowed hard. 'Before, I was always organised and had all of my ducks in a row. But since I decided to do the stay-at-home mom thing, over time it was like I'd lost my ability to function. I could barely get the kids dressed in the morning. Or do simple things – like remember to pay the mortgage, or charge my phone. And even now, the house is always a mess. Sometimes I don't shower until like ten at night. Or at all, because I'm so tired.'

'That doesn't sound like you, at all.'

'I know. It isn't me. And it had all started to come to a head when Mum got sick. I thought Nate and I were OK financially, but then FinTech crashed and all the stock options I had went up in a puff of smoke – along with my confidence, I guess.' This was the first time I'd admitted something like this out loud, and it felt . . . OK. 'But then I found out Nate had . . . a couple of related investments, but didn't tell me in time. Maybe in case I felt pressured to go back.'

Though more than anything I wished my husband had confided in me, that we'd confided our fears in each other. How had we got to that point?

'Oh, and . . . are you two OK now?'

I bit my lip and swallowed back the lump in my throat. 'To be honest, I'm not . . . sure. He's been working away a lot, says he needs to build back up everything we lost, and of course now there's only one salary and our mortgage isn't small . . .' I sat back in my chair, not quite ready to confide in Matt, or anyone, about my suspicion that our marriage might well be over. 'But being here this week, even though I was dreading it, I think it's kind of . . . helped? I honestly thought this year would be unbearable, especially this time of year, when I see her everywhere . . .' My voice broke a little. 'In this house, the decorations and the tree, especially here in the kitchen with the food, the festive songs and so many memories . . . It hurts. So much.' I bit my lip, desperately trying to hold it together.

'But she knew that, Jo,' he said gently. 'That's exactly why she has us doing all this stuff. You understand that, don't you?'

I stared at him, suddenly realising that he was right. Mum's list . . . her Christmas list . . . all these little things, it wasn't *just* about making an effort for Dad, making sure friends and neighbours weren't forgotten, or mindful we'd be twiddling our thumbs all cooped up together in this house . . .

It was about distracting us from the empty chair at the table at Christmas dinner, the presents that would no longer be given or received, the bittersweet memories of so many happy family holidays gone by . . .

How did I not see it?

That this whole thing was the perfect way to distract us all from our pain, a brief escape from the rawness of our grief, and maybe switch the focus away from the huge void that existed without our mother, our friend, our guide.

I blinked, tears brimming in my eyes. In all honesty, I *hadn't* understood that.

I'd latched on to this stuff at first because it was a plan, a to-do list, a road map laid out to work through and tick boxes with ease – all the while ignoring the elephant in the room, the heartbreaking loss we all felt without her. And perhaps most of all, the ultimate way to avoid confronting the fracture that now existed within our family.

'You're right. And Romy is too,' I said, sitting up straight, having realised something else.

I was wrong to hold on to Matt's letter, so wrong. For once in my life, I needed to stop trying to control things, and instead just let the chips fall where they may – good or otherwise.

'About what?'

We had been so engrossed in our conversation that neither of us noticed our little sister walk into the room.

Turning in her direction, Matt and I exchanged a glance. She looked rough, and I wasn't so clueless as to miss that she clearly had the mother of all hangovers.

'About . . . my wanting to get catered stuff for tomorrow night,' I said, thinking quickly. 'It is missing the point.'

Matt winked at Romy. 'Little Miss Corporate finally gets it.'

'But I seriously wasn't suggesting or expecting that you, or anyone else, should do all the legwork, Romy. I hope you know that.'

But she remained silent and, whatever about Matt, I guessed my sister definitely wasn't in the right state of mind for a heart-to-heart.

'Late one last night?' I ventured, when she didn't respond.

'Ugh,' she moaned, collapsing into a nearby chair. 'I feel like hell.' She put her head into her hands and closed her eyes as if daylight was exceedingly painful.

Ah yes – it had been a long time since I'd experienced the dreaded horrors, and I couldn't say I missed it.

I glanced at Matt and saw that he could barely conceal a smirk. While I might have been a bit of a party girl in my time, if there was one thing that we both knew about our sister, it was that she was not nor ever had been much of a drinker. Not in the slightest.

'Hair of the dog?' he offered, chuckling, and I kicked him under the table.

'Oh God no,' she groaned. 'I'm never drinking again.'

'There's some Lucozade in the fridge,' I said and, getting up from my seat, I patted her on the shoulder. 'Stay there. It looks like it hurts to move.'

As she gulped down the rehydrating old reliable, the three of us sat around the table in silence.

'Damien still in bed?' I asked, half hoping that maybe he'd hot-footed it over to bother his own family for a bit, or even better for Christmas altogether.

'Yeah,' Romy answered. 'I was going to wake him, but . . .' Her voice trailed off. 'Do you think Mum would've liked him?' she blurted suddenly.

I swallowed hard, trying to think of a diplomatic response.

In all honesty, Mum would have been appalled by this guy's attitude and behaviour, but she also definitely wouldn't have passed judgement, verbally at least. More likely would've guided Romy to draw her own conclusions about the . . . object of her affection.

'I think she would have welcomed him here, as she did everyone,' I said evenly. 'And of course, encouraged you to never short-change yourself, especially with someone who's supposed to care about you.'

Matt shifted in his seat. 'She's right. Mum would want you to be with someone who treats you the way you deserve to be treated.'

I looked at my brother, wondering now how on earth he'd managed to get caught up in that brawl last year, when beneath the laddish exterior he had always been a gentle soul at heart.

I knew all this too, but had forgotten it until recently.

Romy nodded and I saw her lip tremble a little. She seemed to be on the verge of tears. I reached out and placed my hand on her arm.

'You OK?' I asked, worried now and having an inkling that this was about more than just a hangover. My mind flipped back to Damien's mocking insolence, keeping in mind that not all harm came in physical form.

However, without Romy talking to us about it, there was no way we could truly understand the dynamic in this relationship.

'I don't know . . .' she whispered, unable to meet my eyes.

'Damien didn't . . . do anything, did he?' Matt asked quietly, keeping his voice low as he verbalised my own train of thought.

She shook her head. 'No, he didn't. I mean, not physical or anything. Nothing like you . . .'

A shadow crossed my brother's face and despite my own opinion on the matter, I felt for him that he'd be even inadvertently lumped in with a guy like Damien.

'Are you really sure you're OK?' I asked, offering her an opening, and for a second she paused and I thought she was about to confide in us.

But then, the man himself entered the room.

Speak of the devil . . .

'Morning,' Damien bellowed, making us all wince. 'Jeez, it's like a funeral here. So much for the festive season.' He glanced pointedly at Romy. 'Bad hangover, babe? Worth it, though.' He reached for her Lucozade bottle, and downed it in three gulps.

'Bud . . .' Matt said, distaste in his voice. 'There's more in the fridge if you want it.'

'Nah, I'm grand.'

My gaze was boring holes into Romy's face, willing her to say something, but she remained quiet.

'So, what's the big plan for today?' he asked, smoothly changing the subject. He looked at the table where Matt and I had been working. 'Arts and crafts again? You can count us out anyway,' he added, making the decision for both of them.

'I was hoping you'd come with us on the invite rounds to the neighbours?' I ventured, looking at Romy.

Come on, sis, stand up for yourself. This guy is a dick.

'Ah, you can't be serious,' Damien answered. 'More do-gooder crap?'

But my sister remained mute, and I felt myself wilting. There was no way she could enjoy his company. No way that she could truly like this guy. So what did she see in him?

'It's a family tradition,' Matt said, standing up. 'And important to our mother.'

'Yeah, you lot definitely need to get over this beyond the grave control-freak shite. All a bit creepy, if you ask me.'

I bristled again and out of the corner of my eye I saw Matt clench a fist. 'We didn't ask.'

Romy took a deep breath and stood up. 'I need to shower and change.'

'Understatement.' Damien chuckled at his own joke.

'Back in a bit.' She turned on her heel and walked out ahead of him, leaving my brother and I once again alone.

I felt myself shaking with anger.

'Prick,' Matt spat, reading my thoughts. 'We really should have said something,' he muttered. 'I wanted to deck him there, to be honest.'

I shook my head. 'I know, but if we express reservations, let her know that we don't like him or even answer back, it's only going to drive her into his arms even more. He's no fool, either, he knows what's he doing. She has to come to the conclusion on her own.'

Like the rest of us, and our issues, I added silently to myself.

'Ah, I know I shouldn't even be thinking it, but it would still feel good to punch the fucker.'

'I hear you, but I'd have hoped you've learned your lesson there.' His face fell a little at this and I felt bad. 'So, better get back to our "arts and crafts" . . .' I added with a derisive chuckle, quickly changing the subject.

I sealed another bag of shortbread, this time with a green ribbon, placed it in the pile with the others and reached for the guest list. 'So the Hennesseys, Hartmans, Mrs Mayfield from next door . . . who are we missing? Oh, maybe we should invite Paddy too,' I suggested. 'I'll keep an eye out for him again today.'

'The postman?' Matt piped up. 'So he *did* come yesterday then?' he added, frowning, and my stomach skipped.

And as a guilty blush crept automatically up my face, my brother and I both seemed to realise at the very same time that I'd been rumbled.

Chapter 42

'I just thought maybe it wasn't the right time . . .' I said, handing the envelope to him. There was no avoiding the subject or denying the letter delivery now.

'Do you have any idea how long I've been waiting for this?' Matt said, ice in his tone, his jaw working furiously. 'My God, after everything we've just talked about . . . how dare you keep it hidden from me, Joanna? You had no right.'

I stepped back a little at the vehemence in his tone. 'I'm sorry . . . Paddy had me sign for it. I know I should have given it straight to you when you came down for breakfast. It's just . . . honestly, I don't know what I was thinking. I suppose I just . . . didn't want to ruin things.'

My voice sounded weak and small, even to me.

'Jesus Christ, you just never learn, do you?' he said, echoing Romy's accusation, and I winced, realising I deserved it.

'I'm so sorry . . . I hope it's not bad news. Romy mentioned there was something in the courts.'

Matt shook his head. 'I couldn't understand it when the tracking said it had been delivered and signed for. I thought maybe postal delays at this time of year . . .' He ripped open the envelope, and took a deep breath before reading the contents of the letter inside.

Then, his gaze still on the page, he slumped heavily into the kitchen chair.

'Is it what you were . . . expecting?' I asked tentatively, trying to read his face.

He flung the letter across the table at me, and I reached out and picked it up. It was indeed a solicitor's letter, and scanning through the usual legalese, certain phrases jumped out at me.

Finds in favour of . . . no wrongdoing . . . complaint dismissed.

I looked at him, my heart lifting a little that it seemed to be positive news at least, while at the same time I was deeply confused. 'You've been exonerated of the assault charge? That's good, isn't it?'

He barked a laugh. 'Is it? You tell me. My relationship is ruined, I no longer have a job or a life, and here I am, thirty-seven years old and living back home with my dad. Although to be fair, that's a whole lot easier than having to live with *this* hanging over my head.' He stood up. 'I need a drink.'

I got the distinct sense that I was missing something, while my brother took a wine glass out of the cupboard, filling it to the brim. 'Want one?'

I nodded distractedly. Middle of the afternoon or not, truth be told I could do with taking the edge off too.

'All that . . . stuff last year,' I ventured. 'If you were innocent of any wrongdoing – and don't get me wrong, I'm not suggesting otherwise – how did it come to this?' I pointed at the letter.

'Because, believe it or not, Joanna, you don't know everything. And in this situation especially, you got hold of the wrong end of the stick. You and Romy both.' He looked away. 'I lost the rag at the party last year, yes,' he said, taking a gulp of wine. 'But it had nothing to do with anyone else.' Then my brother looked me in the eye and I realised I was seeing something I didn't think I'd ever seen before in his eyes.

Shame. Embarrassment, even.

My annoying little brother, who drove me crazy and was as bold and brazen as anyone I'd ever known. But shame? Not a chance. Even last year when we'd talked about this entire situation, what annoyed me as much as anything else was how Matt didn't seem to take any of it seriously.

'I didn't . . . do anything wrong, Jo, and I certainly didn't instigate it. *I* was the one who was wronged, had been for a long time, even though I hadn't really been able to get to grips with that reality at the time.' He swallowed another gulp and I frowned.

While I wasn't entirely sure what he meant, I got the distinct sense that this admission, whatever it was, was hard for him, painful even.

'The guy from work, basically my boss . . . had been undermining me for months, piling on the workload, stealing my ideas, shifting the blame on to me for campaigns that underperformed. And for a long time, I put up with it, rolled with it even, because I – the great Matt Moore – should be able to eat this kind of crap for breakfast, yeah? Nothing gets to me, sure isn't life just one big joke?' His gaze flickered to the floor. 'But as time went on, it seemed to get worse and worse, to the point that it wore me down. To the point that I no longer even wanted to go into the office. I'd begun to hate work, and the stress of it was beginning to affect my relationship with Hazel. We'd started to drift apart – much like you and Romy, she misinterpreted the distance between us as me just living up to my reputation and maybe playing away. But those days were long behind me. I love . . . loved her. But we were kind of hanging on by a thread. And I was pretty sure she was going to leave me anyway.'

Now I was worried. 'You really didn't tell Hazel anything – anything at all about the . . . work situation?' It sounded to me like a clear-cut case of bullying, but I knew how emotive that word was so I didn't want to express it.

He snorted a laugh. 'I felt shitty enough being walked all over all day at work, without having to come home and admit to my girlfriend that the guy she'd fallen in love with was actually a loser.'

Putting it mildly, I was floored. To think that someone like Matt could allow himself to . . . but then I stopped, checking my thoughts. Of course he hadn't *allowed* anything. This was something that had happened *to* him, though I had to admit I had a hard time picturing my brother as a pushover or victim.

I couldn't begin to understand the nitty gritty, and I got that there was so much more to all of it than met the eye, but there was no denying the pain in his eyes just now as he opened up to me.

Nor the relief when he'd read the contents of the letter and, I guessed, the findings – which were a validation of sorts of what he'd been through.

'But whatever about Hazel, why wouldn't you confide in us – or Mum and Dad, even?'

He took a deep breath. 'I kind of did to Romy, last Christmas. Or at least I tried to, but evidently the notion that I might not be the one at fault was so unlikely – even to her – that she filled in the blanks on her own. Yes, that night things came to a head and got messy. Like I said, there was a lot of drink taken, and the guy from work . . . ramped it up even more, singled me out in front of everyone, including our boss, a woman . . .' He shook his head. 'Anyway, I know that shouldn't make a difference and it's really hard to explain . . . but it got out of hand, except this time it was a public situation and he made me look stupid and small in front of her and my workmates. And I lost it.' He hung his head. 'It got nasty, there was a bust-up, and I went for him. But his teeth got broken so he came down on me with unprovoked assault, when all I was doing was standing up for myself – finally. I didn't know how else to deal with it. Yeah, I know Mum and Dad always told us that we should never resort to violence in these situations. But honestly, the guy, he just . . . pushed me too far.'

'So that's where the suspension came in,' I clarified, realising that he was right – I had completely gotten the wrong end of the stick.

He nodded. 'When I used provocation as a defence and outed the fucker for what he'd been doing, they put us both on a leave of absence while they investigated, and then he took a separate civil assault case against *me.* To be honest, I wasn't sure what was going to happen, that maybe we might even end up going to court over it. And I was also trying to figure out a way to tell Hazel what had gone down in any case. This kind of . . . stuff is not easy to admit, and I didn't want her to think I was . . . I don't know, weak or something? So last Christmas, I decided I'd maybe talk to you guys about it first, see if maybe you, as a boss yourself, had insight to give, but instead you and Romy automatically assumed I was just up to shenanigans . . .'

I put a hand to my mouth. 'Oh Jesus, Matt, I'm so sorry.'

He snorted a laugh. 'Weirdly? It was almost easier to take. It's expected, *in character* even for the likes of me. Playing to type. How hard do you think it would've been for me to admit to you two that I was being *bullied* – like in the fucking schoolyard? So I decided to just let you think what you liked and not bother going into the finer details yet, especially not with Hazel about to arrive any minute. Then thrash it all out properly with Mum and Dad after. And it was actually a handy out for me, since there was *definitely* no chance Hazel would get wind of anything like what you two thought. And I could always clear things up afterwards. So what difference would it make?'

It was hard to conceive, and also very sad that our brother actually preferred us to think badly of him than admit to the truth, and risk letting the macho image slip.

'But you never did clear things up with us.'

'I was going to, but the timing wasn't right, especially when Mum told us about her diagnosis, and we all had enough to be dealing with. But I will tell Romy now too – if I can get her on her own away from He-Man for a second.'

Despite myself, I had to smile at his wholly apt depiction of Damien.

He refilled his wine glass. 'So, yeah, last year I figured I'd get more of a handle on how I should play things once I'd talked it all through with Mum and Dad. But of course, I didn't expect that Mum would . . .' His voice broke a little. 'Though in a way, it actually made things a little clearer for me. Fuck the job – I could just pack it in and come home, be of some help. All that crap that was happening at work . . . it didn't matter, not really. Whereas being here – with and for Mum in her final days – what else could be more important than that? She knew, though,' he said, his eyes shining, while I felt an all too familiar tightening in my stomach at his words. 'She cottoned on straight away that there was more to it than met the eye. That I hadn't just landed myself in another tricky situation.'

I shook my head, recognising that of course Mum would have realised, would have automatically given him the benefit of the doubt, would have trusted the son she and Dad had raised so well.

Whereas I (as usual) had immediately jumped on my high horse, self-righteously making my mind up without any regard for nuance or, in this case, truth.

And speaking of truth, I looked at Matt. Having only now realised what he'd been through, I could for the first time truly comprehend the strain he'd been under this past year. To say nothing of the even more horrifying implications for him personally, given how I'd outed him to Hazel after our mother's funeral.

As I watched my brother stare forlornly into his wine glass, I couldn't understand for the life of me how he was able to tolerate my presence here right now.

When to all and intents and purposes, I – his own flesh and blood – had behaved no better than a bully too.

Chapter 43

My mind was running a million miles a second as I tried to get to grips with this situation, what to do with it and most of all how to *fix* it.

In front of me, Matt sat slumped in a chair with the bottle of wine, like someone had let the air out of one of those inflatable pumpkins you put out at Halloween.

'So . . . you really did come home to be with – to help – Mum?' I said, feeling deeply ashamed on so many levels for the accusations I'd levelled at him.

How was it that from a corporate perspective I could operate in a cool and decisive manner, but when it came to my family, the people I *loved*, I was a complete disaster?

'Yes, like I said, what could be more important than that? But when it all came out in April, Hazel refused to believe me, was fully convinced that the fact I'd hidden it all was proof enough that I'd betrayed her. Course, I know it was my own fault for not telling her in the first place but—'

'I had no right to accuse you of being underhand, though . . .'

And while I could now appreciate that Matt's secrecy within the relationship had set off a chain reaction of miscommunication, it was still ultimately my fault that everything had exploded.

That day, I'd lashed out – taken my own failings out on him, and indeed Romy.

While Matt had said some stuff to hurt me too, ultimately I should have risen above it. I was, after all, the eldest, the one who should've stepped up to the plate from the get-go, the one who could supposedly handle everything life threw at her. But I'd been too wrapped up in my own issues – my own regrets – to see that.

My failure to do any of those things was primarily the reason our family had become so scattered this year, that my sister had lost her new-found confidence, that my brother's duty and kindness towards our parents had gone unappreciated, and that his wonderful girlfriend had dumped him.

Wonderful, talented, *solicitor* girlfriend . . .

The beginnings of an idea dangled in my brain, so much so that I barely registered that Matt and I were no longer alone in the kitchen, and that Romy and Damien had since returned.

'Whoa, who died?' Damien quipped, as he observed our silent demeanour.

My sister shushed him, and I shot him a glare.

Truth be told, I was by now sick to the back teeth of this man-child.

'Back in a bit, I need to think,' I said abruptly, and headed from the room.

'Hey, who crapped in her cereal?' I heard him say from behind me.

Rolling my eyes, I didn't wait to hear my sister's response.

I needed some space, a quiet spot where I could maybe make sense of all of this, and my feet automatically propelled me to the spot where I knew I could find some balance – my mother's study.

Closing the door behind me, I turned on the table lamp and glanced out of the windows, where the weak light meant that the day was on the verge of ending.

I sat down at the desk, pulled Mum's cashmere sweater around my shoulders and took out my phone.

Wincing, I reflected on everything I had said in April.

I had been so harsh, uncaring, dismissive. And now, when I truly thought about it – again, I'd been looking at everything purely through my default lens.

Quash the threat, shut it down.

In the same way I'd treated Mum's prognosis. I'd been so busy focusing on trying to dismantle the threat that I'd failed to recognise just how dangerous it was.

Until it was far too late.

But maybe it wasn't too late with the others, I thought, my mind racing now.

I could build bridges, mend fences in more ways than one. I owed Matt, and Hazel too, that much at least.

For a start, I could explain, let his lovely girlfriend know that I'd got it all wrong, and back up whatever assertions my brother had tried to make in the aftermath. Do my best to make it right.

Persuade her that he wasn't a liar, a cheat. That he loved her, but was at a loss as to how to go about getting her back.

I could certainly give it a try, though.

I attempted to envisage her reaction at hearing from me – at hearing from us. Was it wildly stupid for me to think that after all this time, Hazel would give a damn about Matt's plight – or my pleas for forgiveness?

I put my head in my arms on the desk, inhaling the smell of furniture polish and the lingering scent of perfume.

'What would you do, Mum? You always seemed to know exactly what to do. About everything.'

As I tried to channel my mother, there was a muffled knock on the door and I jumped.

'Come in,' I called out, expecting Matt or even Romy, if our brother had since filled her in.

'You OK?' Nate asked, concern etched on his face. 'What's going on?'

'Just thinking. Are the girls OK?'

That's right, Joanna, you have kids too, remember?

'Flaked,' he chuckled. 'Your dad has worn them out.'

I smiled. 'Pity we couldn't take him back home with us, put him up in the guest room, maybe.'

'What are you doing in here anyway?' he enquired, stepping further into the room and looking around at my mother's inner sanctum.

In truth, I wasn't sure if he was ever even in this room. I motioned for him to take a seat across from me on the small chaise longue up against the wall.

Then I filled him in on what I'd just learned in the kitchen, bringing him fully up to speed on the situation, and my determination to make amends by trying to fix it.

'You know, it was always so easy to make decisions when I was working. Just to look at the options and what we needed to achieve our optimum strategy, and then just pull the trigger. I was always so good at that.'

And part of me now wondered if my tireless and dispassionate pursuit of such goals had hurt other people too.

When I expressed this to Nate, he didn't have to say a word in reply, because I found immediate confirmation in his eyes. I didn't know if that meant that I had bulldozed our marriage altogether, or if he was just conceding in general that, yes, I had been a bulldozer.

But I felt myself nodding, letting him know I had received the message.

As they say, the truth hurts – but as I already knew, to my deepest regret, there was no way to change the past. All I could do was be better now and in the future.

That was the commitment I made to myself when I first decided to come home this year.

Fix it.

And here was a unique opportunity to do just that.

Help my brother. Make amends by trying to right the wrongs, for him and Hazel especially. Help my sister regain the confidence she so obviously needed to kick the asshole she was with to the kerb.

Be there for my dad and my husband (if he still wanted that) and try to be the best mother I could be for my girls – instead of killing myself trying to chase some ideal that didn't exist.

Find a way to make things right once and for all, so that we could all enjoy the kind of Christmas my mother wanted, one that truly would honour her memory.

And achieve all of this without razing this family to the ground all over again.

Chapter 44

Steeling myself, I scrolled through my contacts and then crossed my fingers, trying to make an effort to send good vibes into the universe.

On the other end of the line, a phone rang two or three times. I pressed the phone to my cheek and wondered if I was hoping Hazel would answer or that it would go to voicemail. If she wasn't answering, it was likely because she saw my name flash on her screen.

'Hello,' a flat voice finally said after the fourth ring and before it went to voicemail. And I felt myself freeze, my stomach clenching in knots.

Finally, I stuttered, 'Hazel? Hi, it's Joanna.' I paused, almost about to say 'Matt's sister' by way of clarification.

Utter silence. I couldn't even hear her breathe. In fact, it was so silent that I wondered if she had maybe ended the call. I looked at the phone's screen to see if it was still connected. It was.

Bringing it back to my ear and glancing at Nate for support, I said, 'Hazel, are you there?'

But then the silence was broken. Her voice was even, and completely devoid of emotion.

'What do you want?'

What did I want? Forgiveness? Absolution?

'Well, it's been a while – and I hope you are well. Merry Christmas.'

I felt so stupid. Me, trying to make pleasantries. My mind automatically travelled back to the last time I'd seen her. I had been less than caring about her health at that point. I had been mean, nasty, vindictive.

'Joanna, I don't mean to be rude but I'm just about to walk into a client dinner, so I don't have a lot of time.'

She was all business, and she was treating me like a stranger. Fair enough.

'Right, OK,' I said. 'Well, the reason I am calling is firstly, I feel terrible about the last time we were together. For everything that happened, and really—'

But she cut me off. 'I'm over it. Go on.'

'OK. Well, I'm calling about the situation with Matt. The real situation.'

'What do you mean, the . . . *real* situation?'

I felt my heart lift just a little. At least she was engaging, even a little.

'The employment . . . situation. It seemed we – *I* was misinformed. Truly, Matt never should have had to leave his job.' I didn't feel there was anything to be gained from going into long and drawn-out explanations on the phone. I could do that if I could somehow finagle a meeting in person. 'Anyway, the thing is, Hazel . . .' I pushed ever so slightly. 'I know this is probably a long shot and maybe I'm wasting my time. But I was wondering if maybe we could meet? So that you might be able to . . . advise?' I added quickly, suddenly deciding to appeal to her professional side.

Deathly silence.

'Look, I'm only asking because I trust you. We trust you. Like I said, I was misinformed about a lot of things, and I am well aware that things ended badly with you two, but Matt, he . . . he has had a really tough time of it this last year. I'm not sure if you know, but he lives here permanently now with my dad, keeping an eye on him and bringing him to all his hospital appointments and everything, pretty much as his carer. And please know, I'm not making excuses for Matt, I'm really not. I know he was at fault in some of this too, for not telling you enough about what he was going through and . . .' I babbled on and on, unable to stop myself. So much for taking control. 'But . . . I'm worried about him just now. And I especially feel you two have some . . . well, a *lot* of unfinished business.'

An even longer silence followed.

'Also . . .' I took a deep breath. 'I know what I said, how *I* acted after the funeral was awful. I shouldn't have landed that on you, shouldn't have implied that Matt was trying to pull the wool over your eyes. I don't expect you to forgive me easily – or him, for that matter. But please know that we all miss you. We all truly hoped you'd be a part of our family one day. And for my part again, I'm really sorry for my role in all of this. But Hazel, we . . . *I* really need you now.'

I took a deep breath and willed the other woman to speak. To say something, if only to tell me to sod off. The silence was almost worse than a flat-out rejection – even more nerve-racking than an outright dismissal.

'Hazel?' I probed, my voice gentle. 'Are you still there? Please say something.'

'Yes, I'm here.'

I bit my lip. 'So, what do you think? Could we meet for a chat? I could come to you, or you could maybe come here over the break . . .'

I heard her suck in her breath before saying, 'Joanna, you're absolutely right,' and all at once my spirits buoyed a little. But she wasn't finished. 'You are wasting your time.'

And she hung up.

Chapter 45

Two days later, the Moore household was once again filled with the festive sights and smells of Christmas.

The tree twinkled prettily in the corner of the living room, which was now fully bedecked in glittering red, gold and green.

Romy had to hand it to Joanna – once her sister decided on something, she really . . . went for it.

Having decided in the end not to call on caterers for their little get-together, Jo had rolled up her sleeves and gone gung-ho on the chopping, basting and baking as if it was a military operation, enlisting the help of the entire family. Even Damien had been roped in (to much grumbling) to clear and sweep the front porch, freeing it up from an overnight snow dusting.

And now the results of everyone's efforts were apparent for all to see.

Mini mince pies, plus the bigger latticed version, shortbreads, caramelised onion quiche, winter berry tartlets, a beautifully arranged smoked salmon platter, as well as Mum's elaborate sausage pastry wreath had all been reconstructed with care, and now plates of their all-time family festive favourites – hot and cold – were laid out all over every available surface, while among other dessert treats, a ginormous sherry trifle chilled in the fridge.

It was, in a word, picture-perfect – apart from the strange, incongruous addition of a gingerbread 'shack', standing sentry in the middle of it all.

In the kitchen, Joanna herself stood sentry too, landing a playful swipe at anyone – mostly Matt – who tried to steal an errant mince pie or attempted to break into the mulled wine.

For her part, Romy too had been completely thrown by her brother's revelation, albeit relieved for his sake that he was now off the hook.

But much like Joanna, she was appalled to think that he'd preferred to let them automatically think the worst of him, and hoped he and Hazel might be able to make up.

She wasn't sure if that was even possible – but, she thought, looking around the sparkling living room while Nat King Cole crooned familiar Christmas tunes in the background, at this time of year, anything was possible.

'Oh my God, berry tartlets,' she gasped then, poking her head over her dad's shoulder and stealing one from the plate. 'I could literally eat a hundred of these.'

Bill smacked her hand playfully. 'Just don't let Jo see you.'

'What can we help with?' she asked her sister, also making it apparent that Damien wasn't going to simply sit on his ass and observe.

'If you guys could just start laying out plates, napkins and whatnot in the living room, that would be great for now,' answered Joanna. 'And then . . .' Her voice trailed off and she furrowed her brow as if something troubling had just occurred to her.

'You OK?' Romy asked. 'You seem a bit . . . distracted.'

'Sorry, just . . . lost my train of thought.'

Right then, Nate came downstairs with the twins in tow. He placed them in the playpen in the corner of the living room, safely away from everything while they ogled, mystified, at all the lights.

'Here to help if you need me,' he called back to Joanna from the doorway, and her gaze flickered over his shoulder.

'You don't have something else to do?' she asked, her voice wary, which Romy picked up on instantly.

But he simply smiled. 'What else would I have to do? It's Christmas Eve and we're going to party.'

Romy considered the pair as she and Damien headed back into the living room to set up plates and other utensils.

Something was up there too – but what? Nate seemed noticeably upbeat, while her sister appeared anxious and distracted – and not just about the upcoming gathering.

What *now*? she wondered, sighing, honestly wishing at this point that she could just wave a magic wand over this family, and she was so engrossed in her thoughts she barely heard her phone when it pinged with a notification.

Damien, who was noisily laying forks and napkins on a nearby occasional table, looked at her. 'Aren't you going to check that?'

'What? Oh.' She pulled her phone out of her pocket and looked at the screen, smiling in surprise as she spotted the sender's name.

It was from Luke Dooley.

Are you sure we're OK to come along tonight? Not sure if you were just being polite followed by a wink emoji.

She vaguely remembered giving him her phone number, along with the invitation to him and his mother for this evening, at the restaurant the other night, and now she flushed automatically with embarrassment at the memory.

As if a guy like him would be interested in her silly family get-together.

Nice of him to double-check, though, and while at the time she was mostly attempting to cover up for Damien's boorishness, Luke really was lovely, and Romy found that she quite liked the idea of having him and his mother join the party tonight, if they wanted to come.

Especially given what he'd said before about this being such a tough time of year for anyone who'd lost someone. And how his sage advice had pretty much given her the inspiration this family so badly needed.

Little distractions . . .

If she hadn't been so preoccupied by the unexpected message and related musing, she might have felt Damien come up behind her.

Or at least have been better prepared to prevent him from snatching the device out of her hand.

'Hey, what are you doing?' she gasped, grabbing for her phone. However, being so much taller, he held it up over his head and way out of her reach.

'What are you being so smiley about? Who the fuck is *Luke*?' he demanded, reading off the sender's username and message, 'and why the wink emoji?' His face contorted with suspicion.

'He's a friend,' she stuttered, trying to keep her voice calm, but for some reason she felt herself trembling at the depth of this unexpected rage. 'You met him actually, the other night after dinner at The Shamrock Lounge, remember? He was with his mother at the next table. We used to go to school together.'

'Right. And what else did you and Mammy's Boy do together?' he snarled sarcastically, and Romy guessed that her face told its own story – that this old school friend was actually someone she liked, a lot. 'Grand, so maybe send a message back telling him that you *were* just being polite and he can feck off with himself if he comes here sniffing around after you.' His voice was venomous and Romy felt her anxiety rising even higher as she watched him type away on her phone, composing a message that would no doubt be equally as nasty as he was being to her right now.

'Stop it,' she cried, raising her voice a little. 'Give that back to me.' She rushed forward and grabbed his arm, pulling at it with all of her might, but he pushed her away as if swatting at a fly. 'Damien, stop it, *please*,' she urged, her voice reverberating off the walls.

Within seconds, the others appeared to investigate the commotion.

'You're gonna want to give my sister-in-law her phone back, bro,' Nate warned, shooting daggers at the other man. 'Right now. Or there's going to be a problem.'

Damien paused, clearly sizing up his odds against Romy's much bigger relative, then he made a decision. Evidently unwilling to take the risk, he handed the phone to her and took a step back.

She looked down at the screen to find the beginnings of an absolutely profane message to poor Luke, but was pleased to note that the intervention had at least prevented him from sending anything.

'You all right?' Nate asked, and she nodded, feeling her eyes tear up as she tried to control her emotions. She didn't want Damien, or anyone, to see her cry – but it was too late.

Joanna rushed to her side. 'Honey, maybe you should . . .' She knew her sister was urging her to make a stand, but right then Romy felt exhausted.

'It's fine, Jo.' Stealing a glance at Damien, who looked satisfied, she added, 'Just a misunderstanding.'

'I'm going for a run,' he said, eyeing her pointedly. 'Need to let off some steam.'

Then he marched out of the room.

Chapter 46

In Damien's wake, I was studying my sister's face, incredibly unsettled by what I'd just witnessed.

'Why did he grab your phone?'

She told me about a seemingly innocuous message from Luke Dooley and I listened without offering any feedback. My mind, however, automatically travelled to my own recent bout of spying on Nate's device, albeit far less aggressive and without intended malice, and I felt terrible.

I wanted to be there for Romy, but what with Matt's recent confession and my inability to set things right, my growing concern that my husband was about to pull the plug on our marriage, plus almost twenty-four hours of baking and party prep, at this point I felt myself teetering on the edge of exhaustion.

Why did I always think I could control everything? Especially when everything I tried to do just ended up in disaster.

As it was, each passing hour made me wonder about what was about to be 'deployed', and if it meant another disaster for my own family's future.

'Thanks for stepping in, Nate,' Romy said, and my husband patted her shoulder kindly.

'You know you don't have to put up with that,' he told her. 'Being steamrollered. By anyone.'

I turned my head sharply in his direction, wondering if there was some kind of double meaning there, and my stomach lurched again, thinking of my own behaviour.

Nate caught the look. 'What?' he queried, frowning.

But I shook my head. 'Nothing. Just . . . nothing.'

'Love, why don't you take a breather – maybe head down the village with me for a little walk,' Dad suggested to Romy, but his eyes were worried. 'A bit of fresh air might do us some good, and we've everything nearly sorted here, haven't we, Jo?'

'Yes, of course. Great idea.'

'Grab your coat, pet, and I'll meet you outside.'

Romy nodded wordlessly and the minute she left the room, the rest of us looked at each other, trying to figure out the best thing to do.

Finally, I offered, 'Mum wouldn't have liked that.'

'None of us liked that,' Dad said sternly. 'So many times, I've wanted to ask that gobshite to leave, but I don't know how I can do that without going over her head, or thinking that I'm treating her like a child. The last thing we need is another falling out in this house.'

I nodded and wearily slumped into a nearby sofa.

'Matt and I had this conversation only recently. I don't think we *can* ask him to leave, Dad. He's here as Romy's guest and she has to learn how to stand up for herself. She has to come to the conclusion on her own that he's a bad egg, otherwise she won't thank us for intruding on her business.'

'I don't like to see anyone mistreat my daughter, though,' Dad said grimly, and was it my imagination or did Nate's face flush at this?

'Hey, let's all just keep an eye on the situation and just get through the rest of the holidays,' he said. 'Given time, this stuff tends to come to a head – one way or the other.'

I squirmed uncomfortably at my husband's words, worried that *our* time would be up all too soon.

But at that moment, we were all interrupted by the ringing of the doorbell, heralding the arrival of a visitor.

I checked my watch, eyes widening. It was only three in the afternoon, not even dark yet. 'I seriously hope someone hasn't got the time wrong. We're not supposed to kick off for another couple of hours and I'm not even dressed.'

'I'll get it,' Matt piped up from the hallway, heading for the door.

But when he didn't immediately return with any party guests, and I wasn't hearing any of the typical festive greetings, I breathed a sigh of relief.

Checking in on the twins, who were now happily playing with yet another shiny bauble, I headed out to the hallway to see what was going on.

And my eyes widened when I saw who was standing in the doorway.

'Hazel?' I muttered, incredulous.

'Uh . . . come in,' Matt croaked, his voice catching in his throat as he stood back to usher his ex inside.

Hazel looked at him, seeming to pause a beat, studying his face as she decided her next move.

'Wow, I . . . thank you for coming,' I babbled. 'After our call, I didn't expect . . .'

She side-eyed me. 'Romy phoned in the meantime, inviting me to the get-together. I'm just here to honour Cathy.'

Of course. I squirmed, inwardly marvelling at my little sister's ingenuity.

Of *course* that was the right way to handle it. Instead of dispassionately seeking her out asking for absolution, of course I should have appealed to her relationship with our family – and respect for our mother – and invited her to be part of this gathering.

As always, I'd misjudged things, while in her own quiet way my sister did what was necessary to help make things right.

Much like Mum would have done.

Now my dad rushed to the door to greet her in a flurry of welcomes. 'Oh, Hazel, pet, it's so good to see you. Come in, come in out of the cold.'

She smiled kindly at him. Whatever her feelings were regarding the rest of us, there was no denying that my father still held a special place in her heart.

'Merry Christmas, Bill. I've been thinking of you a lot this year. How are you doing?'

He patted her on the back. 'Thanks for asking, love. Ah sure, I have my days – some good, some bad. Although I have to say everything's been much better lately, having everyone back under the same roof. It's really lifted my spirits.'

'Can I take your coat, or . . .?' Matt asked, the awkwardness returning as she and my brother faced each other, and there were a lot of forced smiles from me and a little throat clearing by Dad as he went outside to wait for Romy, and I skedaddled back into the living room to give them some privacy, while Matt led Hazel towards the back of the house to the den.

What these two needed to talk about definitely did not require an audience.

Chapter 47

Romy heard the doorbell downstairs and realised her dad was right about getting some air. She needed to pull herself together for the upcoming social gathering, all the while trying to put the image of what had just happened out of her head.

She was completely mortified – not just by Damien's behaviour, but also the fact that her family had borne witness to what he had said and how he had taunted her, and, more than anything, her shame that she hadn't stood up to him.

Her mind automatically turned to Luke Dooley, and how different he had been, so kind, thoughtful and chivalrous. He'd always gone out of his way to help her or make her feel comfortable, even when saying the wrong thing.

He and Damien were night and day.

Wondering why she was even making the comparison, Romy made her way back downstairs, but paused a little as she heard muffled voices coming from the den. Quietly wandering down the hallway, as she neared the door she saw it was slightly cracked open and the light was on.

And from inside, much to her surprise, she heard none other than Hazel's voice, talking softly with Matt.

Despite herself, her heart lifted. Her call had worked; her brother's lovely girlfriend came, just as she'd hoped she would.

At first, Romy had felt a little skeevy using her mother and the fact that the family were treating this year's get-together as a tribute to Cathy and celebration of her memory.

Especially since that had never happened back in April. But she knew Mum wouldn't have minded.

It was the outcome that was most important.

Romy wasn't fooling herself, though; she knew Matt and his girlfriend had a lot to work out. But she also knew that her brother had endured so much, and had truly grown up over this past year.

Most of all, he was miserable without Hazel.

Unlike Joanna, she hadn't called looking for forgiveness or absolution. She'd called because Hazel had once been an important part of this family, and she knew it was the best way to help her brother buy the time he needed.

And Romy also knew it was what her mother would have done.

Turning an ear towards the door a little, she tried to make out some of what they were saying, trying to get some indication that the conversation was at least going well.

But then she chided herself, guilty for eavesdropping. After all, wasn't what she was doing now pretty much the same as what Damien had just done to her?

She thought about it. Well yes, *and* no. She wasn't barging into the room demanding to be told what their conversation was about. She wasn't bulldozing her way into the business of other people. She was just trying to see if her little 'helping hand' was having the desired effect.

'Tell me. Whatever you want, I'll do it,' Matt was saying, his voice growing thick. 'I miss you. I miss us. I was just so afraid of letting you – and everyone else around me – down.'

Romy felt her throat tighten at his words, and her mind turned to these last eight months and the notion of her dad and her brother, both alone in this big cold and lifeless house, each struggling to deal with their own grief and broken hearts.

'There's a lot to work out, though . . .' Hazel paused as if she was searching for the right words in stating her terms. 'You let me think the worst and didn't even try to convince me otherwise. I was so sure you'd betrayed me . . .'

'You're right,' Matt agreed. 'And I should have done that from the start. I got so many things wrong, but I swear I would never . . .'

Romy moved away. At that point she'd heard enough – what was going on now was between her brother and Hazel – and they would either find a way forward, or they wouldn't.

However, as she padded off silently back down the hallway and out the front door, she got the sense that Matt had now faced off his demons and truly learned to stand on his own two feet.

And Romy wondered if maybe it was about time for her to do the same.

Chapter 48

I was a ball of nervous energy.

The food was all prepared and laid out, the mulled wine warmed, all of the Christmas lights both inside and out were on and the entire house was festive, twinkling and gorgeously warm and welcoming, exactly how Mum would have had it.

Now, we just needed our guests to appear – Hazel, of course, being the surprise early arrival.

I finished getting dressed and it felt amazing to glam up in a red sheath midi and a pair of gold platform sandals that I always kept in my wardrobe here in case of any unexpected social occasions – though I hadn't worn a dress or heels on either side of the Atlantic in what felt like forever.

I missed dressing up. I missed this version of myself. Confident, glamorous, powerful; feeling like I could take on the world. That I could do anything.

As I finished applying my make-up in the en-suite bathroom, I came back out to see how Nate was getting on with the girls. He'd offered to make a start on wrestling them into their matching tights and dresses while I got myself ready.

However, when I emerged, I found both toddlers crawling around the room still just in their vests and nappies, and my husband once again distractedly typing on his phone.

And once again my stomach gave an involuntary lurch. It was Christmas Eve, so it couldn't be work. What else could be so important?

'How's it going?' I asked, trying to make my voice sound carefree.

Jumping a little, as if he had been caught in the act of doing something untoward, he shoved his phone in the pocket of his dress pants, and turned his attention back to the girls.

'Sorry, just had to answer an email. Work stuff.'

I willed myself to keep my face neutral, even though I knew damn well he wasn't telling me the truth.

But yet he had been so supportive lately – and much like my own siblings, we were getting along better with each passing day. The two of us had been so much better throughout this trip. Why would he behave like this, being so good to my family, or have even come here with me at all, if he was going to drop some sort of divorce bomb on me?

I had tried googling the lawyers' office in San Francisco from what little I recalled of the details, but hadn't come away any the wiser. There were a lot of lawyers in the Bay Area.

'Hon?' he said, snapping me out of the rabbit hole I had started down in my brain. 'Earth to Joanna.'

I shook my head, trying to clear the fog that had settled around my ears.

'Oh, sorry. Just, um, crossing off lists in my head,' I lied.

He got up from where he was crouched and kissed my cheek. 'This family and lists,' he said, smiling a little. 'I'm really looking forward to tonight. The place looks incredible and the food . . . wow, who knew? And you look absolutely stunning too, by the way.'

My heart flip-flopped once again as I tried to figure out what was going on with him, and I decided to just persuade myself there was nothing to worry about. I'd already gotten so much else wrong this year, had made far too many errors of judgement, that I had no choice but to distrust my own faculties.

What would be, would be.

'Thank you,' I said earnestly, unable to remember the last time he had paid me such a compliment. It made me feel good – it made me feel . . . normal.

Yes, it was just in my head, I decided, as I went to put my arms around him.

As my body pressed against his, however, I felt a vibration against my hip. The damn phone in his pocket again.

My heart dropped into my stomach and outcome be damned – I was about to just come straight out, ask him what the hell was going on, but I heard a strangled cry as one of the girls, Katie, knocked her head against an open drawer.

And suddenly we were right back to the domestic stuff.

Nate dutifully pecked my cheek. 'Better finish up with these two. See you down there?'

I nodded in agreement, feeling as though I was being dismissed.

And as I left the room, my husband once again pulled his beloved phone from his pocket.

Chapter 49

Romy was at the front door with her dad, greeting Eve and Sam Hartman from next door, when Joanna came back downstairs to a chorus of festive greetings and hugs all round.

Matt was already circulating among the guests, and a relaxed-looking Hazel was on duty pouring mulled wine for their visitors (and herself), while Damien had since returned from his run and planted himself on the couch, a decidedly *un*festive bottle of beer in his hand.

'Ah look, here's Joanna too,' said Sam. 'How lovely ye two sisters look. And I see so much of poor old Cathy in both of you.'

Romy murmured her thanks, as another old friend of her mother's commented on the decor, her eyes shining. 'Oh, it's all just how she always had it, too. She would be so, so proud.'

Matt moved to take coats and offer refreshments, and she took a moment to study her brother's demeanour. He appeared calm and happy, as if the proverbial weight had well and truly been lifted from his shoulders.

Hazel, too, seemed content and assured in everyone's company – just like old times.

While she didn't know for sure, Romy smiled inwardly, pleased to think she may have played some small part in their reconciliation.

With Bing Crosby now cooing in the background, the get-together was soon in full swing.

Luke and his mother, Biddy, arrived too, and Romy had to smile when she saw him gallantly lead the older woman, who seemed quite unsteady on her feet but had a wicked twinkle in her eye, to the sofa, settling her comfortably alongside the Christmas tree, while they both laughed and chatted easily with the neighbours.

But when she turned her attention back in her sister's direction, she again noticed that Joanna seemed jittery.

'You OK, Jo? Where's Nate?' she asked as the doorbell rang again, causing Joanna to jump a little.

'Finishing getting the girls ready.' She looked at the door with expectation on her face just as Bill answered, ushering in the Mayfields from down the road, followed by Paddy – the beloved postman greeted like some kind of conquering hero by everyone as he joined the neighbourly gathering.

Her ever sociable dad was in the middle of it all, well and truly in his element and so heartening to see.

Romy looked at her sister, curious as to what was going on now.

'You'd tell me if something was wrong, wouldn't you? I mean, since we're getting everything out in the open now . . .'

'What?' Joanna mumbled distractedly. 'Oh of course, sure. I'm just . . . just nervous, I suppose. Just want to be certain everything is done right.'

Romy placed a hand on her sister's elbow. 'Hey, everything is done. Everything is great. It's time to relax and enjoy it now. Everything is going to be fine. Even if it's not perfect.' She nodded to the rogue gingerbread shack standing comically in the midst of the otherwise picturesque festive aesthetic.

Despite herself, Joanna raised a smile. 'Everything better with you two now?' she enquired, taking a glance at her dad's favourite armchair by the fire, where Damien lazed looking bored and grumpy.

For her part, Romy had tried to engage him, to introduce him to some of their family friends even, but he'd made it more than clear he was uninterested. And evidently still cool with her for not saying anything more about the text, despite the fact that she'd done nothing wrong.

But it really wasn't the time or the place, so instead of poking the bear, she decided just to let him simmer in his own misery and ignore him.

She waved a dismissive hand. 'It's fine.'

Just then Nate entered with a twin in either arm. Both girls were bedecked in red velvet dresses with glittery white snowflakes, and a crisp white bow around the waist. For the moment at least, they were spotless.

'Oh my God, those dresses,' Romy cooed at Suzy in her dad's arms. 'Adorable.'

'Did I get it all right?' Nate asked his wife, as he glanced down at the two of them. 'Bows correctly tied? Shoes on the right feet? Everything perfectly Insta-worthy?' he added wickedly. 'Or are we gonna need some filters and Photoshopping?'

'Perfect.' Joanna walked up to the three of them and kissed each twin softly on the nose, before doing the same to Nate.

Feeling a little bit giddy with happiness at how everything was turning out, Romy headed into the kitchen under the guise of bringing out some more food.

Entering the quiet space, she went to the fridge and lifted up the magnet, freeing the innocuous piece of paper that seemed to have worked so much magic.

Exactly as intended.

Reading again through the particulars on the list, Romy felt a lump in her throat, though this time the feeling was more bittersweet than sad, and she held it to her chest and raised her head, silently thanking the heavens.

We did it, Mum.

'Sexting your new boyfriend?'

Her head shot up to see Damien lurking in the doorway of the kitchen, beer in hand. He brought the neck of the bottle to his mouth and downed what was left of it in one chug, as he strode closer. 'Hiding out in here, waiting for him to join you?'

Romy quickly stuffed the list in her pocket, annoyed that he had interrupted her reverie.

Why had she even invited him here? And what had she ever seen in him in the first place? He was nasty, possessive and narcissistic. He had been dismissive towards her family and, worse, had tried to manipulate their rift by preying on her vulnerabilities.

It was also clear that he had no respect whatsoever for her, or the people she loved. And right then, Romy knew what to do.

What she should have done a long time ago.

'Frankly, it's none of your business,' she said, idly putting both hands in her pockets.

'Like hell it isn't. Give me that phone. Or I'll go back out there right now, and tell the asshole myself how it needs to be.' Before she knew it, he'd closed the distance between them and slammed the empty bottle on the counter.

Then he reached out and grabbed her wrist, pulling it behind her back.

She shrieked in response, and seconds later Luke himself rushed through the door, Matt and Joanna quickly bringing up the rear.

'Get the fuck away from my sister, asshole,' Matt warned.

'And take your bloody hands off her,' Luke put in, his expression murderous.

'It's OK,' Romy said shakily. She turned her attention back to Damien, placed her hands on her hips and narrowed her eyes. 'You do *not* tell me what to do. Nor tell me who I can talk to. You do not control me and you definitely will not threaten me. Nor put your hands on me without my permission. I deserve someone who respects me – and who respects my family. You are *not* that person, and I regret inviting you here. There's clearly a reason you don't talk to your own family. Now get the hell out.'

She glanced briefly at the others, noticing a mixture of relief and admiration written on her siblings' faces, and a small smile of satisfaction on Luke's.

But Romy didn't need anyone to fight her battles for her. She could do that well enough for herself.

Feeling like an unstoppable badass, just like her running bible had always taught her, she turned her attention back to the matter at hand.

'Pack up your stuff,' she said, staring Damien down once and for all. 'There's no room here for you tonight.'

Chapter 50

'You all right, sis?' Matt asked, eyeing Romy, and I noticed how she had started to shake a little once Damien stormed from the room, presumably to pack his things and sod the hell off.

Good riddance.

I figured her adrenaline was starting to wear off, so I went to the sink to get her a glass of water, while she took a seat at the kitchen table.

My dad appeared then, closely followed by Nate and Hazel, and I hoped that somebody was keeping an eye on the twins or there'd soon be even worse ructions to deal with.

Nate obviously caught my questioning look and nodded. 'They're back in the playpen.'

'Yeah, I'm OK,' Romy said, and then she smiled broadly. 'Actually, that felt great. I don't know why it took me so long.'

'You were brilliant,' said Luke, who'd just before that pretty much alerted Matt and I to what was going on in here by jumping to his feet and into the kitchen after Damien. 'And you're right – you deserve much, much better. Nobody should ever make you feel like that again.'

I looked at the lovely guy who I last recalled meeting in the woods with Romy this time last year. And as he gently patted my sister on the hand, I got a glimpse of something in his eyes – a quiet resolve – before he left the room that made me feel certain he meant every word.

Romy sat up a little straighter and took a sip of the water. Once she'd swallowed, she looked at each of us in turn. 'I'm sorry for bringing him here – in the middle of all this. I thought I needed the backup. But I have no idea why, because he was the very opposite of supportive.' She sighed. 'It's just . . . I'd already spent so much time berating myself this last year, I was starting to believe what he was insinuating. That I was . . . useless.'

The silence in the room was pregnant with expectation, and I knew that this was my cue to say what I should have said a long time ago.

'Hon, I realise I'm to blame for that, given what I said, and—'

She cut me off. 'Really, Jo, it's fine, you don't need to—'

'Please – I do. I really do. I love you – you're my sister, and my friend. I treated you terribly back . . . then. I said some incredibly unkind stuff and I regret every word. Awful things to the rest of you too, and I know I caused a lot of pain.'

Then I took a deep breath, and looked directly at Matt and Hazel. 'And you two – well, I should have kept my nose out of your business. I definitely shouldn't have said what I did, no matter how I felt or what I thought was the case. It was completely out of order.'

'Hey, I wasn't exactly an angel myself, Jo.' Matt reached across and squeezed my hand, and at that point I knew he was so happy and giddy with relief that he would have forgiven me anything.

'And Hazel,' I continued, looking at her then. 'I hope you can forgive me too, for being so aggressive, and nasty . . . treating you like collateral damage almost, when you were equally an important part of this family. That was especially shitty of me, and I know that.'

'Thank you.' She smiled uncomfortably, then she and Matt exchanged a glance. 'I should maybe go back out and check on everyone . . .' And as she went to rejoin the party, I raised my eyes to Dad.

'What kills me is that I acted in a way that is directly at odds with how Mum would have wanted me to be. And, Dad, I am doing my best to be better, calmer, more like her. She always had everything under control, and I wanted so much to be like that. But I'm just . . . not.'

He looked at me curiously. 'Love, I'm not sure why you've been operating under the idea that Mum was perfect, or that she always had things figured out, because that's just not possible. That wasn't her at all – sure it isn't anyone, really. There are plenty of times when your mother fell apart, there are plenty of times when the house was a disaster and you kids were driving her up the wall. She locked herself in the bathroom on more than one occasion, just to try to escape the rest of us for a few minutes. I know, because I had to coax her out.' He laughed at the memory and then took my hand. 'Don't get me wrong, your mother was the best person I ever knew, but she wasn't infallible, she didn't live her life on a pedestal. Maybe that's what you thought you saw, but she would want you to know the truth. Being perfect is no way to live, sweetheart. Life is messy. Your mother knew that better than anyone.'

I felt my eyes pricking with tears. 'I think I'm starting to realise that now more than ever. But' – I lowered my head, my face wobbling – 'I know we were all hurting, all grieving, but all I could think about at the funeral, all I could focus on back then, was what you had rightly pointed out, Matt . . . where *was* I? Why hadn't I been there for her last few months, her last days, her last . . . breath.'

I was sobbing openly now, as every emotion I'd been bottling up inside for so long suddenly came pouring out. The real reason for my inner rage at the funeral, and the sore spot Matt's accusation had struck with bullseye precision. 'You were right. I *should* have been there, of course I should, I know that. But . . . I wasn't.' My voice broke. 'I should have moved heaven and earth – not to try and *save* her,' I said, disgusted afresh by the very notion, 'or try to make the problem go away – but to be by her side before *she* went away.' I stopped, needing to take a huge gulp of air, while the words just kept on coming.

'Instead of spending all that time convincing myself that of course she'd beat it, that of course things would go back to normal, that she was *fine* . . . all the stupid nonsense I distracted myself with. While all the while, she was slipping away before my eyes. But I didn't want to accept that, and so I didn't.'

'Ah Jo . . .'

But I could barely hear my brother's plea. The pain of it all was still eating me up inside, as it had been over the last eight months.

'I would give anything to get that time back now, so I could let her know how much I appreciated her, how grateful I was for everything she'd done for me, for *us*. How I loved the very bones of her and how I was so lucky . . . so very lucky to have had her as my mother. She deserved at least that, and so much more. But I didn't get to say any of that because . . . I *wasn't* there.'

'Love . . .'

'For God's sake, Dad, I couldn't even manage to get back in time to . . . to be able to . . .' My voice broke as I struggled to say it, to admit out loud what had been ripping me apart all this time. 'I . . . never got to say goodbye,' I whispered, choking on the words, as tears hurtled down my cheeks and the guilt of it tore me asunder afresh. The hardest truth of all.

My husband put a comforting hand on my arm, while the others seemed at a loss what to say.

They had never seen me like this. I was the one who never faltered, who always knew what to do, who always had it together, who always *held* it together.

The one who could do anything.

And yet, when it came down to it, when it truly counted, I had done . . . nothing.

I shook my head, willing the thoughts and the words and the tears away, and yet still they continued to pour out in unison.

'I never got to say goodbye. That reality – the regret and downright shame of it – has been making me want to tear my own skin off every single day since she left us. And I have to live with that for the rest of my life.' I clenched my hands into tight fists, fresh grief rippling through me as I finally admitted my worst failure – my deepest regret – out loud. 'Because in the end I failed my mother, who deserved so, so much better. And I never got the chance to say goodbye . . .'

Chapter 51

'I suppose I don't need to tell anyone that this has been a rough year for this family . . .' Nate began, while I sat with our two girls dozing on my lap.

When the get-together finally broke up and little by little all the guests had left for home, he'd gathered the family together again in the living room, saying he had an announcement to make.

While I was curious as to what he had in mind, in truth I was also by now completely exhausted. Probably exacerbated by the fact I'd pretty much just poured my heart out (and hopefully) made my peace with everyone earlier.

But it had been long overdue.

In any case, at this stage I didn't think I could take any more angst or drama. And I certainly hoped my husband wasn't going to drop another bombshell now – though after a full and frank chat in the aftermath of my tearful outburst in the kitchen, I knew that yet again, I had overreacted.

While I still had no idea what the mysterious paperwork was, I was sure enough it had nothing to do with me or our marriage, and that was fine by me.

Right then, I just wanted to lie down and sleep for a hundred years.

But it seemed Nate had other ideas.

'It hasn't always been the best of times,' he admitted, meeting my eye now. 'If I'm being totally honest, I wasn't even sure if we would all be right here in this house this evening. If you'd have asked me six months ago, I probably would've said no way.'

He looked around the room and took in all of the faces that stared back at him. 'But that of course would've been wrong, a real disservice to this family and all the good times we've shared. And most of all, a major disservice to Cathy's memory. It would break her heart to know that we weren't together here now at this time of year, or any time really.'

Romy edged up next to me and took my hand, giving it a reassuring squeeze.

'But thankfully, we are all together – *truly* together again now, and I have to give my wise and clever mother-in-law all credit for making that happen. For bringing us all back to one another. For helping us remember, via traditions and through working together, that family truly is the most valuable gift of all. I gotta admit that when I first met Joanna, I didn't really get that. After all, as you know, my own family situation is very different.'

He looked at the floor then and I saw his Adam's apple bob up and down in his throat, and my heart broke a little when I realised his eyes were shining with emotion.

So while I was confident that we had come to some kind of equilibrium and that he wasn't intending to divorce me, just what *was* he doing?

'I am so grateful to the love of my life, my wonderful wife, for showing me what family is all about, and of course for giving me two of the greatest gifts – and terrors – a man could ask for.' He chuckled then, smiling fondly at the girls, and I kissed each of their little heads in turn. 'And even though she is no longer with us physically, my mother-in-law's little reminders of cherished family rituals and traditions was pretty timely in our case, illustrating just how easy it can be for loved ones to drift apart, sometimes because of distance, others because of differences of opinion. Cathy left us that Christmas list this year because maybe she had an inkling we all needed a push, a gentle reminder of how important and special these things can be. I remember how she used to say that all the time – just focus on the little things.

'And as they say,' he said theatrically now, 'often great minds think alike. Over the past few months, I've been working on a project of my own, a way to help everyone to . . . do just that, and most importantly as a tribute to this wonderful family Cathy and Bill have created and nurtured.'

I looked at him, now deeply curious as to what he'd been up to.

What project?

'This originated as a gift for my wife, with the intention of maybe giving her the lift I knew she needed. And now seems like as good a time as any to deploy it . . .' He winked at me then, and I was totally confused, albeit intrigued, that, despite my concern that we were losing each other, instead he'd been working on something to . . . cheer me up?

'Let me introduce you to Momento . . .' He took out his phone and displayed the screen to everyone around the room, pointing at what looked like . . . an app?

O – K . . . I wasn't entirely sure how a freaking app was supposed to work at making me feel better, unless he'd already sold it for a gazillion dollars or something and thus restored our financials.

Though in truth, that stuff meant nothing to me any more. I would give it all away again in a heartbeat if it meant I could turn back time.

'But as I began coding the software and compiling the hardware . . .' Nate went on, and then disappeared off on another tangent. 'OK, so people code stuff every day, upload apps online and whatnot all the time. And if you don't do it correctly, your IP – your intellectual property – can get stolen. Which is why I officially trademarked and copyrighted the app with this family credited as the creators. While basic app utility can eventually be shared if we so decide, it can never be duplicated – kinda like Cathy herself, when you think about it.'

I looked around at the others, wondering what they were making of all of this. An app launch on Christmas Eve right in our front room was an . . . interesting choice of gift, to say the least.

But, I realised then, the copyright thing potentially explained the more recent text from the legal firm I'd discovered. *Ready to deploy . . .*

Nate seemed to realise that he was in danger of losing his audience, though.

'OK, so you're all probably curious about how this works. And I suspect that even though Cathy was a traditionalist, and of course from a whole different generation, she definitely would've appreciated it. There are some other interesting features, but this thing is, in a nutshell – a time capsule of sorts, I guess. An archive or chronicle. Bit by bit, you add the hardware elements, which in this case needed to be after the fact, though from hereon will be in real time.' He turned to the TV and then tapped his phone, apparently using AirPlay to launch the app. 'So the software automatically puts all the pieces together and does this . . .'

We all turned in unison as the TV came alive, and soon a big-screen montage of achingly familiar images kicked off, which I immediately recognised as footage from some of my dad's beloved home movies, now upgraded and transferred to digital format, though with the same comforting flickering graininess. Along with a cheery soundtrack in the background.

I smiled automatically at some of these treasured childhood memories, of Matt and I splashing around in the paddling pool on the lawn, while our long-deceased grandparents looked on in the background, all punctuated by the maniac waving to camera that was practically mandatory when being filmed back then.

Next, a quick flash to my mother holding a brand-new arrival – Romy – her face beaming with delight as she presented our new sister to Matt and me.

But where did he get all this stuff? I looked across at Nate and he winked again, clearly delighted with himself, then turned my attention back to the screen while the rest of the family looked on, rapt.

And after a while, I began to lose myself in the montage of blissful, carefree childhood days, mesmerised by the images of a time when I felt so safe and loved and deeply treasured by my wonderful parents. I glanced at my dad and saw his eyes tear up at these fond familiar memories of his beloved wife, looking so sprightly and alive – lovingly doing what she did, happy as always in the midst of the people she loved.

The years sped by quickly, as I watched the three of us growing up right in front of my eyes, the action moving quickly from first days at school, to Christmas plays, summer holidays, graduation ceremonies, and then onwards to my own wedding day, watching my mother wipe an eye on camera as I walked down the aisle with my new husband and into another life.

Then even more candid shots and reels of the family at various get-togethers and homecomings here in Ireland, and some back home in California, the most recent being the arrival of the twins last year.

And then the action shifted to a more recent memory of this time last year, our final Christmas together – in fact, our final time together as a family, so much of which Nate had been filming away throughout, though I hadn't noticed at the time.

What we were watching now was the ultimate chronicle of my family's life together, all the beautiful little things and precious moments brought together for a highlight reel that was both spellbinding and at the same time so bittersweet to behold.

When I stole a glance around the room at the others, I saw that they too were rapt with attention. Even the twins, having just caught a glimpse of themselves on the oversized screen, seemed interested.

I dabbed my eyes and turned my attention back to the montage, getting a sense that it was shortly to come to an end – and I wasn't ready. And more to the point, I wasn't able. I was fragile enough as it was.

Because of course we all knew how this story ended.

And for me personally, it would forever remain cut short – painfully unfinished, while I grappled once again with regret for all the things I hadn't said or done.

And I wondered why on earth Nate thought that something like this would have given me a lift, when all it was doing right now was reopening an already desperately painful wound.

Until the reel panned forward to a scene that all at once took my breath away and ripped my heart out. My jaw wobbled and finally I broke down, sobbing with the realisation of what I understood my husband was right then trying to illustrate – this part for me alone.

Both my parents in the centre of the camera shot, waving happily on the porch as we drove away from the house, same as they always did at the end of any visit.

And exactly as they'd done a year before, the last time I left.

Before zooming in on my mother's face and her unmistakable, achingly proud smile as I departed, waving me away with so much love in her heart.

Saying goodbye.

Chapter 52

Happy Christmas everyone.

This may well be my last entry, but it is definitely not the last time I will ever think of you all, in this life or the next.

I do hope that my little ramblings might at least have given you a few helpful pointers here and there along the way, although I'm completely mindful that you'll probably just have a great laugh at the very idea that you'd want to carry on all my silly little festive traditions and grand notions.

And I have a sneaking feeling that you'll probably just end up ordering in Chinese for Christmas dinner.

Hey, whatever you decide to do is entirely up to you.

But now the time has come for me to leave you to your own devices.

I hope you have a wonderful Christmas morning. I so wish I could be there in person.

But I will be there.

Give the twins a little kiss from their grandmother? And remind them now and again how much I treasured the time spent with them. I wish it could have been for longer but that wasn't to be.

As of course is the case with you all.

I wish it could have been so much longer, but it wasn't to be. But wasn't it truly wonderful while it lasted?

I don't think any of us should have any complaints and definitely no regrets.

I will love each and every one of you forever, and am so, so very proud to have shared my life with you.

Merry Christmas.

As per the norm on Christmas morning, down through the ages, the floor beneath the Moore family tree was covered with abandoned wrapping paper and torn-off bows and ribbons – the remnants of a very generous Santa visit.

The twins' unwrapping . . . rampage had of course been captured for posterity, the memories of Nate's unexpected gift the night before still fresh in everyone's memory.

The girls had figured out quickly that they were pretty good at opening presents, though Romy thought they seemed even happier about actually being encouraged to make a mess.

Now, the family sat around the tree, laughing, joking, putting together toys that seemed to have millions of pieces and reflecting on the festivities thus far.

'I think it's been a pretty good Christmas, considering,' said Matt, 'thanks to Mum.'

'Thanks to all of us,' Bill reminded him. Her dad shifted a little in his chair. 'And while I think of it, there's a couple of presents left.'

Romy looked around and beneath the tree. 'Nope, I think we've got them all.'

'I was actually supposed to give you these back in April . . .' he admitted, chuckling a little. 'But sure we all know that didn't really work out . . .'

She and her siblings glanced at each other, still somewhat ill at ease about that time, despite having made up.

For her part, Romy was still reeling at the anguish Joanna had been putting herself through, and she wished she'd had the wherewithal to put her own petty grievances aside and maybe reached out to her sister in the interim.

But Jo had always been so strong and resilient that Romy automatically assumed she was, as ever, just taking everything in her stride. Grieving, of course, but unravelling? It was still hard to believe. But she hoped her sister's purge last night had gone a long way towards healing those damaging, albeit entirely self-inflicted wounds.

Now she looked up at her dad, as he continued to speak. 'Your mum had a couple of things tucked away that she wanted you three to have,' he said, 'and sure no better time than now. Hold on a minute and I'll get the box. Or maybe one of ye might give me a hand – Matt?'

'Course.' Her brother hopped up from where he and Hazel had been playing with Katie on the floor, and, now well and truly intrigued, Romy followed.

What now . . . ?

◆ ◆ ◆

Upstairs, inside Mum's study, Romy and Matt watched, perplexed, as Bill picked up a box.

'Need one of us to carry that down for you?' She looked at it, wondering what was in it and if it was heavy.

'Not at all. There's just a couple of things in there for the three of you, but your mother wanted Matt to have something – and I thought it best to give it to you first. You'll understand why.'

Reaching into the box, Bill pulled out a smaller black velvet ring box and handed it to his son. 'Before she left us, she told me that she wanted you to have this when I felt like the time was right. And it feels like the time might be right.'

Romy felt a lump in her throat as Matt tentatively opened the ring box to reveal a platinum band featuring a single princess-cut diamond. They had all seen it on Mum's finger a million times, and now it seemed she was giving him a gentle nod to put it on someone else's.

'Take your own time now, there's no rush,' Bill assured him. 'But I remember putting that ring on your mother's finger and feeling like I had just won the lottery. I hope you feel that way too.'

Matt's jaw was working hard as he struggled to keep it together. 'Thanks, Dad, I know I will.'

Now deeply curious as to what else might be inside the box, Romy followed her dad and Matt back downstairs, and waited as Bill distributed a couple more packages.

'Here you go, something for each of you. From Mum. Don't ask me what – you know I'm not as nosy as she was. This is for you, Jo,' he said, handing his eldest a thick rectangular package. 'And you, love,' he said to Romy, before retreating to his favourite chair.

The sisters looked hesitantly at each other.

'You go first,' Joanna offered, and Romy was only too happy to oblige. The suspense was killing her.

Ripping open the wrapping, she pulled back a layer of tissue paper and found what looked like a rack of some sort, like something you would hang belts or scarves on. Inscribed across the top were the words: *She believed she could, so she did.*

Furrowing her brow, she realised there was also a tiny gift card included and, opening it, she immediately recognised her mother's handwriting.

Sweetheart, celebrate all the races in your life – long or short. Remember, it doesn't matter how fast you are – just that you keep going. And know that I will be with you every step of the way.

Her eyes clouded with tears as she looked back at her gift, understanding.

'It's a holder . . . for race medals.' Romy fiddled with one of the clips. 'She wouldn't have known that I didn't do the marathon, though.' But now she felt even worse for giving up as she contemplated this.

Joanna reached out and rested a gentle hand on her shoulder.

'Yet. That you didn't do the marathon . . . yet. It's not too late, Romy. Do it whenever you're ready – that's if you want to, of course.'

Feeling automatically better, she nodded, determined. 'You're right. I haven't run it – yet. But I sure as hell will get that medal next year. For Mum.'

'For yourself too, love,' her dad put in. 'You wanted to achieve it, so go for it.'

Romy's tears were flowing openly now, and looking back at her sister she urged, 'Open yours, Jo.'

Needing no further encouragement, Joanna tore open the wrapping paper to reveal what looked to be a collection of used notebooks, plus a small gift card for her too.

'My darling Jo, as you know I always kept a diary, but I don't think I ever told you that I actually started the day you were born. Upon meeting you for the very first time, I felt such intense, overwhelming emotion that I knew the only way I could hold on to the experience was to write it all down for posterity. Being a mother has truly been my greatest achievement, but it has also not been an easy one. I hope that through reading this, maybe you will understand that motherhood and indeed life is not always easy, and never perfect. But once your children know how much you love them, it feels like a win. And I hope you already know how much I love and am so very proud of you.'

'They're her diaries . . .' Joanna gasped, and Romy's head snapped up. 'I'd almost forgotten she kept a diary.'

Bill smiled.

'Religiously. I've never read them – she warned me not to. I hope you find what you're looking for in them, sweetheart,' he answered sagely. 'But maybe keep to yourself what she says about me,' he finished with a wink.

Romy saw Joanna's fingers shake a little as she opened the first book and glanced over pages and pages of her mother's handwritten wisdom, and she guessed her sister must feel as if she had just been given the keys to the kingdom.

'What about you, Matt?' Hazel enquired then. 'Didn't Cathy leave something for you too?'

He simply smiled. 'She did. And you'll find out what it is soon enough.'

'Time for a family photo?' Nate suggested then.

'Wait a minute.' Staring at the diaries, Romy stood up with the medal rack still in her hand. 'Just . . . back in a second.'

◆ ◆ ◆

She exited the room and headed down the hallway, the buzz of Christmas morning family chatter still ringing in the background.

Going into Cathy's study, she closed the door behind her and leaned against the door, taking a deep breath. Then she went to the drawer and opened it, taking out the brightly covered notebook she'd discovered a week earlier.

So her mother had gifted Joanna her journals. But only Romy knew that not all of them had made it into the box.

Flicking through the pages and rereading some of her mother's chatty writing, she thought for a few moments and then came to a decision. She picked up the journal and tucked it under her arm.

Maybe this one had also been meant for Jo, but sometimes these things had a way of working themselves out.

This time last year, Romy had told herself and the others that she wanted to achieve something. And thanks to her mother's wise words and helpful pointers along the way, she'd achieved the most important thing of all.

Bringing this family back to one another.

They didn't need to know the hows and whys of the Christmas list and that it had in fact been *her* creation, not Cathy's.

Little distractions . . .

When Romy had first happened across the diary and started to read through her mother's fond festive memories and titbits, written in her trademark intimate style, she realised that she needed to find a way to honour Cathy's hope that some of the family's favourite traditions might continue, as they navigated through this difficult time without her.

This will be a Christmas like no other, but that doesn't mean it needs to be a terrible one.

Her mother would have foreseen they would struggle in any case, but of course she couldn't have known that the family bond had in the meantime become so fractured that they couldn't even *attempt* to carry on as normal.

So, freshly inspired by Luke's comment at the tree farm about the importance of distractions, Romy had distilled her reading of her mother's most deeply felt festive tips and recollections and written them down, in order to compose an actual plan of action. Pinning her hopes on the idea that getting everyone working together for their mother's sake would – at the very least – help distract from the pain of Cathy's absence.

But the list had worked even better than expected, effectively easing the family's path back to one another.

Now, though, this errant diary could potentially rumble everything, and while of course Romy could just come right out and tell them the truth, she figured that they were already grappling with more than enough emotional revelations, and didn't want to risk rocking the boat. And at the end of the day, wasn't it the outcome that was most important?

In all honesty, she still couldn't quite believe that none of them had copped the handwriting difference on the festive to-do list she had compiled.

So she'd just slip this diary into the box with the rest downstairs for Joanna to read in her own time, and nobody need be any the wiser.

It was the best option.

After all, she thought, smiling, in her mum's own words, this truly was the time of year for believing in something. Wasn't it?

When Romy returned to the living room, Nate moved to set up the timer on his phone camera while the family assembled in front of the Christmas tree.

Once all was ready to go, he rushed back, grabbed Katie, plopped Suzy in Joanna's lap and wedged in next to his crouching wife.

Matt and Hazel stood behind them in front of the tree holding hands, while Romy perched alongside Bill on the armchair, her head leaning contentedly on his shoulder.

'Cheese!' they all crooned in unison, as a flash erupted from the device.

'One more, just in case?' Nate offered, jumping up to set up another shot.

But Joanna stopped him. It didn't matter if someone wasn't smiling, or had their eyes closed.

Right then, it was a single family moment in time.

And it was perfect.

Epilogue

ONE YEAR LATER

'Come on, Jo, hurry up!' Nate urged. 'Everything's set.'

'I'm trying, I'm trying, I can only move so fast,' Joanna grumbled, padding awkwardly into the room. 'Where's the fire . . .'

'What fire? Where?' asked her dad, and she burst out laughing at his genuinely worried tone.

'Bill, we can't see you, so just press the silver button on the remote,' said Nate, instructing his father-in-law on how to set up Momento correctly on his TV.

'Sure you know I'll have forgotten how to do all of this the minute ye're gone . . .' his father-in-law grumbled.

'So much for being able to look after yourself, when I'm gone,' Matt piped up jokingly, and Hazel elbowed him.

'OK guys, here we go – the Moore family year in review. Us first,' Nate announced right before a video clip of Joanna appeared, lying on her back as she watched a different kind of screen up above the bed.

'Nervous?' Her husband's voice could be heard from somewhere off camera.

'Trembling like a leaf . . .' she replied. Then another sound, a rapid pitter-patter, like the fluttering of a thousand butterfly wings.

'Can you tell if it's . . . ?' Joanna's question hung in the air.

'Do you want to know?' the ultrasound technician asked.

'I do,' she said. 'You, hon?' she asked Nate.

'Absolutely.'

'OK. It's a little boy. Congratulations.'

At this, the entire family cheered in unison and, now in real time, Nate smiled at his wife. 'I mean, I'm still going to be outnumbered, but at least the score is starting to even out.'

'On the domestic front too,' Joanna grinned, leaning into shot. 'The hotshot CEO of Momento Inc. can only conquer the world if Daddy's sharing the childcare,' she grimaced, as Suzy and Katie crawled all over their parents on the sofa in San Francisco.

Bill slapped his thigh in delight. 'Brilliant! No better woman.'

'Yup. Back in the driving seat, where she belongs,' said Nate fondly.

'And here's us,' Matt said, pride in his voice, when this time a clip appeared of Hazel in a white dress, carrying a bouquet of pink roses.

On her finger sparkled Cathy's engagement ring, and Matt was sliding another ring onto that same finger, as they both said 'I do'.

'You really did look like you'd just won the lottery,' Bill chuckled.

'Sure I wouldn't say no to that either, houses in Galway aren't cheap,' his son joked, and his new wife elbowed him again.

'OK, and . . . cueing up October now,' Nate announced as onscreen the software smoothly navigated to another clip.

This time, the entire Moore clan, the twins included, stood amid the deafening roar of crowds waving flags and holding signs along a crowded Dublin street beneath blue skies on a bright autumn day, an electric sense of celebration in the air as athletes whizzed passed in their dozens.

'Four hours and forty-five minutes.' Joanna gave a thumbs up into the camera, nerves thick in her voice.

Matt was studying a tracking app. 'She's not far, I think, maybe the next wave . . . ?'

More and more people passed by until finally Hazel called out excitedly, 'Here she comes! I see her! Look, girls, hold up your signs, there she is!'

The shot panned shakily to the side until soon enough, a flushed and sweaty Romy approached, a mixture of pain and elation on her face as step by step she edged closer.

'Come on, sis!'

'Go on love, nearly there . . .'

'Go, go, go Aunt Romy!'

'You've got this!'

As she neared where her family were, she seemed all at once to spot the signs and hear their voices. Her eyes widened and she automatically quickened her pace, gritting her teeth as she pushed through the pain barrier and onward towards the final few yards of road.

And then raising her arms to the sky as she ran onto the mat, Romy crossed the finish line as the overhead clock reflected four hours and fifty-one minutes. And 26.2 miles.

Elated, she lifted a tired hand to her chest as she finally allowed her feet to stop moving, while a race volunteer handed her a precious, hard-earned Dublin Marathon Finisher medal. Clutching at it with tears streaming down her cheeks, she looked up at the sky, uttering a silent prayer to the heavens.

The family cheered afresh both on and off screen then, when Luke Dooley, who'd finished the race a little earlier, joined her for a shared celebration just beyond the finish line.

Whereupon a tearful and breathless Romy threw her arms around him, and the pair stood locked in an embrace while uproarious crowds cheered behind them.

'You know, I could watch that a million times,' Joanna sighed dreamily. 'Talk about a finale . . .'

From her dad's living-room sofa, Romy grinned and squeezed Luke's knee, while he pulled her close and kissed her on the head.

'How's long-distance working out for you guys so far?' Hazel asked. 'A few months married to your brother, and I'm starting to wonder if maybe that was the better way to go . . . ouch!'

Romy looked fondly at Luke. 'Well, and I never thought I'd say this, but technology helps,' she said.

'Ha!' her sister laughed. 'Finally – a convert.'

'So what do you reckon, Bill?' Nate asked then, evidently proud of the app he'd dreamed up and brought to fruition so successfully pretty much a year to the day before. 'By the time your daughter's done, this thing is going global. Nice way for us all to mark the important moments, right?'

Bill's eyes shone with emotion as he looked between the happy faces of his beloved children in California, Galway and – in Romy's case for now – the sofa opposite.

'It's absolutely brilliant. And definitely the kind of thing your mother would've been thrilled with.'

And somewhere in the universe, as her precious family gathered as always for Christmas, in separate locations this year yet still very much together . . . Cathy was.

ACKNOWLEDGMENTS

For me, the very best thing about being a writer is connecting with readers. Thank you for reading my scribblings and I very much hope you enjoyed this story, which is incredibly close to my heart. Please do let me know your thoughts via my website, www.melissahill.ie, social media, or even just say hello! I love hearing from you.

Huge thanks to lovely Sammia Hamer, Victoria Oundjian, Celine Kelly and all at Lake Union for being so brilliant to work with, and as ever the wonderful Sheila Crowley and gang at Curtis Brown for continued support, especially throughout such a challenging year.

And finally, to my own family – while missing so much time together in 2020 was very hard, it was also a reminder of the importance of all our shared little moments, and to never take them for granted.

Melissa xx

ABOUT THE AUTHOR

Melissa Hill is a *USA Today* and international bestselling author living in Ireland's beautiful County Wicklow. Her page-turning contemporary novels of families, friendship and romance are published worldwide and have been translated into twenty-five languages.

She is the author of *Irish Times* bestsellers *The Summer Villa*, *The Charm Bracelet* and *Something from Tiffany's*. Her novel *A Gift to Remember* has been adapted for TV by Hallmark Channel USA, along with a sequel, *Cherished Memories*. *The Charm Bracelet* has also been made into a film in the USA and multiple other titles are in development for movies and TV.